"HIII-EEE-HAHHH!"

He screamed the panther scream of the Oglala Sioux and climbed up on his horse. Tracy had no course but to ride out and into the Arapaho, one way or another. The paint stud was nose-close to Knaska's rump in two jumps.

With both ponies going at a yellow-lather clip, the scout threw every ounce of his weight backward against Knaska's hackamore, literally pulling the mare's forefeet off the ground, haunch-sliding her to a stop that took half the skin off her hocks. The paint stud couldn't match it; his sliding stop carried him ten feet past Knaska, leaving him off-balance for all the time Tracy needed.

Before either chief or studhorse could recover and wheel, the scout drove Knaska crashing into the Indian pony's rump. It was a jarring, twisting impact, sending the Indian pony hock-over-fetlock down the bank of the Arkansas. Horse and chief cascaded into the swirling waters ...

Nine Lives West

Clay Fisher

BANTAM BOOKS · LONDON · TORONTO · NEW YORK

NINE LIVES WEST
A Bantam Book / October 1978

ISBN 0-553-10085-8

Published simultaneously in the United States and Canada

Bantam Books are published by Bantam Books, Inc. Its trade-
mark, consisting of the words "Bantam Books" and the por-
trayal of a bantam, is registered in the United States Patent
Office and in other countries. Marca Registrada. Bantam
Books, Inc., 666 Fifth Avenue, New York, New York 10019.

PRINTED IN THE UNITED STATES OF AMERICA

For TEX AVERY,
my friend

Contents

Foreword

THE GAMBLERS

Nowhere was the game of human survival more dangerous than in the American west.

There, the players could not buy in, or out, with simple markers of paper money. Neither would silver stack the deck, nor gold guarantee the pot. Life itself was the ante, the price of a pile of blues. It was the hard and sole reward for the winning hand. There were no nickel chips, and the losers cashed-out in blacks.

Each day in that harsh land was a last-chance bet to see the sun again.

So it is with the gamblers herein.

A life is laid upon the line in each of the nine games dealt. No player wins without bucking the black tiger. And even then the victory may smell more of bitter ashes than taste of heady wine.

But the winners *would* stay.

They would not quit.

That was the way of the Old West and of the old westerners.

They knew the price of life.

Nothing came free. No man won who did not buy in. The players paid for their chips, they asked for their cards, and they knew it was sudden death that smiled and cut the deck.

Nine Lives West

A Mighty Big Bandit

It was a real nice day. Early fall, wood-smoke hazing the air, nippy in the shade, dozing-warm in the sun, quiet as cotton both in and outside town. For me, I wasn't fighting it. A man doesn't get many vacations in my line and I was making the most of this one. It was up in Minnesota, a fairly decent piece from the Chicago office, my idea being to get as far away from my work as possible for a Pinkerton. Trouble was, some friends of mine from Missouri had the same idea—with trimmings. They not only wanted to get as far from their work as possible, but as fast. When that rattle and slap of gunfire broke loose in town, it brought me bolt upright in the old fishing skiff that was drifting me down the little Cannon River, just outside Northfield.

I stand something like six-four with my boots off, which they were right then. Stretching, I could see over the road bridge, down toward the square. There was a shoot-out going at the First National Bank, and it looked to me as if the local folks had ambushed themselves a couple of tinhorn bank robbers. I have been more wrong, but precious seldom.

Bank robbers, yes. Tinhorns, not quite.

I thought I recognized the last man out of the bank, even from the distance. Big fellow, rough-cut, burly, yet graceful and quick as a buck deer. Time he and his pals had cleared the doors and were mounted up, two, three of them had been knocked clear out of their saddles and the remaining six of

1

them, the big man riding last, were hitting it on the flat gallop for the Cannon Bridge.

It occurred to me, along about that time, that this was the same bridge I was drifting toward. Now I had no sure way of knowing who they were, even though the burly one looked familiar. But I did know one thing; since I was in the same business—on the other side—they might know me. It took me rather strongly that it would be a profitable idea if I rowed like crazy and skinned in under that bridge until they had pounded across it. Pinkerton or not, I was on vacation. What's more, my gun was in the spare room out at the farmhouse where I was staying, and furthermore my mother had raised a cautious son. Not bright maybe, but outstandingly careful. I went under that bridge like a water skater looking back over his shoulder at a walleye pike.

I will say that I have done very few smarter things in my time.

The five lead bandits hauled up at the bridge not ten counts after I disappeared under it. They sat there reining and holding down their lathered horses, waiting for the big man to come up. He didn't keep them long, and I had, sure as sin sells high, recognized him right. It wasn't anybody but Thomas Coleman Younger, and what he had to say to the little squint-eyed fellow leading the bunch would have frozen the ambition even of Horatio Alger. Cole had a voice like a he-bear with a bad cold, anyway. I will tell you that it surely came through to me clear and meaningful that fall day in Northfield, Minnesota.

"Dingus," he said, "no posse in sight yet, what's your hurry? Now you want we should split up, or stick together?"

Names are certainly interesting. It all depends where you hear them. In some places, like the boys' privy back of the old schoolhouse, a dingus was one thing. Here, in Northfield, right atop a shoot-out bank robbery, it was another. Like, say, a pet nickname for Jesse Woodson James.

Yes sir, that was it. The James gang. And the better part of seven, eight hundred miles from Missouri. I will tell you, mister, I was sweating like a 2:01 trotter in the third heat.

"Split up," whined Jesse, in that reedy, wild voice of his, which all us Pinkertons had heard described a hundred times. "We'll meet, like planned, back at the slough. Six o'clock, sunset. Come on, let's ride!"

They put the spurs in deep, going over that board floor bridge to beat Pickett's last charge. When the dust died back, they were gone and I crawled out from under the bridge shaking fit to shed my teeth.

Well, sure enough, six professional friends from the Show Me state, and any one of them would have struck me dead quicker than a cottonmouth water moccasin. I had to get into town pretty fast, then. Positive identification of its members within five or ten minutes of the robbery, could put the James-Younger gang out of business before nightfall. I knew only Cole personally, but the others were familiar to me from wanted flyers. Far as I knew, I would be the only man in Minnesota who could say for certain who had busted the Northfield Bank. Vacation or not, I had to put what I knew on the wire, or start looking for other work. Being a detective for twenty years sort of warps a man's morals. He gets to thinking he's got to do right.

The telegraph office was next to the bank. A pretty good crowd was already jamming up in front of it by the time I puffed in from the river. I used a few elbows and squeezed in the door, which, being held shut from the inside by two shotgun guards, wasn't easy. The guards were surprised enough that they let me get up to the telegrapher, who jumped up and had at me as if I'd insulted his wife's cooking.

"Hold on there, buster!" he yelled. "Just who the hell you think you are?"

"Special Investigator, Pinkerton, Chicago Office," said I. "Got something important I'd like to put on that wire of yours."

"Not a chance, mister," he growled. "We're holding the key open. Just had a bank robbery here. Gang's headed south."

I gave him my bone-dry look.

"So I noticed," I said.

That sharpened him up. "You notice anything else, mister?" he asks, mighty suspicious. The two shotgun guards moved in on me, right then, too. So I gave them all an innocent nod and straight, sober look.

"Seems I did, now you mention it," I answered.

"Yeah? Like what maybe?"

"Like who robbed your bank maybe."

"All right, Mr. Smart-alec Special Investigator: like who maybe robbed our bank?"

"Oh, like Jim, Bob, and Cole Younger maybe. And Frank and Jesse James. Maybe."

He walled his eyes and got a little desperate, at that.

"Mister," he said, "if you're trying to be funny—"

I gave him a bobtailed nod.

"You put it on that wire," I told him, "and see how funny it sounds."

Having said which, I excused myself and started for the door. There I had to hold up and add a PS.

"And when you've put it there," I said, "sign it 'Yancey Nye.' "

That put up all of their eyebrows, and gave me the chance to shoot them a proper sneer of superiority. But you can't trust those Scandinavian hayseeds.

"Well, by damn!" said the telegrapher. "*The* 'Yankee Nye'?"

"Naw," I soured up quick, "you're thinking of Yankee *Bligh*. He's another fellow. Works down to Kentucky and that way. Always playing up to the boss and getting his name in the papers. I said 'Nye,' N-Y-E, Yancey Nye, you got it?"

"Sure," he said. "Hell, we thought you was somebody."

Well, that's the way it goes. I huffed on out of there and up to the livery barn, where I had my rented rig. It was not over fifteen minutes after I'd climbed out from under the Cannon River Bridge that I was ambling that old buggy horse back out to the Nils Swenlund farm, where I was boarding. Past getting a little nap before the evening fishing, I hadn't a plan in the world. There wasn't any Pinkerton accounts in the bank losses, and I was still on vacation. That's what I thought. But I hadn't consulted with my six outlaw friends from Missouri. Nor with one little seven-year-old Swede farm girl from Minnesota; a little girl who had more pure nerve than any outlaw or gunman I ever went up against in my whole life.

Jenni Swenlund was her name, cute as a blond mouse with her taffy braids and peasant jumper. Half an hour later I was standing with her in the barn lot saying goodbye to Nils and Mrs. Swenlund, who were setting out to be with a neighbor woman whose time it was that day. The good folks were some worried about me and the kid getting on by ourselves, so I was easing them off about it.

"Now you all run on," I smiled. "Take all the time you need with that new baby over yonder. Me and Jenni will make out just dandy. Likely, she can show me where that big lunker is hiding out down by the bridge."

Mrs. Swenlund was still fretted, but gave in some.

"Well, if you're sure now, Mr. Nye."

"Sure, I'm sure," I waved. "Now you all get a move on. That baby'll be old enough to vote before you get started."

That got a smile out of her, and away they went, them waving back and the little girl throwing them kisses and goodbyes until they were lost down the county road. With that, she turned to me, all business.

"Come on, Mr. Nye," she tells me. "Thank goodness they're gone. Now maybe we can get some work done around here."

"Work?" I dug in my heels. "Now, whoa up, there, Princess. I didn't contract to farm this forty."

"All right, you want me to show you where that old lunker is down by the bridge, or don't you?" she demanded.

"Why, sure," I stalled, "but—"

"No buts, Mr. Nye. You just come along and help me hay the mules and get in the afternoon eggs —or else."

I threw her a quick grin and a surrender wave. "Yes, ma'am!" I said. "Show me the way. I'd rather pitch hay to mules than kiss a pretty schoolteacher."

Well, we got into the barn and went to work, me haying the mules, Jenni shagging the old hens around and looking for floor eggs. Hearing an extra loud squawk from one of the barred rocks, I looked around and saw Jenni trying to get it down off a high roost.

"What's the matter, Jenni?" I grinned. "That old biddy giving you more argument than you come prepared to handle?"

She stopped reaching and fetched me a disgusted look.

"Not if I get my hands on her, she isn't!" she told me. "She's broody and doesn't belong in here." She made another dive for the bird, which flopped off the roost and out the nearby front window of the barn. Jenni made a last grab for her as she sailed out the opening. Then she stopped short, threw a scared glance out the window, and ducked back down below its frame. "Mr. Nye," she says, low-voiced, but calm as custard, "come here and look out yonder."

Well, I started over to her grinning half foolish and wondering what little-girl something had gotten her all stirred up about that old chicken.

"What'd she do?" I said, coming up to the window. "Lay an egg on the jump?"

I hadn't any more than gotten this empty-headed remark past my grown-up's grin, than I took my own glance out the window. I pulled back from it as though somebody had jabbed me in the eye with a hayfork. I grabbed Jenni and clamped a hand across her mouth and plastered her and myself back against the barn

wall. Then I whipped a second look out the corner of
that window just to make sure I'd seen what I'd seen.

I had.

It was Cole and Bob Younger and the sixth man
of the gang, the only one I didn't know, riding their
sweated horses up the Swenlund lane, slow and watchful yet desperate and strung-up as wounded game. I
could see they must have seen the Swenlunds take off,
and figured the place was deserted. Since they were
watching the house mostly and not the barn, I was
sure they hadn't seen Jenni and me. But there was
doubt enough to wring me wet before they pulled their
horses to a halt in the barn lot, midway of us and the
house.

Bob was real bad hit. Cole and the other man
were siding him, holding him on his horse. Cole, that
great bear of a man with his gray eyes, curly brown
hair, pleasant look and friendly way, was showing
blood in half a dozen places, but still sitting straight
and bossing the retreat. The other fellow, swarthy as a
foreigner, with a heavy black beard and forehead no
higher than a razorback hog's, didn't look to be hit
any place. Cole was first to speak, his voice, even
though he was hurt so serious, gentle and soft as ever.

"All right, boys, looks like them folks did come
from this here farm. We'd best look around to make
sure, though, that there ain't nobody else to home."

"Well, let's not be all day over it," snarled the
unwounded man. "We got to meet Frank and Jesse and
your brother Jim come sundown. You heard Jess."

Cole clutched Bob closer.

"Pitts," he said, "Frank and Jesse will wait. That's
why I sent Jim with them; to see that they did."

Charlie Pitts! I ought to have recognized him. I'd
seen that mean-animal face on a dozen wanted flyers.
I was slipping. But Pitts wasn't. Again, he snarled at
Cole.

"Your brother Jim! Bushway! He ain't going to
hold Jess and Frank up none. He's bad hurt as Bob,
here. Maybe worse." He paused, then added with a

sneer, "By the way, how come you Youngers took most of the lead back yonder?"

Cole withered him with a hard stare, and a soft reply.

"Could be, Pitts," he said, "that we waited for it a mite longer than you other boys."

Pitts scowled back stupidly. He was a human brute, not up to the outlaw class of the Jameses and the Youngers.

"Go on," ordered Cole. "Check the house. Find what you can of bandages and medicine for Bob. I'll hold here with him and the horses till you get back. Hop it."

Pitts slid off his mount and went cat-footing it up to the house. Jenni pushed my hand away from her face, giving me a big-eyed look that made me cold inside.

"What's the matter, Mr. Nye?" she whispered. "Are they real bad men?"

"They're not men, honey," I murmured. "They're animals, hunted animals. You understand?"

"Yes, but they're hurt, Mr. Nye. They need help." She shook her head. "Can't you see they're wounded, Mr. Nye?"

"Sure enough, honey," I said, desperate to get it through to her what danger we were in, "that's right. They're wounded, and a wounded animal will kill you. Now don't you argue with your Uncle Yancey, Jenni. You just show me where that hayloft ladder is. I don't see it, and we're going to need it, powerful bad."

"But, why—" she began, femalewise.

I grabbed her hard and talked the same way.

"Now you look out that window again and you tell me what that man looks like that's coming from the house. You're only a little girl but I want you to look at that man real good. Careful now; don't let them see you."

She nodded and peeked out. I could see Pitts coming toward Cole and the horses, and I could see

Jenni watching him. He was walking with his bent-kneed crouch and his silent snarl. He came up to his horse and pulled his Winchester from its scabbard, putting his revolver back in his belt.

"All right," said Cole, "now the barn. And hurry it; Bob's bleeding terrible."

Pitts growled like a feeding dog, wheeled and came toward the barn doors, not ten feet from where we crouched at the window. Here came a killer. Even a child knew it.

"Come on, Mr. Nye," whispered Jenni. "The loft ladder is yonder back of the feed room."

We scrambled up that ladder and lay down in the deep hay on the loft floor just in time. There was a two-inch crack in the loft floorboards, through which we could watch below, and my eyes were as big as Jenni Swenlund's, as we both did so.

"Don't even breathe loud," I told her. She bobbed her braids and gave me a pale-small grin and a pat on the hand. I never knew a kid like that, before or since. She had more sense and spirit than any grown-up I ever worked with.

Down in the barn, now, it had got so quiet you could hear the manure flies buzzing around the mules. Of a sudden there was a crash of splintering wood and the doors, hasp and all, flew apart. Charlie Pitts, who had kicked them in, came stalking forward levering the Winchester. He looked behind the feed room and into the mule stalls, turned to the door and called to Cole.

"All clear, bring him in; nobody here, neither."

Cole came in carrying his young brother, Bob, in his arms like a child. Behind him, the trained Missouri thoroughbreds walked in quick and close as hunting hounds.

"Shut the doors," said Cole, "and give me them things you got from the house." He put Bob down in the clean straw of the stall beyond the mules—the one square under where Jenni Swenlund and I lay in the loft. "Easy, now," he said to Bob, "we're going to get you cleaned up, now. Lie quiet, boy, it may hurt some."

Bob, barely conscious, groaned his reply, and Cole went to work on him. Pitts, having seen to the horses, came and stood over them, breathing hard and nervous. Up above, Jenni and I lay flat as two mice with the cat walking past. The stillness got so deep there was no chance even to whisper any more, and I had to pray the little girl would know to go on keeping stone-still. That she finally couldn't, was no fault of hers. A short straw got under her nose, and it was either move a hand to brush it away, or give a loud sneeze. She made the right choice but in shifting her arm to use the hand, her elbow brushed a little streamer of hay dust down through the crack in the floor. I grabbed her and rolled sideways, just as Charlie Pitts flashed his .44 Colt and drove three shots through the boards where we had been.

I looked at Jenni. She was all right, but had both hands over her mouth to hold in her fright. This was all to the good; now she *knew* that death was standing down there below. I gave her a squeeze, a nod, a pat and the best grin I could manage under the circumstances. She returned the nod, her eyes bigger than a brace of china-blue milk saucers.

"All right!" snarled Pitts, "whoever's up there, come on down. And come mighty careful."

I didn't know what to do but put finger to lips, warning Jenni to make no answer.

"You coming down," asked Pitts, "or am I coming up?"

For me to reply, and to start down that ladder, would draw me certain death. Somehow, Jenni sensed that. Before I could clap a hand over her mouth, she called down.

"Just a minute, mister, I'm coming—"

I had to let her go, then, but I did it knowing that Cole Younger would never let harm come to a little child. But Cole was still bent over Bob. The minute

Jenni appeared at the head of the ladder, Pitts, the crazy man, fired blind, just at the movement of her bright little dress. By grace of God it was a clean miss, and the next instant Cole had leaped across Bob and hit Pitts so hard it drove him clean across the stall and over a tool bin, flat-sprawled.

"You feebleminded idjut," he roared, "it's only a little bitty girl!"

Pitts got up, wiping the blood from his mouth.

"She ain't too little to talk," he snapped.

As he said it, he raised up his revolver to fire again. Cole near broke his arm taking the gun away from him.

"You'd shoot a *kid?*" he said incredulously.

Pitts bared his teeth.

"I'd shoot my own kid, were it come down to him or me. We ain't leaving no witnesses behind, Younger. You know Jess's orders on that."

Cole turned him loose, called up to Jenni real soft.

"Come on down, honey. Be tolerable cautious, now. Them ladder rungs look looser'n a old horse's teeth."

Jenni smiled sort of palelike, and started backing down. Pitts moved in, took hold the ladder, gave it a vicious shake.

"Get a move on, you little brat!" he rasped.

Jenni gave a low cry, lost hold of the ladder, fell clear to its foot. Cole jumped Pitts like a mad grizzly. He very nearly mauled and beat him to death before he was stopped from it by Jenni asking him to please not hit the man any more, as he likely hadn't meant to hurt her!

Cole dropped Pitts and crouched over her. He dug out his bandanna awkward and fumbling.

"Here, honey," he said, "leave me wipe away them great big tears."

Noticing an old piece of shaving mirror nailed to the stall partition, he reached it down and held it up for Jenni to see her face.

"Lookit, there, at what them streaks of salt water are a'doing to your dimples!" he grinned.

She grinned back, but Cole lost his smile the next minute. He was seeing something else in that mirror, and it was me peering over the edge of the loft above. I could see his face, too, the way the angle of the glass was, and our eyes met for one dead-still second. Then, Cole just shook his head and muttered soft as ever.

"My, my, the things a person does see when he ain't got his pistol cocked."

Pitts, limping over just then, scowled black and ugly.

"What'd you say?" he demanded.

"Nothing," answered Cole, "to you."

Pitts glared.

"Well, then, I'm a'saying something to you. Same as I said before. We ain't leaving this kid here."

Cole got up from Jenni's side, his gunhand shifting.

"You're dead right we ain't, Pitts. Not bad hurt the way she is. I'm staying with her."

Pitts shook his shaggy head, small eyes glittering.

"All right, you're welcome to stay, Younger. Stay and get strung up by your lonesome. Me, I'm making it on to Frank and Jess while there's yet time. Stand aside."

Now it was Cole's head that shook slowly.

"Not without Bob, you ain't going no place. He's fixed good enough to ride, now, and you're taking him along."

Here, Bob raised up in protest, but Cole put him down.

"Hesh up, Bob. You're going. I'll meet you all at the slough come sundown, like planned. The little girl's my affair, though. You ain't putting your neck in no rope for me, nor her."

Bob knew the lateness of the hour, both his and the gang's.

"All right, Cole," he said. "We'll wait for you."

"Yeah," sneered Pitts, "at least five minutes."

Cole put hand to gun butt, gray eyes nailing Pitts.

"Get Bob on that horse and get him out of here," he said.

Pitts, too, knew the time of day by now. He only nodded and helped Bob up on his mount. Bob swayed, then steadied. He said, "I'm all right, Cole," to his brother, and Cole said, "Move out, Bob, and God bless you." The two outlaws walked their horses to the lane, then put them on the lope and were gone down the county road in seconds. Cole, turning away from the barn doors, looked up and said quietly.

"All right, mister Pinkerton man, come on down and come friendly—"

When I had got down, he looked at the empty place my pistol ought to be.

"Why, Yance," he said, "I'm surprised at you. You don't hardly look decent without your working tools on."

I winced and grinned. "I'm supposed to be on vacation."

"Oh. Well, now, I'm a heap relieved, Yance. I thought maybe you had retired."

"Looks like I ought," I answered, pretty dismal. "You mind if I have a look at the little girl, Cole?" He nodded it was all right, but I held up a minute. "One thing," I said. "You recognized me in that mirror just now. How come you didn't let on to Pitts?" He shrugged, embarrassed.

"Aw, now, Yance, you know we was in the same Missouri outfit. I cain't turn on a fellow Confed'rate soldier."

"Cole," I said, "you're in the wrong business for a man with normal sentiments like that."

"Now, shecks, you know what I mean, Yance. Cold-blood murder like that damn Pitts was a'talking for that pore little thing yonder. Why that's downright sinful!"

"It sure is," I agreed. "Let's look to her before you bust out bawling. She's passed out cold."

"Sure, Yance, sure." He went with me, and we both got down beside Jenni Swenlund. I gritted my teeth when I saw the leg. Cole looked at me, frightened.

"It's broke compound," I said. "That means when the bone shoves out through the skin like this. Give me your bandanna."

He border-shifted his Colt to his left hand, dug out the bandanna, passed it to me.

"You going to put a twist on her, Yance?"

"Got to. She'll bleed out, if we don't. First we got to get that bone back in if we can. Lay hold her ankle. She may twitch pretty sharp."

As Cole put his big hands on the little leg, Jenni opened her eyes and looked up at him.

"He won't really hurt me, will he, mister?" she asked.

Cole glared at me. I thought he'd drill me then and there.

"She heard you!" he accused. Then he patted her braids careful as though they were glass. "Now, now, honey, he was only funning," he said. "Why, if he was really to hurt you, Uncle Cole would blow his head off." He glanced up at me, nodding softly. "Go ahead, Yance. And, remember, 'Uncle Cole' ain't funning!"

It was maybe an hour later. We had her on the bed in her folks' room up to the house. She was unconscious again and looking pale as a ghost. Cole was patting and stroking her hair, scared half-sick. He still had his cocked Colt in his off-hand, keeping it on me while he fretted over Jenni. I knew I had him where the hair was short, no matter.

"Well, Cole," I challenged, "what you going to do?"

He just groaned with his helplessness.

"Yance," he confessed, "I purely don't know."

"Well, you better do something, and pretty quick."

"You mean about her, don't you, Yance?"

"And *you,* Cole," I answered. "Can I see you out-side?"

Cole Younger was not a brainy man, but a gentle-humored big bear, simple in both mind and imagina-tion. Decisions were beyond him, but he understood warnings. He got up.

"Rest easy, now, honey," he told Jenni. "I got to be gone a bit, but I ain't leaving you. Don't have no fears."

Outside the door, I looked at him hard as bedrock.

"You notice that fresh bandage?" I said. "It's all blood again. Soaked knee to ankle in thirty minutes. She don't have a doctor, Cole, she's going to die."

He was in a place where his own life was on the line, too, yet he didn't take two breaths with his an-swer.

"Yance," he said, "happen I let you ride inter Millersburg and fetch back a doctor, will you guaran-tee you won't tell I'm out here?"

I had to tell him, no, and he agreed.

"I reckon not," he said sadly. "It wouldn't be no different nor lying, and I never knowed you to lie in your life."

"It's not your life we're talking about, Cole," I reminded him. "You better think of something fast."

He cringed as if I'd hit him with a whip. Turning, he went back in the room, staring around it in des-peration. I watched him and, of a sudden, saw his face light up when he spied an open wardrobe full of Mrs. Swenlund's things.

"Yance," he said, whirling on me, "you ever get married up? I disremember."

"Nope," I said warily, wondering what was in his slow mind. "Why you ask?"

He beamed happy as though he had proper sense.

"Well, then, your wife won't mind seeing you in the company of a strange woman, will she?" He jabbed the Colt toward the wardrobe closet. "Start handing me out them female unmentionables!"

I looked at him, then at the farmwife's clothes.

"My God," I said, "you really mean a *strange* woman, don't you?"

"Heavens to mercy, no!" he vowed, widening his catfish grin. "We'll make a mighty handsome couple, you'll see." He flicked his glance to the bed and saw that little Jenni had come awake. Swinging his herd bull's bulk between me and the girl, he growled with deadly coyness. *"Won't we,* Yancey dear?"

Since he had shoved the Colt three inches deep in my belly with the question, all I could do was grunt and give in. "Whatever you say, *dear,"* I agreed, and started handing him the unmentionables.

Now it was the main stem, Millersburg, Minnesota; a typical dirt-street hick town. Up the center of the road, creaking in from the farm country, came the narrow, high-side corn wagon, canvas cover laced over its bed. I was driving. On the seat with me was Cole Younger, dressed in Mrs. Nils Swenlund's Sunday best. The outfit was complete with starched petticoats, over-shawl, flowered print dress, poke sunbonnet. Yet despite the heat of the day, Cole had a buggy blanket over his knees and was snuggled up to me like young love with the lights turned off. Also snuggled up to me, under the blanket, was the snout of his Navy Colt. The two old mules plodded steadily. Ahead, the shingle we were looking for loomed up: I.V. BERQUIST, M.D. Cole gave me a delicate nudge with the Colt.

"Turn in," he cooed.

"Yes, ma'am," I said, and gee-ed the mules down the right-hand alley, to the doctor's rear yard. There was a back door to the office, and Cole slid down off the seat and knocked on the panels. Dr. Berquist opened the door a moment later and Cole put the long Colt barrel under his nose and asked,

"Can you sew up a thirty-six-caliber hole through a man's head, Doc?"

That thick, hairy arm coming out of that print

dress was more than Dr. Berquist had been ready to write a prescription for. "Why, no!" he gasped. "Of course not!"

Cole tapped him on the shoulder with the Colt barrel.

"Then don't make a sound," he said, "and you won't have to try." He shoved him back into his office, following him in. In a moment he was back. "All clear, Yance; bring the little tyke in," he told me. I lifted Jenni out of the straw-filled wagon bed and carried her in. Inside, the doctor ordered me to put her on the table. I did and Cole and me bent over, with him, watching like hawks to see what news showed in his face. Right away we could tell it was bad. But still he didn't say anything.

Cole shot a nervous look at the clock on the wall. It was five P.M. He put his huge hand on the doctor's arm.

"We're short on time, Doc. How long will it take?"

Berquist shook his hand off, scowling.

"It can't be hurried. Not with a fracture like this."

Cole brought the Colt above the tabletop.

"How long, Doc?" he repeated softly.

Berquist stared at him defiantly.

"A half hour at least. Perhaps longer."

"Damn!" said Cole, still soft. "That's dismal!" Yet he never hesitated. Going to the front door he turned the "Doctor-Is-Out" sign to the street, pulled down the shade, came back to the table, looked again at the clock on the wall, said quiet as spider silk, "Go ahead, Doc; and don't make no mistakes."

When Berquist finally put down his instruments and tied off the last bandage, it was five minutes till six P.M. Cole, long out of his woman's clothes, grabbed him and spun him around rough and hard. "She all right?" he growled.

"For now, yes," answered the doctor.

"What you mean, for *now?*"

"Precisely what I said. She will be all right if kept perfectly quiet. If she is moved suddenly, or handled in any way roughly—"

Cole shoved him aside.

"That's enough, Doc. Nobody's going to be rough with her. Thanks for your help. You'll get your reward in heaven, unless you want it soooner. One peep out of you that we've been here and—"

Berquist interrupted him, showing no fear at all.

"I doubt you need worry about me following you, Mr. Younger," he said. "Descriptions are out on all of you, and others will recognize you as easily as I. Further, every law officer and local posse in southern Minnesota is already in the field looking for you and the others. You will never get out of this state alive."

Cole scowled, tapped him out with the Colt again.

"Just remember that if I don't, Doc, neither does the little girl. You savvy them sentiments?"

This Berquist had a heavy skull, like all those Scowegians. He wasn't going to buckle one inch to Cole, and I moved in quick.

"He means it, Doctor," I told him. "Don't give any alarm before we're well away. These Missourians are killers." I gave Cole a special look. "*All* of them," I added.

Cole admitted the compliment courteously.

"Regretful, sir," he said to the doctor, "but true." Then, to me, "Move, Yance. No more palaver."

I picked up Jenni Swenlund and went out the back door. Cole followed. He never looked back at Dr. I. V. Berquist. Outside, Jenni safely stowed in the bed under the tarp, him and me back up on the seat, he poked me with the Colt.

"Mind what I told the Doc, Yance. Remember I'll be back here under the tarp with the little tyke." Saying which, he slid off the seat and beneath the canvas cover behind me. All I could see of him was the Colt's nose. "All right," he concluded, "let's go. You drive one mile south on the Madelia Road. Turn left at the Hanska Slough signpost. You got that straight?"

I took a look back at the doctor's office. I thought I saw the rear shade stir a bit. Taking the hairiest chance of my life, I repeated his directions in a too-loud voice.

"*Yes sir! One mile south on the Madelia Road. Turn left at Hanska Slough sign!*"

He very nearly put that Colt through my kidneys.

"Keep your big mouth shut, Yance," he rumbled, "and dig!"

"What's the great rush, Cole?" I said, mad at being poked so hard and knowing, anyway, he wouldn't dast shoot me just now. "Jesse said six o'clock. That still gives you five minutes."

"Which is four more than *you* got, Yance," he promised, "happen you don't light out, right quick."

I nodded meek enough, and whipped up the team.

So it was we set out from Madelia, my only hope the slim one that Dr. Berquist had heard those loud-repeated Hanska Slough directions and would figure out what they meant. It wasn't much of a hand to back against the likes of Cole Younger. Not to mention the James boys. I've bluffed bigger pots with a busted flush going into four aces. But my real bet was still on Cole, and on what he would do about that little girl under the wagon-tarp with him, when the chips were down. One thing sure. I was going to find out.

The country was desolate, heavily wooded. The slough was brackish, lonesome-looking. Through the ground brush I could see the crude wickiup the outlaws had made. I got only the one glimpse of it. I made out two wounded, much-bandaged men lying inside. Crouched over the fire outside was Charlie Pitts. In the brief look, I saw no sign of the others. If Frank and Jesse were there, they were out in the brush some-where. As soon as Pitts heard the crunch of our wagon wheels on the slough road, he jumped for his rifle and dove out of sight.

At that time we were maybe a scant furlong from
the camp. Coming to the wickiup moments later, we
had to pass under a big, low-limbed hardwood. I never
thought to look up. The next thing I knew, that crazy
Pitts had jumped down off the overhang and hit me
with his boots between the shoulder blades, sprawling
me clean off the seat and onto the ground. He lit the
seat and braced himself to finish me off with his rifle.
He didn't get a fine sight drawn. From under the wagon
tarp behind him, up reared Cole and laid his pistol barrel across the back of Pitts's hat. Pitts, he just caved
in and slid off the seat. Cole slid onto the driver's box,
picked up his rifle, stepped to the ground, covering
both of us.

"All right, Yance," he said, "get up real careful.
Pitts—throw a rope on him."

As the latter growled and went about tying my
hands, Cole noticed the two men in the wickiup to be
his brothers Jim and Bob, and that there was but three
horses on the picket.

"Three horses!" he barked at Pitts. "Where's
Frank and Jesse?"

"They've cut out on their own," mumbled the
hangdog Pitts. "Said to tell you they wasn't needing no
more wounded Youngers to hold them back."

Cole nodded, as though to expect no more from
his famous friends. "How come you didn't turn tail with
them?" he asked.

"Fat chance! They was gone when I got here.
Left the message with your brothers. Real question is,
what're we gonna do?"

"Light out after them, I reckon. Saving for one
thing; I got the little girl in the wagon yonder."

"You ain't!" Pitts was absolutely bashed in by it.
I took a hunch it was time for me to horn in, but Pitts
recovered and reached for his belt gun before I could
make up my opening speech. "Well," he said, "we're
getting out of here right now and the kid ain't going
with us. I'll see to that, and if you try to stop me I'll
cut you in two."

He had the drop on Cole. Moreover, Cole was trapped another way. His own life was at stake and he knew Charlie Pitts was right. To fool around a minute longer with mother-henning Jenni Swenlund was to put them all, including his two wounded brothers, Bob and Jim, in the shadow of the noose. He watched Pitts head for the back of the wagon, that same dumb, desperate look on his face I had seen in the Swenlund bedroom. And in the same way as then, he got a happy light in his eyes at the last second.

"Hold it, Charlie!" he yelled. "We *got* to take her with us. She's our hostess!"

Pitts whirled around. "Our what?" he said, surprised, and giving me my chance to buy into the game.

"Your hostage," I translated for him. "You know, that's somebody you hold a gun on, so's the other side don't dast shoot. You remember, like in the war."

"Yeah, Charlie," Cole pushed it, "sort of like a pass through the enemy lines. Get the idea?"

Pitts grinned. "Sure," he said, "you bet I do." He shifted his Colt to cover Cole again. "And I'll be the one using that pass. Fetch her out'n the wagon."

With no choice, Cole did it. Meanwhile, I got the three horses off the picket, also given the same option. Pitts turned the third horse loose, hitting him viciously across the haunch with the revolver barrel. He galloped off into the timber. Pitts now mounted one of the remaining two.

"All right!" he snapped. "Tie the kid on this other horse, hard and fast."

"You wouldn't do that!" gasped Cole. "Not even you, Pitts!"

"Put her on that horse," said Pitts, "or I'll blow her brains all over your vest."

Cole and I looked at each other and knew we had to do it. We laced her on real careful, the splinted little leg sticking out straight. She was brave as ever, and smiled and told us not to be afraid, that Pitts wouldn't hurt her. Cole couldn't take that. He moved in close to Pitts's stirrup, starting to plead with him. Pitts lashed out with his spurred boot, catching Cole, full-face, and ripping him like a saber blade. But the act took his gun off me, and I went up onto the wagon seat and jumped from it, at him. He got the Colt on me in mid-air. The big .44 bullet took me across the meat of my shooting arm, turned me half around, slammed me into his horse's ribs and down onto the ground. He never looked down at me but only yelled, *"Hee-yahh!"* at his horse, and took off leading poor little Jenni's mount behind him on the flat gallop.

They didn't get five jumps on the way to the woods.

Out of that heavy cover came a blasting of posse gunfire that drove Pitts out of his saddle and cut his horse down like it was both done with a mowing scythe. Cole, quick as a cat, ran out and grabbed Jenni off her loose horse and got her back to the wagon and wickiup, the posse not daring to fire, of course. But while he was doing it, I thought I saw a chance, and reached for Pitts's rifle lying on the ground. Out of the brush beside me came a spurred boot I recognized, kicking the gun away. The boot was followed by what was still in it, and its mate; Pitts was again on his feet, only lightly wounded, and having got back to the wagon while the posse was watching Cole and Jenni.

Now there was double hell to pay.

With Jenni put in the wickiup and me ordered in there to look to her, Cole and Pitts overturned the Swenlund wagon and, with the wounded Bob and Jim Younger crawling out to fort up back of it with them, put up a hard return fire, pinning the posse down just about as tight as the posse had them pinned down. Pretty quick a white handkerchief waved from a shotgun barrel across the way. Cole rasped, *"Slack off!"* to his comrades, and a silence thicker than swamp fog settled in.

"Mr. Nye," called a voice, "are you and Jenni Swenlund all right? This is Sheriff Glispin of Madelia."

"We're all right, Sheriff," I answered. "How many men you got?"

"Fifteen. Plus Dr. Berquist from Millersburg. Who are the men with you, other than Younger?"

"His two brothers, Bob and Jim, and Charlie Pitts."

"Will they surrender?"

I looked out at Cole, under the wagon. He shook his head.

"They say not," I replied.

"Well, will they permit you to bring out the Swenlund girl under a flag of truce?"

Again Cole shook his head, again I answered in negative.

"Do they mean to use the little girl as a hostage, then?"

"Yes, Sheriff, that's it I'm afraid."

There was a long, ominous pause then before Glispin spoke again. And when he did, the pause only got more ominous.

"All right, Mr. Nye," he said. "Do your best."

The last daylight was going. No sound came from the silent woods. Behind the overturned wagon, Bob and Jim Younger lay with their terrible wounds, but with rifles waiting for the posse to move. Out beyond the wagon a stride, Charlie Pitts lay up back of the dead horse. In the entrance of the wickiup, where he could watch everything, crouched Cole Younger. Darkness would be down in minutes. With it, they had a hairline chance to slip away. But Charlie Pitts, crazed and brutal as ever, could not wait. Leaving his dead horse, he got behind the wickiup without Cole seeing him. Next moment he had broken through its thin back-wall of brush and had his Winchester aimed between Cole's shoulder blades.

"You move," he said to the big Missourian, "I'll drill your backbone. You!" he snapped at me, "get that kid up and bring her over to me." I did it, as I had to. Pitts got a brawny arm around her little waist, lifted her off the ground, back to him, as a shield. Backing out of the wickiup, he stepped clear of it and the wagon. "Sheriff!" he yelled across at the posse, "I'm coming through. Get me a good horse ready. One funny move and the kid dies. You got ten seconds."

As he held up, waiting for Glispin's reply, Cole looked at me, nodded quickly, drew and handed me his revolver.

"All right, Yance," he said. "I'll take his attention; you try to come at him from behind. Good luck, old soldier."

"Cole," I answered, dead straight, "the same to you."

We went out, then, me through the back wall, him by the front opening. Pitts was through waiting for the Sheriff. He threw down his rifle, pulled his belt gun, put it to Jenni's head.

"All right, Sheriff!" he shouted, "I warned you!"

His yell was still echoing when Cole moved in on his left flank, stabbing just one word at him.

"Pitts!"

Charlie whirled to face him. Cole began walking slow toward him. Pitts fired into his big body, one, two, three shots, all plain hits. Cole kept coming. Pitts broke. He dropped Jenni and began to run blind. He picked the wrong way to go—straight into me. I came up from behind my bush and put five of the six slugs in Cole's gun into his belly. The jolt took him like sledge blows, driving him by steps clean back to the wagon, where he finally fell. It wasn't a shoot-out, it was an execution. When it was over, I walked up to where Cole was hunched down on the ground, cradling little Jenni in his arms. I stood there looking down at them.

After a minute, Cole glanced up and smiled tired-like. His own wounds, later found to be eleven bullets lodged in that bear's body of his, finally had him anchored. He could not get up, and had to hand Jenni up to me. I took her from him and said quietly, "So long, Cole."

He made a funny awkward little wave in reply. When he did, Jenni smiled and called back to him.

"Goodbye, 'Uncle Cole.'"

He winced like he'd been knifed. Then looked guilty to right and left, as though to make certain nobody had heard the kid, or was listening to him, or watching. Then he blew her a kiss with his huge paw and muttered roughly.

"Goodbye, little honey, goodbye."

He pulled out his old calico bandanna, the one he'd used to wipe the tears off Jenni's face in the Swenlund barn, and took a swipe at his powder-grimed eyes. He didn't even seem to realize he did it, but sat there staring off after us as we went toward the posse's line, as though he was seeing into another world, and a better one. Maybe he was, I never found out. When Jenni and me passed through the posse line, the firing began again, and I didn't wait to see the end of it.

Later, of course, my line of work being what it was, I did hear about it. It wasn't a good thing, any way you want to look at it, but I wonder just how bad it was, too.

Under Minnesota law of the day there couldn't be any death penalty. After weeks of suffering from their wounds, Jim, Bob and Cole were given life sentences in the state penitentiary at Stillwater. History will say they were outlaws, thieves and murderers. Well, maybe they were. It wasn't my job to say. But I know one little farm girl up near Millersburg who will give you a mighty big argument about one of those three condemned bandits. But, then, why not? He was a mighty big bandit. Thomas Coleman Younger. In my book, as in that little farm girl's, they don't come any bigger.

The Streets of Laredo

Call him McComas. Drifter, cowboy, cardsharp, killer. A man already on the road back from nowhere. Texas of the time was full of him and his kind. And sick with the fullness.

McComas had never been in Laredo. But his shadows, many of them, had been there before him. He knew what to expect from the townsfolk when they saw him coming on, black and weedy and beardgrown, against the late afternoon sun. They would not want him in their town, and McComas could not blame them. Yet he was tired, very tired, and had come a long, tense way that day.

He steeled himself to take their looks and to turn them away as best he might. What he wanted was a clean bed, a tub bath, a hotel meal and a short night's sleep. No women, no cards, no whisky. Just six hours with the shades drawn and no one knocking at the door. Then, God willing, he would be up in the blackness before the dawn. Up and long gone and safe over the border in Nueva Leon, Old Mexico, when that Encinal sheriff showed up to begin asking questions of the law in Laredo. They very last thing he wanted in Texas was trouble. But that was the very last thing he had ever wanted in any place, and the very first he had always gotten. In Laredo it started as it always started, everywhere, with a woman.

Still, this time it was different. This time it was like no trouble which had ever come to him before.

27

Somehow, he knew it. He sensed it before his trim
gelding, Coaldust, set hoof in the streets of Laredo.

Those border towns were all laid out alike. Flat
as a dropped flapjack. One wide street down the middle, running from sagebrush on one end to the river
on the other. Some frame shacks and adobes flung
around in the mesquite and catclaw, out where the
decent people did not have to look at them. Then, the
false fronts lining the main street. And, feeding off
that, half a dozen dirt allies lying in two lines on either
side like pigs suckling a sow asleep in the sun. After
these, there were only the church, school, and cemetery.
It was the latter place, clinging on the dryhill flanks of
the town, where the land was even too poor for the
Mexican shacks, that McComas and Coaly were presently coming to.

It lay to their left, and there was a burying party
moving out from town, as they moved in. McComas
had to pull Coaly off the road to let the procession pass.
For some reason he felt strange, and hung there to
watch the little party. It was then he saw the girl.

She was young and slim, with a black Spanish
reboza covering her head. As the buggy in which she
was riding with the frock-coated parson drew abreast
of McComas, she turned and stared directly at him.
But the late sun was in his eyes and he could not see
her features. Then, they were gone on, leaving Mc-
Comas with a peculiar, unpleasant feeling. He shook
as to a chill. Then, steadied himself. It was no mystery
that the sight had unsettled him. It was a funeral, and
he had never liked funerals.

They always made him wonder though.

Who was it in the coffin? Was it a man or woman? Had they died peaceful or violent? What had they
done wrong, or right? Would he, or she, be missed by
friends, mourned by family, made over in the local
newspaper, maybe even mentioned in the San Antonio
and Austin City papers?

No, he decided. Not this one. There were no
family and friends here. That girl riding in the preach-

er's rig wasn't anybody's sister. She just didn't have the look. And the two roughly dressed Mexican laborers sitting on the coffin in the wagon ahead of the buggy were certainly not kith or kin of the deceased. Neither was the seedy driver. As for the square-built man on the sorrel mare heading up the procession, he did not need the pewter star pinned on his vest to tag him for McComas. The latter could tell a deputy sheriff as far as he could see one, late sun in the eyes, or not.

The deputy could tell McComas too. And he gave him a hard looking over as he rode by. They exchanged the usual nods, careful and correct, and the deputy rode on, as any wise deputy would.

Directly, he led the buggy and the wagon into the weed-grown gate of the cemetery, and creaking up the rise to a plot on the crown of the hill. There, the drivers halted their horses, let down their cargoes. Still, Mc-Comas watched from below.

The two Mexicans strained with the coffin. It was a long coffin, and heavy. A man, McComas thought. A young man, and standing tall. One who had been taken quick, with no warning, and not long ago. No, this was no honored citizen they were putting under. Honored citizens do not come to boothill in the late afternoon with the town deputy riding shotgun over the ceremony. Nor with only a lantern-jawed, poor-bones preacher and a leggy young girl in a black Mexican shawl for mourners. Not by considerable.

McComas might even know the man in that cof-fin. If he did not, he could describe him perilously close. All he had to do was find the nearest mirror and look into it.

Again, he shivered. And again controlled himself.

He was only tired and worn down. It was only the way he felt about funerals. He always felt dark in his mind when he saw a body going by. And who didn't, if they would be honest enough to admit it? Nobody likes to look at a coffin, even empty. When there is somebody in it and being hauled dead-march slow with the wagon sounding creaky and the people not talking and the cemetery gates waiting rusty and half-sagged just down the road, a man does not need to be on the dodge and nearly drunk from want of sleep to take a chill and to turn away and ride on feeling sad and afraid inside.

In town, McComas followed his usual line. He took a room at the best hotel, knowing that the first place the local law will look for a man is in the second- and third-rate fleatraps where the average fugitive will hole up. Laredo was a chancey place. A funnel through which poured the scum of bad ones down into Old Mexico. If a man did not care to be skimmed off with the others of that outlaw dross, he had to play it differently than they did. He didn't skulk. He rode in bold as brass and bought the best. Like McComas and Coaly and the Border Star Hotel.

But, once safely in his room, McComas could not rest. He only paced the floor and peeked continually past the drawn shade down into the sun haze of the main street.

It was perhaps half an hour after signing the register, that he gave it up and went downstairs for just one drink. Twenty minutes more and he was elbows-down on the bar of the Ben Hur Saloon with the girl.

Well, she was not a girl, really. Not any longer.

Young, yes. And nicely shaped. But how long did a girl stay a girl at the Laredo prices? She was like McComas. Short on the calendar count, long on the lines at mouth and eye corners. If he had been there and back, she had made the trip ahead of him.

Pretty? Not actually. Yet that face would haunt a man. McComas knew the kind. He had seen them in every town. Sometimes going by in the young dusk on the arm of an overdressed swell—through a dusty train window at the depot—passing, perfume-close, in the darkened hall of a cheap hotel. Not pretty. No, not ever pretty. But always exciting, sensuous, female and available; yours for the night, if you could beat the other fellow to them.

Billie Blossom was that kind.

Her real name? McComas did not care. She accepted McComas, he did not argue Billie Blossom.

She came swinging up to him at the bar, out of the nowhere of blue cigar smoke which hid the poker tables and the dance floor and the doleful piano player with his two-fingered, tinkly, sad chorus of "Jeannie with the Light Brown Hair." She held his eyes a long slow moment, then smiled, "Hello, cowboy, you want to buy me a drink before you swim the river?" And he stared back at her an equal long slow moment, and said, "Lady, for a smile like that I might even get an honest job and go to work."

That was the start of it.

They got a bottle and glasses from the barman, moved off through the smoke, McComas following her. She had her own table, a good one, in a rear corner with no windows and facing the street doors. They sat down, McComas pouring. She put her fingers on his hand when he had gotten her glass no more than damp. And, again, there was that smile shaking him to his boottops.

"A short drink for a long road, cowboy," she said.

He glanced at her with quick suspicion, but she had meant nothing by it.

"Yes," he nodded, "I reckon that's right," and poured his own drink to match hers. "Here's to us," he said, lifting the glass. "Been everywhere but hell, and not wanting to rush that."

She smiled and they drank the whisky, neither of them reacting to its raw bite. They sat there, then, McComas looking at her.

She was an ash blonde with smoky gray eyes. She had high cheekbones, a wide mouth, wore entirely too much paint and powder. But always there was that half curve of a smile to soften everything. Everything except the cough. McComas knew that hollow sound. The girl had consumption, and badly. He could see where the sickness had cut the flesh from her, leaving its pale hollows where the lush curves had been. Yet, despite the pallor and the wasted form, she seemed lovely to McComas.

He did not think to touch her, nor to invite her to go upstairs, and she thanked him with her eyes. They were like a young boy and girl; he not seeing her, she not seeing him, but each seeing what used to be, or might have been, or, luck willing, still might be.

McComas would not have believed that it could happen. Not to him. But it did. To him and Billie Blossom in the Ben Hur Saloon in Laredo, Texas. They had the bottle and they had the sheltered corner and they were both weary of dodging and turning away and of not being able to look straight back at honest men and women nor to close their eyes and sleep nights when they lay down and tried to do so. No-name McComas and faded Billie Blossom. Outlawed killer, dancehall trollop. In love at first sight and trying desperately hard to find the words to tell each other so. Two hunted people locking tired eyes and trembling hands over a bareboard table and two unwashed whisky tumblers in a flyblown cantina at sundown of a hell's hot summer day, two miles and then minutes easy lope from freedom and safety and a second beckoning chance in Old Mexico, across the shallow Rio Grande.

Fools they were, and lost sheep.

But, oh! that stolen hour at sunset in that smoke-filled, evil-smelling room. What things they said, what vows they made, what wild sweet promises they swore!

It was not the whisky. After the first, small drink, the second went untasted. McComas and Billie Blossom talked on, not heeding the noise and coarseness about them, forgetting who they were, and where. Others, telling of their loves, might remember scented dark parlors. Or a gilding of moonlight on flowered verandas. Or the fragrance of new-mown hay by the riverside. Or the fireflies in the loamy stardust of the summer lane. For McComas and Billie Blossom it was the rank odor of charcoal whisky, the choke of stogie cigars, the reek of bathless men and perspiring, sacheted women.

McComas did not begrudge the lack. He had Billie's eyes for his starry lane, her smile for his summer night. He needed no dark parlors, no willow-shaded streams. He and Billie had each other. And they had their plans.

The piano played on. It was the same tune about Jeannie and her light brown hair. McComas feared for a moment that he might show a tear or a tremble in his voice. The song was that beautiful, and that close, to what he and Billie were feeling, that neither could speak, but only sit with their hands clasped across that old beer-stained table in the Ben Hur Saloon making their silence count more than any words. Then, McComas found his voice. As he talked, Billie nodded, yes, to everything he said, the tears glistening beneath the long black lashes which swept so low and thickly curled across her slanted cheekbones. She was crying because of her happiness, McComas knew, and his words rushed on, deeply, recklessly excited.

He did not remember all that he told her, only the salient, pressing features of it: that they would meet beyond the river when darkness fell; that they would go down into Nueva Leon, to a place McComas knew, where the grass grew long and the water ran sweet and a man could raise the finest cattle in all Mexico; that there they would find their journey's end, rearing a family of honest, God-fearing children to give the ranch over to when McComas was too aged and saddlebent to run it himself, and when he and Billie Blossom had earned their wicker chairs and quiet hours in the cool shadows of the ranchhouse *galeria,* "somewhere down there in Nueva Leon."

It went like that, so swift and tumbling and stirring to the imagination, that McComas began to wonder if it were not all a dream. If he would not awaken on that uneasy bed upstairs in the Border Star Hotel. Awaken with the sound of the sheriff's step in the hallway outside. And his voice calling low and urgent through the door, "Open up, McComas; it's me, and I've come for you at last."

But it was no dream.

Billie proved that to McComas when she led him from the table and pulled him in under the shadows of the stairwell and gave him the longest, hardest kiss he had ever been given in his life. And when she whispered to him, "Hurry and get the horses, McComas; I will pack and meet you in the alley out back."

McComas pushed across the crowded room, the happiest he had been in his lifetime memory. But he did not allow the new feeling to narrow the sweep of his restless eyes. Nor slow his crouching, wolflike step. Nor let his right hand stray too far from the worn wooden grip of his .44. He still knew his name was McComas, and that he was worth $500, alive or dead, to the Encinal sheriff and his La Salle County posse. It was the price of staying alive in his profession, this unthinking wariness, this perpetual attitude of *qui vive*. Especially in a strange town at sundown. With the hanging tree waiting in the next county north. And a long life and new love beckoning from across the river, from two miles south, from ten minutes away.

He went out of the batwing saloon doors, glidingly, silently, as he always went out of strange doors, anywhere.

He saw Anson Starett a half instant before the latter saw him. He could have killed him then, and he ought to have. But men like McComas did not dry-gulch men like Anson Starett. Not even when they wear the pewter star and come up on your heels hungry and hard-eyed and far too swiftly for your mind to realize and to grasp and to believe that they have cut you off at last. You do not let them live because they are gallant and tough and full of cold nerve. You do it for a far simpler reason. And a deadlier one. You do it for blind, stupid pride. You do it because you will not have it said that McComas needed the edge on any man. And while you do not, ever, willingly, give that edge away, neither do you use it to blind-side a brave man like Sheriff Anson Starett of Encinal.

What you do, instead, is to keep just enough of the edge to be safe. And to give just enough of it away to be legally and morally absolved of murder. It was a fine line, but very clear to McComas. It wasn't being noble. Just practical. Every man is his own jury when he wears a gun for money. No man wants to judge him-self a coward. All that has been gone through when he put on the gun to begin with. Perhaps, it was even what made him put on the gun to begin with. What did it matter now? Little, oh, very, very little. Almost nothing at all.

"Over here, Anse," said McComas quietly, and the guns went off.

McComas was late. Only a little, but he was late. He knew and damned himself, even as he spun to the drive of Starett's bullet, back against the front wall of the Ben Hur, then sliding down it to the board-walk at its base.

But he had gotten Starett. He knew that. The Encinal sheriff was still standing, swaying out there in the street, but McComas had gotten him. And, he told himself, he would get him again—now—just to make sure.

It took all his will to force himself up from the rough boards beneath him. He saw the great pool of blood, where he had fallen, but it did not frighten him. Blood and the terrible shock of gunshot wounds were a part of his trade. Somehow, it was different this time, though. This time he felt extremely light and queer in the head. It was a feeling he had never had before. It was as though he were watching him-self. As though he were standing to one side saying, "Come on, McComas, get up; get up and put the rest of your shots into him before he falls; drive them into him while he is still anchored by the shock of that first hit. . . ."

But McComas knew that he had him. He knew,

as he steadied himself and emptied the .44 into Starett,
that he had him and that everything was still all right.
But he would have to hurry. He could not stay there
to wait for Starett to go down. He had to get out of
there while there was yet time. Before the scared
sheep in the saloon get their nerve back and came
pouring out into the street. Before the sound of the
gunfire brought the local law running up the street
to help out the sheriff from Encinal.

He thought of Billie Blossom. . . . The good Lord
knew he did. But she couldn't do anything for him
now. . . . It was too late for Billie Blossom and gunfighter McComas. . . . They had waited and talked
too long. . . . Now he must get out. . . . He must not
let the girl see him hurt and bleeding. . . . She must
not know. . . . He had to get to his horse at the hitching
rail. . . . Had to find Coaly and swing up on him and
give him his sleek black head and let him go away up
the main street and out of Laredo. . . . Yes, he must find
Coaly at the rail . . . find him and get up on him and
run! run! run! for the river . . . just he and Coaly, all
alone and through the gathering dusk. . . .

He could not find Coaly, then. When he turned
to the hitching rail in front of the Ben Hur, his trim
black racer was not there. He was not where he had
left him, all saddled and loose-tied and ready to run.
McComas was feeling light and queer again. Yet he
knew he was not feeling that queer. Somebody had
moved his horse. Somebody had untied him and taken
him, while McComas was on the boardwalk from
Starett's bullet. Somebody had stolen Coaly and Mc-
Comas was trapped. Trapped and very badly hurt.
And left all alone to fight or die on the streets
of Laredo.

It was then that he heard the whisper. Then, that
he whirled, whitefaced, and saw her standing at the
corner of the saloon, in the alley leading to the back.
Standing there with a black Mexican *reboza* drawn
tightly over her ash blonde hair, shadowing and hiding
her hollow cheeks and great gray eyes. McComas could

not distinctly see her face. Not under the twilight masking of that dark shawl. But he knew it was her. And he went running and stumbling toward her, her soft voice beckoning as though from some distant hill, yet clear as the still air of sundown—*"Here, McComas, here! Come to my arms, come to my heart, come with me—!"*

He lunged on. Stumbled once. Went down. Staggered back up and made it to her side before the first of the murmuring crowd surged out of the Ben Hur to halt and stare at the great stain of blood spreading from the front wall of the saloon. The moment her white, cool hands touched him, took hold of him and held him up, he felt the strength flow into him again. The strength flow in and the queer cold feeling disappear from his belly and the cottony mist dissolve from before his straining eyes. Now he was all right.

He remembered clearly, as she helped him along the side of the cantina, looking down at his shirtfront and seeing the pump of the blood jumping, with each pulse, from the big hole torn midway between breastbone and navel. He remembered thinking clearly, "Dear Lord, he got me dead center! How could it have missed the heart?" Yet, he remembered, even as he heard his thought-voice ask the question, that these crazy things did happen with gun wounds. A shot could miss a vital by half a hair-width, and do no more harm than a fleshy scrape. There was only the shock and the weakness of the first smash, and no real danger at all unless the bleeding did not stop. And McComas knew that it would stop. It was already slowing. All he had to worry about was staying with Billie Blossom until she could get him to a horse. Then he would be able to make it away. He could ride. He had ridden with worse holes through him. He would make it. He would get across the river and he and Billie would still meet on the far side.

She had a horse waiting for him. He ought to have known she would, a girl like that, old to the ways of Texas strays and their traffic through the border towns. He should even have known that it would be his own horse, saddled and rested and ready to run through the night and for the river.

Yes, she had slipped out of the Ben Hur before the others. She had seen how it was with McComas and Anson Starett. And she had untied Coaly and led him down the alley, to the back, where McComas could swing up on him, now, and sweep away to the river and over it to the life that waited beyond. To the life that he and Billie Blossom had planned and that Anson Starett had thought he could stop with one bullet from his swift gun. Ah, no! Anson Starett! Not today. Not this day. Not with one bullet. Not McComas.

There was no kiss at Coaly's side, and no time for one.

But McComas was all right again. Feeling strong as a yearling bull. Smiling, even laughing, as he leaned down from the saddle to take her pale hand and promise her that he would be waiting beyond the river.

Yet, strangely, when he said it, she was not made happy.

She shook her head quickly, looking white and frightened and talking hurriedly and low, as she pressed his hand and held it to her wasted cheek. And the tears which washed down over McComas' hand were not warm, they were cold as the lifeless clay, and McComas heard her speak with a sudden chill which went through him like an icy knife.

"No, McComas, no! Not the river! Not while there is yet daylight. You cannot cross the river until the night is down. Go back, McComas. Go back the other way. The way that you came in this afternoon, McComas. Do you remember? Back toward the cemetery on the hill. You will be safe there, McComas. No one will think to look for you there. Do you hear me, McComas? Wait there for me. High on the hill, where you saw the open grave. You can watch the Laredo road from there. You can see the river. You can see the sheriff and his posse ride out. You can see when they are gone and when it is safe for you to ride out. Then we can go, McComas. I will meet you there, on the hill, by that new grave. We will go over the river together, when it is dark and quiet and all is at peace and we know no fear. Do you understand, McComas? Oh, dear God, do you hear and understand what I am telling you, my love——?"

McComas laughed again, trying to reassure her, and to reassure himself. Of course, he understood her, he said. And she was thinking smart. A sight smarter than McComas had been thinking since Starett's bullet had smashed him into that front wall and down onto the boardwalk. He got her calmed and quieted, he thought, before he spurred away. He was absolutely sure of it. And when he left her, turning in the saddle to look back as Coaly took him out and away from the filthy hovels of Laredo into the clean sweet smell of the mesquite and catclaw chapparal, he could still see her smiling and waving to him, slender and graceful as a willow wand moving against the long purple shadows of the sunset.

It was only a few minutes to the cemetery. McComas cut back into the main road and followed along it, unafraid. He was only a mile beyond the town but in some way he knew he would not be seen. And he was not. Two cowboys came along, loping toward Laredo, and did not give him a second glance. They did not even nod or touch their hat brims going by, and McComas smiled and told himself that it always paid to wear dark clothes and ride a black horse in his hard business—especially just at sundown in a strange town.

The rusted gates of the cemetery loomed ahead.

Just short of them, McComas decided he would take cover for a moment. There was no use abusing good luck.

Down the hill, from the new grave on the rise, were coming some familiar figures. They were the long-jawed preacher and square-built deputy sheriff he had passed earlier, on his way into Laredo. They might remember him, where two passing cowboys had shown no interest.

Up on the rise, itself, beyond the deputy and

the parson's lurching buggy, McComas could see the
two Mexican gravediggers putting in the last shovelfuls
of flinty earth to fill the fresh hole where they had
lowered the long black coffin from the flatbed wagon.
And he could see, up there, standing alone and slightly apart, the weeping figure of the young girl in the
black *reboza*.

McComas thought that was a kind, loyal thing for
her to do. To stay to say goodbye to her lover. To
wait until the preacher and the deputy and the gravediggers and the wagon driver had gone away, so that
she might be along with him. Just herself and God and
the dead boy up there on that lonely, rocky rise.

Then, McComas shivered. It was the same shiver
he had experienced on this same road, in this same
place, earlier that afternoon. Angered, he forced himself to be calm. It was crazy to think that he knew this
girl. That he had seen her before. He knew it was
crazy. And, yet—

The deputy and the preacher were drawing near.
McComas pulled Coaly deeper into the roadside brush,
beyond the sagging gates. The deputy kneed his mount
into a trot. He appeared nervous. Behind him, the
preacher whipped up his bony plug. The rattle of the
buggy wheels on the hard ruts of the road clattered past
McComas, and were gone. The latter turned his eyes
once more toward the hilltop and the head-bowed girl.

He did not want to disturb her in her grief, but
she was standing by the very grave where Billie Blossom had told him to meet her. And it was growing
dark and Billie had wanted him to be up there so that
he could see her coming from town to be with him.

He left Coaly tied in the brush and went up the
hill on foot. He went quietly and carefully, so as not
to bother the girl, not to violate her faithful sorrow.
Fortunately, he was able to succeed. There was another
grave nearby. It had a rough boulder for a headstone,
and a small square of sunbleached pickets around it.
McComas got up to this other plot without being seen
by the girl. He hid behind its rugged marker and tot-

tering fence, watching to be sure the slender mourner had not marked his ascent.

Satisfied that she had not, he was about to turn and search the Laredo road for Billie Blossom, when he was again taken with the strange, unsettling chill of recognition for the girl in the black *reboza*. This time, the chill froze his glance. He could not remove his eyes from her. And, as he stared at her, she reached into a traveling bag which sat upon the ground beside her. The bag was packed, as though for a hurried journey, its contents disordered and piled in without consideration. From among them, as McComas continued to watch, fascinated, the girl drew out a heavy Colt .41 caliber derringer. Before McComas could move, or even cry out, she raised the weapon to her temple.

He leaped up, then, and ran toward her. But he was too late. The derringer discharged once, the blast of its orange flame searing the *reboza*. McComas knew, from the delayed, hesitating straightness with which she stood before she fell, that it had been a death-shot. When he got to her, she had slumped across the newly mounded grave, her white arms reaching out from beneath the shroud of the *reboza* in a futile effort to reach and embrace the plain pine headboard of the grave. McComas gave the headboard but a swift side glance. It was a weathered, knotty, poor piece of wood, whipsawed in careless haste. The barn paint used to dab the deceased's name upon it had not even set dry yet. McComas did not give it a second look.

He was down on the ground beside the fallen girl, holding her gently to his breast so that he might not harm her should life, by any glad chance, be in her still.

But it was not.

McComas felt that in the limp, soft way that she lay in his arms. Then, even in the moment of touching her, the chill was in him again. He *did* know this girl. He knew her well. And more. He knew for whom she mourned; and he knew whose name was on that headboard.

It was then he shifted her slim form and slowly pulled the black *reboza* away from the wasted oval face. The gray eyes were closed, thick lashes downswept. The ash blonde hair lay in a soft wave over the bruised hole in the pale temple. It was she. Billie Blossom. The girl from the streets of Laredo.

McComas came to his feet. He did not want to look at that weathered headboard. But he had to.

There was only a single word upon it. No first name. No birth date. No line of love or sad farewell.

Just the one word:

"McComas"

He went down the hill, stumbling in his haste. He took Coaly out of the brush and swung up on him and sent him outward through the night and toward the river. It was a quiet night, with an infinite field of gleaming stars and a sweet warm rush of prairie wind to still his nameless fears. He had never known Coaly to fly with such a fleet, sure gait. Yet, swiftly as he went, and clearly as the starlight revealed the silvered current of the river ahead, they did not draw up to the crossing. He frowned and spoke to Coaly, and the black whickered softly in reply and sprang forward silently and with coursing, endless speed through the summer night.

That was the way that McComas remembered it.

The blackness and the silence and the stars and the rush of the warm, sweetly scented wind over the darkened prairie.

He forgot if they ever came to the river.

The Skinning of
Black Coyote

Tracy eased the little line-back dun out of her shuffle-walk and put her to a stiff lope. Ahead of him, three miles, the Big Bend of the Arkansas glinted dull silver in the brassy noon sun. Behind him, six miles off across a country flat as a spinster's chest and near as uninteresting, crawled the snaking line of Conestogas he was trail-guiding to Bent's Fort.

Tracy swept the wide valley of the Arkansas with constant quick-swinging glances as he let the mare take her own gait toward the river.

A big man, Tracy Higgins, lean as a weather-split hickory post and near onto as hard. About the same color, too. Tracy would allow his pedigree was as white as they came—but his history was something else again.

Snatched out of a burning log fortress up on the Medicine Road when he was a rising six-year-old, he'd been reared up by the same Oglala Bad Face band of Sioux that had put the flame to the frontier trading post of which his father had been chief clerk. Later, as a teen-age young one, looking a sight more the Oglala Bad Face he'd been reared than the Ohio Irish he'd been born, he'd taken to guiding wagon outfits from Independence and Kansas City to Bridger's Fort up by Salt Lake. With the booming of the Santa Fe trade, he'd switched trails and gone to work for Bent and St. Vrain, guiding freight outfits on the Santa Fe.

Right off he'd liked the New Mexico Trail a heap better than the old Medicine Road. The country was all new to him and the outfits were mostly small professional freight trains, like the one he had behind him right now. And the Santa Fe Trail had been a good one for Tracy. In three short seasons, he'd made stake enough to buy and load the bright new Conestoga that rumbled along in the train behind him.

And that big freight wagon meant the main heap to Tracy Higgins. His heart ought to have been high-noted as a meadowlark's morning song, just thinking about that wagon. With the profits from the trade-goods it carried, he would go into settled-down business and he and Dolores could finally say the words in front of old Father Junipero, at the church in Taos. *Que cosa feliz! Que bienaventurado!*

It had been a long wait, but one Tracy had insisted on. It was the pride he had in Dolores. He would only ask her hand as a solid merchant of the town. He would never do it while they still called him "that *Yanqui* squawman of a scout." Or said that he was "only a busted-down *gringo* wagon guide, with not *dos centavos* to clink together, let alone the gold-piece to pay the priest."

But that would be all in the past, this trip.

And for certain sure, Tracy Higgins ought to have been meadowlarking the prospect in his heart.

But he wasn't.

Right now Tracy was about as unhappy as he'd been in a long spell. Let a man tie up his whole future in a wagonload of goods, like he had his tied up in the last wagon of that train back there, and he was bound to run into a sign that would read unhappy to him.

Only yesterday, where they'd been mired in at Cow Creek, Tracy had picked up that sign. It was just a little thing, and mostly a scout wouldn't have paid any heed. After all, when you're in Indian country it sure isn't anything to find an old worn-out moccasin lying around a heavy-used crossing like Cow Creek.

Hell, the country from Turkey Creek on was crawling with Kiowa and Comanche.

Only trouble was, this wasn't any Comanche or Kiowa moccasin. It was Arapaho.

Tracy had been just as unsettled by that as if he'd spied a Comanche arrow broke off in a Powder River buffalo carcass. An Arapaho moccasin was that much out of place on Cow Creek in Kansas Territory. And it wasn't only the moccasin; looking around, he'd found other signs.

First off, there'd been a mess of them—upward of two hundred, way too many for just a hunting party. Then, the ashes of their cook fires hadn't cooled clear out at the time he'd dug into them. So they were a big bunch and they were close. That much was plain. But something else that he saw made his backbone bust out with pimply-flesh high enough to hang your hat on. This something else had a whale of a lot less right being smack-dab in the middle of an Arapaho campsite than the old moccasin.

It was a clean print of a big foot, the edges of the impression sharp-cut in the damp earth, the square toe and cross-cutting heel mark taking away all question of Indian origin.

That print was as plainly white as the crude cowhide boot that'd put it there. And the only set of boots with that peculiar toe cut that Tracy knew were anywhere within a hundred miles of Cow Creek were around the size-twelve stompers of Big Tate Barker.

The little additional thought that struck Tracy with such a peedinger of a wallop was that Big Tate just *happened* to be wagon-bossing the train that was following him right now!

What Big Tate had been doing in the Arapaho camp and how he had managed to get there without Tracy's knowing about it were the questions that turned on the restless spit of the scout's mind as he swung down off the dun mare and let her muzzle-out into the milky waters of the Big Arkansas.

The night before Cow Creek, they had camped at the Little Arkansas. It must have been sometime during that night that Big Tate had slipped out of camp and night-ridden to Cow Creek. Since it was a round trip of thirty-five miles, it must have taken the wagon boss the best part of the night. How in tarnation had he managed it without anybody wising up? What was he up to?

Crooking his mouth, Tracy made a sound in his throat that only an Indian or another frog could have detected from the dry "r-r-rack-rack! rack-rack!" of the little spotted frog found in any prairie wet spot bigger than a bucket.

Out of the stream, belly-deep in the five-mile current, the barrel-ribbed little mare left off her sucking at the opaque water, raised her keg-sized head, muzzle dripping, to stare at the talented six-foot croaker on the shore.

"Ho! Ye, Knaska! Come on outta thar. Ye've had yer gutful and we got ourse'fs some Arapaho to run down."

Knaska was the Sioux word for frog, and truly no horse could have been more aptly called. The dun mare was no more than thirteen hands, rib-sprung and bench-legged as a bulldog in front, broad-beamed and cow-hocked as a Holstein behind. She was unquestionably the ugliest mare ever foaled—and the fastest.

Swinging aboard her, the scout headed due west, up the right bank of the Arkansas. It was eight miles to Walnut Creek, their camp for that night. Tracy meant to scout every mile of the eight, up and back, before Big Tate got the wagons past the Arkansas.

The valley along Tracy's side of the river was broad and open, spotted here and there with a lone snaggle of a cottonwood, slashed occasionally by the low ridges of red clay and yellow sandstone. Otherwise, the two-inch buffalo grass was the only obstruction to limitless vision.

The other side of the stream was another story. Across there, the ridges became considerable bluffs, high and frequent enough to have hidden ten thousand Arapaho. It was these bluffs that the scout's worried gaze searched for the next two hours of his journey. But he didn't see so much as the wisp of a feather tip, or the sun-glance off a lance blade.

By the time he reached the fork where Walnut Creek spilled into the Arkansas, he was beginning to wonder if he'd plumb lost his "Injun Sniffer." And judging from his next actions, his smeller wasn't all he'd lost. Any man who'd been Oglala-raised that would go for a swim in midafternoon in the wide-open gut of hostile Indian country must have had a head as mushy as a scalped settler's.

But give a boy, be he two, twenty, or three times twenty, a long dusty ride ahead of where a pretty creek fork rambles into a fine wide river, the mixed waters running cool and chuckling over a clean sand bottom, and you've got yourself a swimming party.

It took Tracy maybe ten seconds to shuck out of his buckskins, crotch his Hawkens in a convenient cottonwood, turn the mare loose to graze, and splatter his hide into the Arkansas.

The first idea Tracy had that he wasn't the only human within shouting distance of the Arkansas was when a chance glance to check Knaska's whereabouts showed him the little mare standing tense and prick-eared.

Tracy made a great show of resuming his splashing and wallowing, but he threw one eye-corner look at the bank behind him. Instantly, every nerve in his body went catgut tight. The bank off which he'd plunged was about six feet high. Atop it grew the cottonwood whereon he'd so neatly draped his skins and hung his Hawkens. Two minutes before, that cussed cottonwood had been the loneliest tree in Kansas Territory. When he looked at it now, it was no longer so.

Sitting their shaggy ponies utterly motionless, gravely studying the antics of the naked white idiot in the Arkansas, were two dozen Arapaho braves. Those red sons were no friendlies! Their gargoyle

faces were smeared black with charcoal grease paste.
Blazing bands of ocher and vermilion slashed across
their broad cheekbones, zebra-striped their low fore-
heads, cornered their wide mouths.

They were in full headdress—lances, bows, ponies, and persons decked and hung with war feathers.
A hunting party would be plain-shirted, unfeathered.

One man stood out over all the rest. He was tall
and angular, sun-blacked, with a great flatboned face,
a tremendous jutting jaw, and an ear-to-ear knife slash
of a mouth; the whole adding up to about the rough-
est-looking redskin Tracy had ever seen. And Tracy
knew he had seen him before!

This beauty was no subchief, no local nabob.
The snow-flash of bonnet feathers, cascading down
his back and foaming across his pony's flank, trailed
almost to the ground—seven feet of them, a hundred
coup claims at least, maybe more. Where, oh, where in
the hell had he seen that face before?

For one detail and one alone, Tracy thanked his
trained eye: there hadn't been a gun visible in the passel
of them. These were bow-and-arrow and buffalo-lance
Indians. The fact gave Tracy his solitary chance for escape. Saying a desperate prayer to the Sioux gods of
his Oglala boyhood, the big wagon guide took that
chance. His method fascinated the Arapaho war party.

In the midst of the porpoise snorts and buffalo
bellows issuing from the white maniac in the river, now
came a series of spotted frog croaks. "R-r-r-rack, rack-
rack. R-r-r-rack, rack-rack."

The slit-eyed watchers on the shore nodded, the
one to the other. Very good imitation. Very creditable.
As skilled, almost, as an Indian's. They paid little
heed to the frog-headed pony ambling into the stream,
splashing through the hock-deep shallows toward her
master. This was a good situation. Cut just to size for
the red man's love of the dramatic. Just wait till this
white fool turned shoreward to retrieve his gun and
dress skins. Aii-ee! That would be the time. Let him
turn and look. Wait till then. Don't shoot now. Let his

eyeballs pop out along his cheekbones in terror. That was it. Hold the arrows till he turned around. Gently now, the mare is close to him. Don't hit her when he turns to see us. Be careful of the mare. We want her. So, so. Gently, now.

The minute Knaska came within hand's reach, Tracy went aboard her. His heels pistoned into her ribs, and the panther scream of the Oglala Sioux exploded in her pinned-back ears.

"Hiii-eee-hahhh!"

Ahead of Tracy, if he were to cross it, lay three-quarters of a mile of Arkansas—shallow, it was true, but as deep as four feet in places. And four feet was plenty deep to slow up Knaska enough to let the red scuts plumage-up his back with arrow feathers.

His best chance was downstream, and he took it. Swinging the mare hard left, he sent her buck-jumping down the shallows along the shelving bank.

He was in luck. All the Indians but one had plunged their ponies into the stream after him, and they could make no more speed than he. But that one, the snow-feathered chief, had sent his gaudy paint stud-horse pounding down the bank to cut Tracy off, when he came out of the stream. He was full-abreast of Tracy as the latter kicked Knaska in toward the bank.

As he came showering out of the water, Tracy got a split-second's relief from the fact that the chief's bow was not unslung. In its stead, the tall Arapaho brandished a polished hardwood skull cracker—a toy that was four feet long and crotched a six-pound cannon ball in its forked end.

Tracy had no course but to ride out and into the Arapaho, one way or another. He came out at an oblique angle, sheering away from the Indian's charging mount, as though in panic. The paint stud was nose-close to Knaska's rump in two jumps.

With both ponies going at a yellow-lather clip, the scout threw every ounce of his weight backward against Knaska's hackamore, literally pulling the mare's forefeet off the ground, haunch-sliding her to a stop that took half the skin off her hocks. The paint stud couldn't match it; his sliding stop carried him ten feet past Knaska, leaving him off-balance for all the time Tracy needed.

Before either chief or studhorse could recover and wheel, the scout drove Knaska crashing into the Indian pony's rump. It was a jarring, twisting impact, Knaska's right shoulder smashing into the stud's left haunch, sending the Indian pony hock-over-fetlock down the adjacent shelf bank of the Arkansas. Horse and chief cascaded into the swirling waters in a tangle of thrashing hoofs and wildly scrambling rider.

But the delay gave the other Arapaho time to get their ponies out of the river and galloping swiftly to the aid of their warchief. They very nearly caught the big white man. But again the old Oglala gods were with their adopted son. Neither the latter's scalp, nor his dreams of the dark-eyed Dolores, were just yet shortened.

Still, it was cold-sweat close.

Arrows were whistling close around Tracy when, in response to his inspired Sioux yelling, Knaska flattened out and belly-skimmed the short grama grass.

When the fall-off in the drumfire of the barefoot pony hoofs behind him and the increasing arc of the trajectory of the passing arrows let him know that Knaska had opened up breathing space between herself and her pursuers, he turned and shouted insults after the Indian fashion:

"*Wa klure! Wa klure!* Loafers! Loafers! *Nohetto, keyokas!* There you are, you clowns! *Canniyasa!* You are failures, all of you!"

The Arapahos set up a yammer of return coin for these insults, and Tracy sent them a parting gesture as readily translatable in the hand language of the Shacun as in that of their white brothers, the Wasicum. With the gesture, he gave out a last yell of defiance:

"Remember, who has done this to you, you dog-eaters. It is I, To-Ke-Ya, the Oglala. *Wagh!*"

It is the natural fortune of the Trail for those

hardy souls assigned to ride the head of a line of Santa Fe freighters—in this case the brooding giant, Tate Barker—to ride up on many a strange sight.

"Fer the luvva Gawd!" muttered Big Tate, reining in his horse and waving the wagons behind him to a halt. "That damned son of a Sioux musta go'd crazy."

There were grounds for the wagon boss's doubt of Tracy's sanity. Six-feet-two of heel-hammering white scout, aboard a bandy-legged yellow mare, belly-stretching to a flat gallop, with nothing between the two of them and the afternoon sunshine but a horse-hair hackamore and a saddle—it was enough to give the oldest prairie hand a pause.

"Whut in the name of hell happened to ye?" Big Tate shouted as Tracy haunch-slid the dun mare to a dirt-showering stop.

"I got jumped by a scout party of Arapaho. Up by Walnut Fork." Tracy talked fast. "I wuz takin' a swim jest below the Fork when they rode up on me. Lucky fer me I got this mare call-broke. I played dumb like I ain't seed them yet, whistled the mare up, and clumb aboard. They give me a run fer a space, but I had the most hoss under me."

"Waal, ye fer sure air a spectacle 'thout yer skins on. How many of the red scuts wuz thar?"

" 'Bout twenty braves, one real salty chief," Tracy answered.

"Whut'd the chief look like?"

Tracy noted Big Tate's sudden interest. He watched him narrowly, as he said: "Big devil. Tall fer a Injun. Broad, bony face. Biggest jaw I ever seen. White heron feather bonnet trailin' nigh into the dust. *Woyuonihan!* He was a real chief. *Wagh!*"

"Never heard of him." Big Tate's denial was short, but Tracy saw the quick shift of the pig eyes. "And quit gruntin' like a damn Sioux. I don't cotton to Injuns and I don't savvy their lingo."

Tracy had it in mind to call him a damned liar right there, but he hadn't lived with the Sioux ten years without he'd learned to run all the tracks out before he hollered his hand. Right now he had only two cards on Tate; he didn't aim to tip his mitt before the deal was done. "I 'low ye know enough of 'em to know thet a scout band in black grease and feathers totes up to trouble," he said, eyeing the wagon boss.

"How ye figger to be so sartin they wuz a scout band? Mebbe thet wuz all thar war of 'em," Tate scowled.

Tracy's mouth, wide as any Oglala's, clamped down tight. "As I come out'n the valley, I seen a cloud of riders headin' in toward Walnut Fork. Thar wuz a passel of 'em. I figger 'em fer the main bunch —two, three hundred of 'em, I'd say. Leastways enough so's we'll hafta corral-up at Big Bend 'stead of goin' to Walnut Crick."

"The hell you say!"

"The hell I don't. Ye roll this train a axle-turn past Big Bend and ye'll roll her agin my report."

"Waal, git out'n the way then, mister." Big Tate's face stiffened. " 'Cause I'm rollin' 'er!"

"Hold up a minute, Barker. I reckon ye didn't hear me. I said thar wuz a couple hundred hostiles foggin' around beyond Big Bend."

"I heered ye. We're makin' Walnut Crick tonight."

"That ain't time. It'll darken on ye 'fore ye kin git camped."

"Whut of it? Ye ain't afeered of Injuns, be ye?"

"Ye damned betcha. How 'bout ye?"

"Me, I'm tellin' ye we're makin' the Crick tonight. I got a schedule."

Tracy looked at him long enough to wear down a lesser he-bear than Big Tate Barker. "I 'low ye have," he said, "but I reckon it ain't the one Bent and St. Vrain give ye."

The big man went stiff all over. "Ye peep one word 'bout them Injuns to the skinners and I'll gut-shoot ye. I aim to git up to Walnut Crick tonight, and I don't mean to have ye gittin' my drivers all jumped-up 'bout a war party trailin' us. Ye understand thet, damn ye?"

Tracy felt the anger in him well up, but when he spoke, his drawl was as pleasant as a May breeze. "I 'low I do, Mr. Barker. Mebbe-so a lot better than ye think."

He saw Tate flinch as the hook went into him, and he knew that he'd declared a war that could end just one way—with one of them no longer enjoying the privilege of sucking good air into live lungs.

They made Walnut Fork a good hour after dark. Big Tate said not a word to the company about the hostiles, letting a normal camp be set up, including carelessly bright cook fires and just the regular two-hour guard shifts.

The camp got quiet about ten, the fires going to pinpoint coals about eleven. Half an hour later, Tate rolled out of his blankets, listened intently, came noiselessly to his feet, and drifted out toward the loose herd of saddle stock.

Behind him, Tracy Higgins glided on a pair of feet that had learned to step quiet where a noise as big as a mouse's breathing might mean the difference between whether a man's hair was worn or torn.

At the edge of the horse herd, Big Tate paused, whistling low and easy in as perfect an imitation of a sleepy whippoorwill as Tracy had ever heard. When he heard the horse's answering whicker, the scout knew how Tate had worked the Cow Creek slip—and knew also, he had a very scratchy customer to accompany.

He let Tate mount up and get a start before following him, dogtrotting on moccasins that hit the earth as loud as fat snowflakes.

After ten minutes of powder-footed going, Tracy had worked in to where he was a bare twenty yards behind the sound he trailed—the muffled plop-plop of a shod horse going in deep dust. For another five minutes the sound continued, then stopped. Tracy waited a dozen slow breaths, then started working in closer. Finding a proper gully, he slid into it and poked his eyes above the lips. Beyond there, easily seen in the starlight, Big Tate sat his horse, waiting. This must be the place of the meeting—if there was going to be one.

A bull bat twittered harshly out on the prairie: Big Tate answered it. Ear to the ground, Tracy picked up the shuffle-walking approach of several barefoot ponies. In another few seconds, their shadows bulked up out of the darkness and halted some yards out from the waiting wagon boss.

A single shadow detached itself and drifted up to Tate. Tracy recognized the rider. It was the chief he'd dumped in the river.

"Ha-a-u!" called the Arapaho, softly, his tones as deep and guttural as a muttering bear's. "We meet again."

That voice! Once heard a voice like that was remembered. Watan-goa, the Black Coyote! Tracy had seen him in a dozen boyhood war camps. *Aiieee!* A man would almost rather have any hostile on his hands than this one. *Woyuonihan. A-ah!* Respect this one. Look out for him!

"Ha-a-u," answered Big Tate. "Is your heart good?"

"Our hearts are good. Watan-goa's heart is good. We are ready. When we talked at the Creek of the Cows, you told us that one goddam in your train carried big medicine for Watan-goa."

In his gully, Tracy had to smile at that "goddam." It was the Plains Indian's name for the Conestogas, taken from the favorite word of their cursing white drivers.

"I told ye right," growled Big Tate. "Thet goddam is totin' the biggest medicine that is."

"How big?" grunted the Arapaho in impatient tones.

"Mazawakan," snapped Big Tate. "Plenty *mazawakan.*"

Tracy's hair lifted again. *Mazawakan.* Holy irons. Rifles! God Almighty! Guns! So Big Tate was running guns. But where were they? Tracy knew the goods in that caravan. He'd seen the loading in Independence.

There wasn't a gun set aboard any of the wagons, to his knowledge. Where the hell did Tate have them, then?

"How many?" Watan-goa's question came hard and hoarse.

"We have dealt before," answered Big Tate. "Our hearts are good. Ye will do as I say with the *mazawakan?*"

"*Ha-a-u.* I will do it."

"Ten *mazawakan* fer ye, Chief, if you do your part," Tate said.

"How many all *mazawakan?*" the Arapaho wanted to know.

Tracy sensed Big Tate's hesitation and, knowing Indians, appreciated it. They were harder to hold to a deal than an axle-greased eel.

"A hundred," said the wagon boss finally.

"Good. What does Watan-goa do?"

"Ye take the guns to Pawnee Rock. I'll meet ye thar in three suns and we'll make the divvy. Ten *mazawakan*, ye. The rest, me. Is it agreed?"

"It is agreed. Where *mazawakan* now?" Tracy thought the chief's assent came too fast and wondered how Big Tate had the guts to try a deal like that with Watan-goa. Apparently, the wagon boss knew the Black Coyote better than Tracy did. He himself wouldn't trust the slit-eyed devil any farther than he could pitch a bull buffalo.

"Ye know thet big goddam with the red wheels? The bright blue one? The spankin' new one?".

Tracy's hair was getting used to standing up. His Conestoga was the only *new* one in the caravan. Its wheels were as red as saddle sores, its bed as blue as a summer sky.

"*Ha-a-u.* The one that eats the dust?"

"Ye got it. Thet's the one. The last one in the line. Waal, it's loaded with five thousand pounds of bolt calico—" Tracy silently amended the boss's figure. Five thousand, two hundred and fifty pounds. He ought to know, by God. He'd paid for every pound.

"—but it's carryin' six thousand pounds, now. That's a hundred ten-pound rifles in thar, as wasn't when she rolled from Independence."

"Ha-a-u! Ha-a-u!"

"Me and Taos McFarland, the skinner whut's drivin' thet blue goddam, loaded 'em in on the sly at Council Grove. Now, air ye all straight on whut ye do tomorry?"

"Watan-goa remembers well, but would hear once more."

"All right. In the mornin' we cross the crick early. The new goddam will cross first, 'stead of last. I'll be drivin' the second goddam, and I'll mire her in the middle of the crick, so's the other wagons cain't get past me. That'll hold 'em up long enough fer ye to do yer work. Soon's ye see me stuck, ye jump the first goddam, grab the guns, and skee-daddle. Ye got thet, now?"

"Ha-a-u. It is clear."

"All right, then. Ev'eything's all set?"

"No." The chief's disagreement was quick and blunt.

"Whut the hell's the matter?"

"The scout. The Wasicun who calls himself To-Ke-Ya, the Fox, and who speaks with the tongue of the Cut-Throat People. What of him? He is a warrior. What of this one?"

"Don't worry 'bout the Sioux cub. He's goin' to git his 'fore we roll in the mornin'."

"How will this happen?"

"In the mornin' I'll accuse him of dealin' with the Injuns to jump the train. The boys'll buy the bluff on account of him comin' in naked yestiddy with thet yarn 'bout bein' jumped by your war party. When he talks back I'll gut-shoot him. Thet satisfy ye?"

"Ha-a-u," growled Black Coyote. "Good hunting."

Tracy had heard plenty more than enough. Even as the Arapahos faded back into the darkness out of which they'd come and Tate headed his horse around, he was legging it for camp as fast as his long limbs would take him.

When Big Tate snuck back into the darkened camp, he found Tracy rolled in his blankets tight as a tick in a dog's tail. Weary from his own two nights of night riding, the big man lost no time getting into his own bedroll. In seconds, he was snoring fit to shake the lice out of his blankets.

Tracy waited a full hour, and when, at last, he rolled out of his blankets, midnight was far past. When he went cat-footing it through the dark toward Big Tate's bedding ground he carried three objects of tangible value. Item One: a beltful of buckskin laces, three feet long and strong as a boar grizzly's gut. Item Two: two small squares of soft, mending doeskin. Item Three: a short-barreled Ames Navy Pistol, model of 1843, just the thing for sapping hard heads on dark nights.

Big Tate was breathing a little rough when Tracy moved in over him, but following the soft "tunk" of the pistol butt behind his ear he relaxed into a rhythm as nice and easy as a breast-fed baby's. In twenty seconds, the scout had gagged and trussed him neat as a suckling pig ready for the roaster.

With the remaining scrap of doeskin and the unused laces, Tracy faded away toward his own wagon. Taos McFarland, the breed mule skinner he'd hired-on to drive his wagon, was ventilating his tonsils as thunderously as Tate had been. Tracy had to grin as he thought back to how he'd asked the wagon boss to recommend a skinner and Big Tate had steered him onto Taos McFarland. Perhaps the memory sped the pistol hand, for the swinging butt of the Ames cracked into the side of the sleeping teamster's skull with a smack that nigh knocked him clean out of his blankets. For a bad mintue Tracy thought he'd killed him, but Taos started to breathe again after a spell, and the scout stuffed the doeskin in his mouth and tied him, hard.

Slinging the inert form over his shoulder, Tracy started back toward Tate.

"Whut the hell's goin' on 'round h'yar?" Tracy recognized the complaining voice, testy with years, as that of old Dan Masters, dean of the Bent and St. Vrain teamsters. "Sounds like a couple of buffalo wuz breedin' or suthin'."

"It's me, Dan." Tracy's voice was low. "Tracy Higgins."

"Waal, what the tarnal hell ye doin'? Holdin' a war stomp?"

"Dan, lissen. We got big trouble. Git the rest of the boys and meet me over by Tate's bedroll. No lights and no noise. And move fast!"

"Whut's up?" Too long on the South Trail, Dan Masters, to be stampeded by a nervous wagon scout.

"We got a couple hundred Injuns layin' fer us to cross Walnut Fork in the mornin'."

"What Injuns?"

"Arapaho."

"'Rapaho? The hell ye say. Who's headin' 'em?"

"Black Coyote."

"I'll git the boys," was all the old man said, and Tracy, nodding, carried Taos's body on over to dump it alongside Tate's.

In ten minutes the skinners had all come up. Tracy let them have it, short. "Boys, I got Tate and Taos trussed up h'yar and I 'low ye're all hankerin' to know whut in tunket's goin' on. This bear-brain, Tate, him and this yaller breed, Taos, wuz fixin' to let us get our sculps lifted."

"The hell!"

"The hell, yes. Lissen. Last night Tate snuck ahaid up to Cow Crick to palaver with a big bunch of Arapaho thet war camped thar. Then he snuck back into camp 'thout ennybody seed him. Waal, tonight he snuck out and palavered with the same bunch again. I follered Tate and heered him talk to the chief. It war the same redskin I knocked into the river this afternoon. I didn't remember him then, but soon's I heered his voice tonight, I did."

"Yeah? Who wuz it? Whut chief?" The interruption came from one of the teamsters.

"Watan-goa!" snapped Tracy.

"Black Coyote!"

"The one and only. Now, git this. Tate and this h'yar Taos McFarland snuck in a hundred rifles at Council Grove. They loaded 'em in *my* wagon. Tonight I heered Tate dealin' with Watan-goa to turn them guns over to him, on a percentage."

Short and sweet, then, he gave them the whole dirty deal.

"Whut ye aim to do 'bout it, Tracy?" Old Dan acted as spokesman for the teamsters.

"I got a leetle scheme that might pollute Black Coyote's taste fer free guns fer some spell to come. But first I gotta know whether all of ye believe my side. Tate's gonna claim I'm the Sioux-raised black in this red woodpile. Jest like I told ye he done told Black Coyote he wuz fixin' to do. Tate's woke up now from thet tap I give him. I'm gonna cut his mouth loose and let him talk."

"Hold up, thar." Old Dan's voice was quick. "Iffen ye free his flap he jest as apt to yell out to his red friends. Me, fer one, I buy yer yarn. Happen I warn't sleepin' well thet night back thar at the Leetle Arkansaw, afore Cow Creek. I seen Tate ride out and I seen him ride back. He war gone most of the night."

The old man's support was enough for the others. One after another they spoke up.

"Yeah, the hell with it. Leave his yap stuffed."

"Sure, leave him be the way he is."

"He ought to be kilt outright."

"No," Tracy broke in. "I 'low we ain't gonna kill him. We'll let the Arapahos do thet."

"Whut ye mean? How's yer idee work?" Old Dan was questioning again.

"Waal, she shapes up thisaway. As long as them Injuns knows 'bout them guns, they'll come arter us,

Tate er no Tate. Ye all see it thetaway?" A chorus of quick agreement ran around the invisible ring of listeners.

"All right then. I figger it like this. Long as Tate and Taos was fixin' to delivry them guns, I reckon we'll let 'em. After all Black Coyote's bin give the white man's word on the deal and we gotta make good on it. Let's put thet first wagon over the Crick and stick the second one in the crossin', jest like Tate promised them. We'll have them guns in thet first wagon, accordin' to the agreement. When old Watan-goa shows up to claim 'em, why we'll jest let 'em have 'em, thet's all. Is thet clear 'nough?"

"It's beginnin' to be!" Old Dan's dry chuckle was picked up and spread quickly among the other mule skinners. "And I 'low if we delivry them Holy Irons to the Injuns like ye aim to delivry 'em, we got a mort of wagon reloadin' to do 'fore daylight."

"Yeah." Tracy's assent was laconic. "And we ain't got more'n a hour of plumb dark left to us."

"Ye and the boys go to it. I'll set h'yar and wet-nurse these infants fer ye." Old Dan's tones were as easy as Tracy's. "Ye'd best leave me thet Iron Medicine ye give 'em afore, case they git to needin' another dose of head-slappin' 'fore mornin'."

By 4:30 A.M., the last of the reloading of the smuggled rifles was done. The ghost-grey of predawn was putting its sick tinge along the rim of the prairie as Tracy and Dan Masters squatted by the off-wheel of the lead wagon.

The Conestogas still stood in their hollow square, tongues out like they'd been part the night before. Nothing had been moved, with one peculiar exception. Every wagon stood team-hitched, its three span of patient mules full-harnessed, ready to roll. A mighty close eye, given broad daylight, could have seen one other thing: the lead team in each hitch was picketed down, hard and fast.

There was riskful reason for that; all of the wagons except for the lead-off pair of Conestogas involved in Tate's original deal with Watan-goa, plus a third decoy wagon, were to stay right where they were—parked and picketed, in camp—when the three bait vehicles rolled for Walnut Fork crossing, with murky first light of day.

It was the one rut in the smooth track of Tracy's plan, but there was no way around it. The mule drivers who would ordinarily have been guiding those twenty-three Conestogas had something tougher than a mule to skin that morning. They had a coyote. A black one. Name of Watan-goa.

The minutes were crawling after one another so slow you could almost hear them sucking their feet out of the mud of that last half-hour. The start had to be just right: enough light to see an Arapaho across an iron sight, not enough for an Arapaho to see tie ropes and picket pins across a creek.

"I 'low we wuz all-fired lucky to git onto Tate 'fore he let them red sons down on top of us." Old Dan's whisper jumped a little with understandable Indian-nerves. "Onct they had them guns they'd never hold up at jest runnin' off with 'em. Not with all thet powder and shot we found Tate had cached in yer wagon along with 'em. Them Injuns would've had 'nough ammunition to smoke us deeper than a Mizzouri ham."

"They won't hold up, ennyways, even *not* knowin' 'bout the powder and slugs. Bow and errer Injuns'll do ennything to git a gun. We wuz lucky, all right, to git on top of Tate. But we'll be a damn sight luckier if we git out from under Watan-goa."

Tracy was silent a long minute, listening intently. "Whut'd ye hear?" asked Dan, tensely.

"Shet up!" whispered the scout. "I thought I heered Injuns talkin'." In answer to his statement, a fox barked sharply, about three hundred yards up the creek. Its mate yapped back from an equal distance downstream. Out on the plains, directly across the little stream, the sleepy pee-weet, pee-weet! of a prairie plover made known its owner's awakening. The querulous whirring chuckle of a disturbed prairie hen answered the plover.

"It's light enough." Tracy's announcement came abruptly. "Let's roll."

The two figures arose, slipping along the sides of the wagons, away from the creek. At the third Conestoga, Old Dan climbed up and took the reins. "All set, Tracy."

"Ye got it straight, now?"

"I'm to wait till the second wagon starts into the crick, then come on along like I wuz leadin'-off the remainin' wagons."

"Thet's right. Don't stall too long 'fore ye start, er happen they'll smell a mouse."

Leaving the old man, Tracy returned to the second Conestoga. On the seat, bolt upright, by virtue of a four-foot Hawkens' barrel planted in his kidneys, sat Big Tate Barker. The owner of the Hawkens crouched under the canvas sheeting of the wagon cover, just back of the driver's seat, hidden from all but the most inquiring eye.

"All set, h'yar?"

The rifleman nodded as Tracy loomed up. "Good." The scout's answering nod was hurried. Flicking his grey eyes from the hidden rifleman to the ramrod figure on the driver's seat, he went on. "Now remember, Tate, yer feet air strapped onto thet brake-bar and ye've got a Hawkens set in yer back ready to separate yer spine if ye even breathe wrong. Ye drive this wagon spang into the middle of the crick and hold her up thar, exactly like ye told Black Coyote ye would. Thet's all ye do. Not another damn thing. Ye got it?"

The glowering wagon boss licked his lips and muttered thickly, "I got it, Higgins, but lissen. I ain't got a chancst settin' up h'yar like a damn pigeon. They'll—"

"Hey! Ye, in the wagon, thar—" Tracy ignored Tate.

"Yessir, ye betchy!"

"One eyewink out'n this overgrowed slob on the

seat and ye leave him have it 'tween the liver-lights and the kidneys."

"I gotchy."

"All right," snapped Tracy, "we're goin' acrost."

At the lead wagon, his own bright Conestoga, Taos McFarland was sharing Tate's role, feet lashed to the brake-bar, a rifle barrel from inside the covered wagon none too gently nudging the backside of his pelvis. "Ye know whut to do now, Taos? Jest drive her acrost and up onto the flat over thar. Ye foul up in enny way and ye'll git yer bottom blowed off."

The fear-sick breed, too miserable to find his tongue, nodded like a dumb thing that didn't have any. Stepping up on the near-wheel, Tracy leaned into the interior of the wagon, talking through the puckered hole in the Osnaburg sheeting just back of the seat. "Ye all set in thar?"

"All set in h'yar, Mr. Higgins." The answer came cheerily from the man holding the Hawkens in Taos's back.

"Waal, then, h'yar goes to delivry them hundred guns to brother Watan-goa!"

The Conestoga took off with a jangle of trace chains that was all but drowned out by Tracy's roar to the rest of the wagons: "All set! All set! Stretch out! Stretch out! Hooray fer Santy Fee!"

Tate's wagon lumbered into motion, following the track of the one driven by Taos. By the time Old Dan was shouting and lash-popping his teams into their collars, the breed's wagon was lurching and hulking up the far bank of the creek. Behind it, Tate was just carefully heading his mules into the water. In the sand hills beyond the crossing, not a noise louder than a grass sparrow's chirrup was heard. The whole prairie lay as still and as peaceful looking as a clear lake bottom on a quiet day.

Now! Tate had his teams stopped as ordered in midstream. Taos McFarland was already ten yards out on the prairie beyond the crossing, with Tracy's bright blue Conestoga.

Tracy put his heels into Knaska's ribs fit to knock the wind out of her. The clay-colored mare shot into the creek toward Tate's stalled wagon. As if on signal, the sand hills beyond began puking out more Arapahos than there were wheel spokes in the whole caravan.

The warriors—upwards of one hundred fifty of them—bore down directly upon Taos McFarland and the brightly painted Conestoga of Tracy Higgins. They knew the guns were in that blue wagon, and it was like the taste of blood in their mouths. They were right about the guns, but the blood was more than a taste, more than merely in their mouths.

As the wild horsemen rushed up, the halted Conestoga shed its white canvas top like some great red-wheeled rattlesnake. Inside the wagon's bed were crammed all twenty-three of the mule-drivers who the red men believed were still with the wagons in the camp across the stream. And each of the teamsters was firing one of the smuggled rifles point-blank into the faces of the massed Indian riders.

The Arapaho began to fall like strychnined sheep.

Even as Tracy leaped to the driver's seat of Tate's wagon, in midstream, he saw the terrible harvest of the teamsters' rifle fire strewn about his own wagon on the far bank. Seizing the reins from Tate, the big scout sent the snorting mules out of the stream and up the bank, toward the blue Conestoga. He reached it just as the Arapaho, shouted on by Watan-goa, came storming back at the wagon-borne white marksmen.

Their second try was better than the first, half a dozen of them actually scrambling into the wagon bed of the blue Conestoga. But twenty-plus salt-tanned mule skinners, with a hundred new rifles stacked and loaded to hand, could down a sinful lot of redskins, especially when they had them so close they could practically spit them to death.

With a brevity of decision that spoke well for his reputation as a field commander, Watan-goa suddenly remembered a previous engagement elsewhere, and he led his surviving followers in a retreat that was aimed at piling up as many sand hills as possible back of the flying heels of the last pony.

There were five injured mules and three still-crawling savages left over. These were quietly singled out and humanely shot—the mules first, as befitted their prior places in the hearts of the skinners.

Taos McFarland had got himself mortally gut-wounded with four arrows, and he was dumped into the empty Conestoga to wait for the end that had come with so much more mercy to the seventeen red brothers sprawled on the ground around the lead wagon.

Then the skinners waded back across the creek to drive the rest of the wagons over before gathering around Tracy's Conestoga to hold a Trail Court over Big Tate Barker.

Tracy made the winning proposal.

"I 'low," he announced soberly, "we ain't none of us got no right to set ourse'fs up to votin' no man's life away in cold blood. If we go to blowin' the back of Tate's haid off, it'd be jest plain murder. Ain't no other name fer it. And me, I won't take a hand in no sech a deal. Ner will I set still fer nobody else tryin' it. We've give Tate a fair trial, and I 'low we're goin' to give him a fair sentence."

"Whut ye aim to do, Tracy?" Old Dan sounded anxious. "Ye cain't jest turn a hydrophoby skunk like Tate loose."

"Thet's precisely whut I aim to do, Dan'el."

"By God, Tracy, ye ain't a gonna do it. We won't stand fer it. Tate's gotta git whut's comin' to 'im!" Several of the others were alongside the old man, muttering rough assent to his demurrer.

Tracy's interruption stopped the muttering. "Look over thar on thet sand hill," he said, quietly. "Thet low, red un, past thet yeller saddleback—"

The men, following the scout's pointed arm, broke into a running fire of oaths.

Lining the crest of the sandstone ridge, black

against the morning sun, the Arapahos sat their ponies, not even the stir of a prairie breeze to ruffle the hardcut profile of their motionlessness. Even at the distance, the tall figure and seven-foot warbonnet of Watan-goa picked him out from his fellows.

"Dad blame my hide!" cried Dan. "I thought them red scuts would be in Wyomin' by now!"

"No, they ain't gone and they won't be, till we trail into Bent's Fort." Tracy's answering drawl was slow with thought. "In the meantime they ain't gonna hit us agin. Ye kin tie on thet. But whut they'll do is foller us—they'll foller us all the way—every step."

"Waal, whut's thet got to do with Tate?"

Tracy let his eyes wander along the distant ridge. "Oh, nothin' in particular. I wuz jest thinkin' mebbe-so Watan-goa might have a few questions to ask Tate 'bout whut went wrong with the gun delivry. Seein's how Tate set the deal up with the chief in the first place, I wuz figgerin' the fairest thing we could do fer him would be to give him the chancst to explain the sitchyashun to Watan-goa. The best way to arrange thet is jest to turn Tate loose."

For a long minute there was silence. Finally Old Dan spoke up, his narrowed eyes watching Tracy, his tones caustic. "I thought ye wuz agin murder."

"It ain't murder," said the young scout, quietly, "so long as we don't pull the trigger."

Old Dan nodded thoughtfully. "I 'low ye got a point, Tracy. Fer a minute thar, I thought ye'd gone soft."

"Like a mule's mouth," said a dark-bearded Texas skinner. "Whut'd'ye say, boys? Shall we let Higgins talk us into showin' Tate the Christian mercy of turnin' 'im loose? I'm fer it. Me, personal, I cain't stand to do no cold-blood harm to a feller white man."

A grunted chorus of agreement was the Texan's answer, and as soon as it came, Tracy stood up.

"If thet's the way you vote it, boys, thet's the way it's gonna be. Let's get set and stretch the hell out of h'yar. We got nineteen miles to roll to Ash Creek, and I aim to boil my coffee thar tonight!"

"Hee-yahh!" the Texas skinner answered, going for his wagon. "You heard Mr. Higgins, boys; roll 'em out fer Santy Fee—!"

And that, Bent's Fort folklore insists, was the way in which Tracy Higgins parlayed seventeen dead Indians, a hundred smuggled rifles, his Irish luck, and one dark-eyed Spanish damsel named Dolores into the mercantile firm of J. T. Higgins & Sons, Santa Fe, "Freighters to the Entire Southwest Territory & the Coasts of California."

There was nothing to it, Tracy always said.

If God was on a man's side, he could thrash grizzly bears with wet thread tied to toothpicks.

Or, coming to that, skin a black coyote at Walnut Fork of the main Arkansas River.

With nothing but his bare brains.

And a bit of Oglala persuasion.

For Want of a Horse

Through the prairie dusk the five riders approached Hatpin, Kansas. Hatpin was a waterstop on the Missouri & Western mainline between Kansas City and Denver. The mounted men were wary but confident, old professionals all: Clell Miller, Charlie Pitts, Bill Chadwell, Frank and Jesse James. These were the Missourians, the raiders of Lawrence and Centralia, Kansas, and the latter state was enemy territory to them. But the stakes were high this night—$35,000 in unsigned banknotes aboard train number 1608, due through Hatpin at twelve midnight.

The plan to take number 1608 was Jesse's, naturally.

The blinking-eyed killer maintained there was no risk whatever, in the hard terms by which he and his men defined the word, and that it would be the perfect job.

There was no law worth worrying about within a hundred miles. Escape lay open to every point of the prairie compass. Their matchless Missouri thoroughbreds were fresh and eager to run. The beautiful animals moved impatiently beneath them, wanting to go, to race the wind and beat it. But Frank James was nervous nonetheless, and was beginning to show it. He kept looking around through the gusty twilight. Licking his lips repeatedly. Shifting in the saddle every few rods of their advance. His uneasiness got to the watchful Jesse.

"You turning hunchy on us again, Frank?" he

demanded. "Why, this here rube town is as easy to kick over as a dry buffler chip. Now, slack off. I've got her all figured."

"Could be," admitted Frank, glancing around once more. "I remain saying she's too still all about. I don't trust these jawhawk farmers. It smells to me like they've got us spotted. I mean it, Jess."

"Sure you do." Jesse nodded. "But quit your squinching around, will you? You're getting the others edgy. Besides, Buck, who do we know in Hatpin, Kansas?"

"Ain't the question, Dingus." Frank frowned, returning the exchange of boyhood nicknames. "Question is, who might know *us* in Hatpin, Kansas?"

"Hell," said Jesse softly. "That could hold for any town in a thousand miles. Keep moving easy."

They were into the deep dust of Main Street now, only a hundred yards out from the town's first buildings. "Bill," said Jesse to Chadwell, "start whistling. You, Charlie, you and Clell get to talking out loud enough to be heard. We don't want anybody thinking we're dishonest."

They were among the buildings. The street, ahead and behind, seemed deserted. Here and there a cracked window reflected a greasy halo of inner lamplight. But no soul was on Main Street. It was spooky. Only the faint jingle of their own bit and spur chains, the squeak of their saddle fenders, the snuffling and blowing of their slender thoroughbreds, accompanied their passage of the town heading out for the railway depot at street's end.

"Damn!" muttered Jesse. "We'd best spread out."

Frank nodded and threw a hand signal to the three men behind. The latter unbooted their carbines, reined mounts wide to cover the station as flankers, Frank and Jesse riding on in to the hitchrail below the raised baggage platform. Halting their horses, they narrowed keen eyes. Within, they saw only the night telegraph operator at his desk beneath a solitary oil lamp. The man was sound asleep. Jesse gritted a word to his older brother. Frank turned in the saddle and waved the three flankers forward. The men swung their horses in, slid off them at the rail.

Chadwell, the horse-holder, gathered all the reins and crouched below the platform behind a trash barrel. Clell Miller and Charlie Pitts joined Frank and Jesse on foot. The four men stepped up on the platform, drew guns, glided toward the station door and the lone telegrapher.

The horses became nervous as their riders departed.

They began to hipshift and to step around on Chadwell. "Be still, blast you!" the latter hissed at them. "There ain't nothing here to turn you jumpy." But the sensitive animals were pricking their ears and rolling dark eyes toward the now-impenetrable dusk blanketing the railway station. Chadwell cursed them again. But his own eyes joined theirs in probing the darkness of the windy night, and it was not the prowling gusts which stirred his neck hairs. Could be old Buck was right. Maybe these rubes had spotted them outside town. Wait a minute. Was that something moving toward him and the horses from behind that stack of empty chicken crates and hogshead barrels yonder? No, it must be only wind shadows. Nightspots. The fantods pure and simple. But why were the horses so itchy?

The telegrapher in the Hatpin depot was awakened from his drowsy after-supper nap by the kiss of steel lips behind his left ear.

"Don't touch the key," advised Jesse, cocking the big Colt for emphasis.

"Yeah," annoted Frank. "If we want any messages sent, we'll compose same."

The telegrapher, a man of peace, bobbed his pate in eager assent. Ducking his head gingerly out from in front of Jesse's revolver muzzle, he swiveled in his creaking chair to peer beneath green eyeshade up at his accosters. What he saw decided him in his determinations for love and brotherhood.

Frank James was a sadly handsome man, with clear gray eyes, drooping, sunfaded moustache, the look more of a preacher than a train and bank robber. Young brother Jesse was also a fine-looking man. Not so tall and spare as Frank, his face was more square-cut, with a black spade beard, the eyes a bright blue, albeit bloodshot and continually blinking, and the general outlook that of a cattle buyer or fine horse broker, both of which he indeed was in those areas of his time not blocked out for armed assault and the swifter gains of gun and mask.

No, it wasn't Frank and Jesse that worried a man.

It was those two abysmal brutes who stood behind the brothers James waiting to be loosed upon any such innocent and defenseless citizens as Cyril Peebles, Hatpin's telegraph operator, railroad agent, baggageman, and night clerk for the old reliable M&W's main line for Denver, Colorado.

Those two looked to Peebles as if they would enjoy slitting their own mothers' throats, or kicking crippled children, or, for the present matter, gut-shooting important railroad employees. The telegrapher cleared his throat to announce his love for all men. Before he could get this philosophy, inspired in the main by the Neanderthal glares of Clell Miller and Charlie Pitts, enunciated, a sudden neighing of the outlaws' horses carried in from the outside.

Frank and Jesse traded dark looks.

Jesse was crouching like a big cat about to spring, the blue eyes twitching. Brother Frank spoke first.

"Ding," he said. "I don't care for that. I had best see to the horses. We got to get us a new holder one of these days. Since he's got married, Bill ain't steady."

Clell Miller, the primal brute among them, literally slobbered at the mention of Chadwell's new status. "Hell." He grinned. "Iffen any one of us had us a witch-bodied woman like old Bill to think on, we'd all be worried about getting back home without no lead in our ramrods. Ha! Ha!"

"Wait a minute, Buck." Jesse ignored the crudity of Clell. "Chadwell's all right." He did not want to show indecision or doubt in front of his men, much less to demonstrate uncertainty of purpose to the Hatpin night clerk. He spun about now on the latter. "Friend," he said in his high-pitched voice, "you had better discover where at is your tongue, and gulp out fast what's going on around here." He slid the long, cold Colt barrel about four inches into the gaping mouth of Cyril Peebles. "Did we walk into something, or not, neighbor?"

The telegrapher commenced to sputter around the Colt barrel. Jesse removed the obstruction.

"You can do better than that." He nodded. "And if you don't, we'll teach you how in a hurry." At his words, the bestial Pitts and Miller slunk in behind the Jameses, each pulling, not a gun, but a glittering eight-inch knife. In his skinny belly, Cyril Peebles knew a fearful chill.

"Wait, wait!" he cried. "I'll tell it all!"

Outside the Hatpin depot, the troubles of horse-holder Chadwell multiplied. "Whoa-up, whoa-up!" he snarled at the head-tossing Missouri thoroughbreds. But the horses saw what they saw, the shadows moving swiftly in toward the man who held them, and they renewed their snorting and rearing.

Now suddenly the holder heard the creaking behind him of a sun-dried station-platform board. He whirled in time to find the shadowed figure of a large assailant almost upon him. The latter held a sawed-off shotgun. Chadwell, nonetheless, went for his holstered Colt. But it was an off-balance draw, demanded by the fact that he held the reins of five powerful saddle mounts in the left hand, while attempting to pull and fire with the right. In the fraction of time so lost, a second shotgun-armed figure ran up out of the night behind Chadwell. The second man did not shoot the horse-holder, but instead struck him in the back of the head with the butt-stock of the shot-gun. Chadwell's jaw went slack, his body sagged, the hand holding the reins of the horses loosened.

But now half a dozen new figures raced up through the darkness. Some took Chadwell's slumping body, hand-and-foot, and carried him off. The others seized the horses before they might escape, but the Missouri-bred animals kicked and reared anew, neighing sharply in alarm.

Inside the depot, the sound carried to Jesse and the others, breaking off the interrogation of the telegrapher. As one, the gang ran for the stationhouse door. Bursting out upon the loading platform, they were in time to see their prized horses disappearing down Main Street and around its far dusty corner into the endless night beyond Hatpin, Kansas.

"Jess," said Frank James. "What will we do?"

It was a moment to try the nerves of any outlaw band. In the quiet way that the older brother had shown the instinctive trust in the judgments of Jesse James, he had also demonstrated the source of the gang's great strength. But before Jesse could reply to Frank's question, they all distinctly heard a loud groaning emanating from the stack of empty barrels on the far side of the loading platform.

Carbines and Colts at the ready, they rushed the barrels. But it was only Bill Chadwell struggling to get to his feet. The holder was grasping his wounded head and trying to explain what had happened to him and to the precious charges in his care.

"Get him inside!" rasped Jesse, catching Chadwell by one arm, as Frank caught the other. Pitts and Clell Miller covered the retreat back into the depot, but no sight or sound of the hidden enemy pursued them.

Within the stationhouse, the telegrapher was making good his departure through the opposite door giving onto the trackside loading dock. Jesse stretched him coolly with one crack of his revolver barrel. Cyril Peebles fell with a thud to the rough planks of the floor. His body blocked the townside door. Clell Miller kicked and rolled his unconscious form out of the way, slammed shut the street door and barred it from the inside with a propped chair.

Pantingly, the gang crouched, eyeing one another.

This could be the big trouble, or it could be only a matter of searching out the town to locate their stolen mounts and retrieve them from the sap-headed farmers who had made off with them.

Jesse saw the signs of fear beginning to shadow the faces of his fellows, and moved to halt its spread. Panic was the surest enemy of the trapped.

"Now, let's stand easy," he ordered. "All we got to do is figure out what's the most likely thing these rubes have done with our horses, then go and fetch them back. Frank, what you say?"

Frank, who had been peering out one of the windows, did not answer with words but with action. Leaping to Peebles' desk, he seized up the station lamp and blew it out. As its acrid smoke coiled through the darkness of the depot, he said, "It ain't what I *say*, Jess, it's what I *see*." He paused, and the men moved in behind Jesse, but looked to him. "Them farmers not only took our damn horses, they've took up ambush posts all about out there to make the horse-lift stick. I can see them all around the depot. We ain't just set afoot, Jess, we're cut off!"

Clell Miller growled a curse. His comrade Charlie Pitts told him to "hesh up and look to Jess."

Jesse, meanwhile, sprang to the window Frank had abandoned. He held himself flat to the wall, craning head to peer out into the stillness. He seemed reassured. Slipping to the other side of the window, he repeated the performance in the opposite direction, the bloodshot blue eyes blinking rapidly. In a moment he was back.

"I don't see nothing out yonder." He frowned. "You certain sure you wasn't shagging wind shadows, Buck?"

"No mistake," Frank replied. "I seen them moving into place. They're just a-laying low and waiting now."

Jesse shook his head like a dog with a wrongsized bone. The men scowled, demanding some action of their young leader with their very silence. Jesse threw one more glance out the window, wheeled on Frank.

"We got to get them horses back," he said in that tightly worded way of his which permitted no discussion. "Come on, all of you."

The men looked to their weapons. Carbines were levered, Colt cylinders spun. Levi's were hitched up, dry lips licked, Stetson hats set down hard on shaggy heads. They moved as one toward the door, following Jesse. The latter pulled the chair away, swung the plank door creakingly open, nodded tensely. "All right, here we go."

Jesse went first, Frank next, the others flanking him.

Three steps onto the platform and they were met with a blast of gunfire that withered their number like flame, drove them staggering back into the fortress of the depot.

Frank had been right; they were cornered.

Gunfire from the surrounding citizens of Hatpin continued sporadically. Its ricocheting lead whined through the stationhouse. The gang, holding its fire, watched the station clock tick away the minutes, and possibly their lives with them. Clell Miller had one arm in torn bandage and sling. A blood-soaked rag bound up the head of Charlie Pitts. Whatever of disdain any of the Missourians may have felt for the Hatpin farmers was now long extinct. There was no question remaining: they were in final trouble.

"Near ten P.M.," muttered Jesse, again checking

the station clock. "Number 1608 is just about pulling out."

"I wisht we was on it," averred Bill Chadwell honestly.

"I wisht *you* was on it," Charlie Pitts told him pointedly. "In a damn pine box."

"Yeah," sided Clell Miller. "Next time I need a horse helt, I'll hire me a hitching post."

"That's enough of that," Jesse ordered quietly. "Bickering amongst ourselves ain't going to get us out of Hatpin."

At his guard post by the front window, Frank James, the educated outlaw, quoted softly. " 'A horse, a horse, my kingdom for a horse.' That's from *Richard the Third*. Feller named Bill Shakespeare writ it."

"Ain't that just grand?" sneered the wounded Charlie Pitts. "Quote me something I can saddle and straddle in Hatpin. Never mind old Bill What's-his-name."

"Yeah, nor old Richard, neither," agreed his friend Clell. "You got any idees yet, Jess?"

The leader only scowled and blinked the harder.

Frank James snapped a shot at a shadow in Main Street, ducked as an answering shot nearly beheaded him. "You'll think of something, Dingus," he said in simple faith. "You always do."

As he spoke, the receiving key of the telegrapher's instrument began to chatter with an incoming message.

Jesse leaped to the side of the telegrapher, whom they had bound in his swivel chair. Cutting the man free, he spun him around to face the desk. "Take it down, friend," he grated. "Get it percisely as it comes over. Every dot and dash of it. Change one click of that key, and your wife's a widow."

The white-faced hostage nodded, began taking down the message: . . . REGARDING YOUR EARLIER INQUIRY FOR HELP IN APPREHENDING JAMES GANG SAID TO BE IN HATPIN, CAN VERIFY YOUR INFORMATION REGARDING MOUNTED POSSE READY HERE,

AND AVAILABILITY YOUR NEEDS HATPIN. PLEASE GIVE YOUR SITUATION NOW. CONFIRM GANG'S IDENTITY. URGENT. TIME EVERYTHING. J. W. WHICHER, CHIEF DETECTIVE M&W RR, KC MO DIV.

When these words appeared, read aloud by Frank James from the telegrapher's pad, Jesse's eyes took fire. His dark face was literally alight when the message had ended. His men sensed his deep excitement, all watching him.

"Buck," he said to Frank. "Are you remembering what I am? About 'Whicher's Posse'? That inside report we got from our spy at the M&W? The one about the special James Gang Posse gathered together in Kansas City by old Whicher? The ready-mounted bunch?"

Frank's gray eyes widened.

"You meaning that stretcher we was told about the railroad fixing up a baggage car into a horse car and keeping it all set to roll? To hook on to any train? Get to the scene of any robbery quick as a sheep dog on a coyote?"

"That's the one; named special in our honor."

"But we don't know nothing for real about that posse, Jess." Frank was frowning now. "We ain't never seen it. Far as we know, it's just a story."

Jesse eyed them all.

"Supposing it *ain't* just a story," he said softly, but with clear implication, and the light came on belatedly for Frank and the others. All of them gaped at their leader.

"Ding! You ain't actually meaning to find out?"

It was brother Frank. Neither he nor the others, even thinking they knew Jesse, could have imagined such a daring outlaw gamble. No, only Jesse James could have thought of it. Who else could have figured out *this* possible escape from the deadly trap of aroused citizenry in Hatpin, Kansas? But Jesse *had* thought of it, and Jesse *did* mean to give it his best try.

For the last time his Navy Colt swung to cover Cyril Peebles.

"Mister." He blinked. "Take a message: TO J. W. WHICHER, CHIEF DETECTIVE M&W RR, KANSAS CITY, MISSOURI ..."

In the home office of the Missouri & Western, the night operator took down the message with a yawn. Suddenly his eyes bugged. Tearing loose the message sheet, he sprinted across the hallway into the office of J. W. Whicher, chief of railroad detectives. The latter took the message sheet: JESSE JAMES HERE HATPIN NOW ... GANG SET TO BOARD TRAIN 1608 WITH DENVER UNSIGNED NOTE SHIPMENT ... MIDNIGHT HATPIN TIME ... ACKNOWLEDGE YOUR RESPONSE, URGENT.

Chief Whicher gave a strangled cry, leaped up from his desk. He was a man on the verge of a purple stroke.

"Any answer, Mr. Whicher?" asked the telegrapher.

Whicher did not reply. He ran out of his office, down the hallway, and out into the switch yard, waving the message sheet and shouting desperately, "Hold Sixteen-Ought-Eight!" Then, changing directions: "Shunt the posse-car, shunt the posse-car!"

The switch yard became instant bedlam. Somehow, out of the confusion, order emerged. The special express car fitted out to hold saddled horses stood upon its siding already hooked to a caboose similarly of special fitting to accommodate the riders. Its side ramp door was now let down and the horses loaded with precision into its narrow confines. A group of very hard-looking possemen showed up, trotting on the double. Lanterns were awave throughout the yard, and trainmen shouted everywhere. Train number 1608, halted in time, was backing onto the posse-car siding. It hooked onto the horse car and caboose with a banging jolt, as the last of the mounts were run up the ramp. The ramp was drawn up, the door slid shut. J. W. Whicher puffed into view.

Seizing a lantern from a switchman, Whicher

mounted the caboose steps, waved the lantern frantically ahead to the brakeman. Number 1608's whistle blasted shrilly. Sand screeched on steel as the drivers of 1608 bit into the rails. Horse car and caboose started to roll.

The Jesse James Special was under way.

In Hatpin, midnight neared. Jesse and his men were still pinned down in the depot by citizen sniper fire. But all were busy, and there was no grumbling now. In the bandit life, bullets were a part of the natural environment. Bad luck hit everyone alike, even Jesse Woodson James. It was the way a man responded to these chancy breaks which marked him what he was, or ever hoped to become, in the minds of his fellows.

And Jesse was responding with all his cunning.

He was at the moment drawing a can of coal oil from the drum in the depot. Frank was hefting a sledgehammer, getting ready for his part. Clell and Charlie Pitts were slicing open sacks of wheat, spilling the grain out upon the station floor. Bill Chadwell was on lookout at the windows, firing first out of the Main Street side, then running to blast at the other farmers hidden across the tracks.

Far down the track, just then a whistle screeched. Number 1608!

Frank handed Jesse the sledgehammer. With a glance at the wall clock, then showing a minute till midnight, he grinned and said, "Right on time; good luck, Ding."

His younger brother picked up the can of coal oil and snuck out of the station by way of the small swinging door which serviced the depot's woodbox from the outside. Old guerrilla fighter that he was, he managed to slip through the citizen lines and on down the track toward the train's whistling. A short distance beyond the station he found the stack of creosoted cross-ties that he had prayed he remembered being there. Piling these on the tracks, sweating and grunting at the labor, he doused them with the coal oil, just as number 1608 rounded the near bend east of the Hatpin water stop. Jesse scraped the match on his haunch, tossed it into the coal-oiled timbers. They burst into smoky flame, and number 1608's engineer fed the sand to the rails and clamped on his brakes. Number 1608 screeched to a halt, sat steaming and chuffing.

Up into its cab swung the bearded desperado, with the sledgehammer in one hand, a Navy Colt in the other.

"Get down, get down!" he shouted. "It's Jesse James!"

With the dread name, he fired over the heads of fireman and engineer, both of whom went to the floor of the cab and remained there praying. Jesse swarmed up on the coal car, and from there to the rounded tops of the passenger coaches, to race down them toward horse car and posse caboose. As he approached, the loading ramp of the horse car came open and down to the ground with a great slam. Out galloped the possemen, ready-mounted and hell-bent to ride. With a company yell signaling doom to the James gang at last, all spurred their animals uptrack toward the halted locomotive.

Laughing aloud, Jesse dropped down between cars and with the sledgehammer began to drive out the coupling pin between caboose and horse car.

The excitement of it fired him through and through. By God, Jesse had a plan! He always had a plan! Whicher, the Pinkertons, the private bank dicks —none of them could think along with Dingus James. Just let them try!

At the head of the train the special posse thundered by, firing into the night, and at nothing. The engineer yelled down from the cab that it "was so" Jesse James, and he had dashed off with his entire gang "of near a dozen desperate murderers" into the open prairie off to the north.

Away went the posse, cursing and firing.

At the depot, the Hatpin citizens, hearing this

wild bursting of gunfire, broke their ambush to run
down the tracks and join in the kill. Watching them
abandon their stations about the depot, Frank James
said dryly, "All right, boys. Fetch along the coal oil
and the gunnysacks."

Once free of the stationhouse, he led the others
westward along the tracks, in the opposite direction of
Jesse's halting of number 1608. "Keep a-coming, keep
a-coming," he urged his panting fellows. "Who's got
the matches?"

Back down the line, in the glare of 1608's head-
lamp, the posse had returned from the prairie, to mill
in disgust under the beginning jeers of the Hatpin
men.

Big-city lawmen, humpfh!

Kansas City railroad detectives, hah!

But then they remembered, suddenly, their own
deserted posts about the stationhouse. Too late, they
stumbled back to the depot. It was as dark and empty
as the outer night.

It was now the Kansas City posse's turn to curse
the local vigilantes and tell them they were full of jay-
hawk corn and that heads would roll for this false
alarm. A red-faced J. W. Whicher vowed personally
to see to it that the track was ripped out and relaid
wide around Hatpin, Kansas.

Returning glumly down along the stalled train,
they reloaded the sweat-caked horses, and number
1608 shortly pulled on out for Denver. In the caboose,
short-tempered possemen swore a vengeance upon
whoever could be nailed for the fiasco they had just
performed. But even as they took oaths, one of them
looked out the caboose and yelled, "What the hell! We
ain't moving. Yonder goes the train with our horse
car!"

The startled lawmen rushed as one out of the
motionless caboose. All of them remembered the jeer-
ing figure waving to them with the sledgehammer from
the disappearing roof of their famed horse car, just

then sweeping out of sight around the Hatpin depot bend.

It was Jesse Woodson James.

Number 1608, all innocent of the detached posse caboose, gained speed quickly. Hatpin and its feeble lights were soon a pinpoint on the black prairie. Hearts grew lighter.

"Well, anyways," the engineer consoled his recovering fireman, "we still got the Denver banknotes aboard and safe."

He was entirely correct, justifiably gratified.

For about four minutes and three-quarters of a mile.

Then a second pile of oil-soaked cross-ties was blazing in the right-of-way, and another James brother was leaping to the locomotive's cab as the engineer again poured sand to steel and brought his train to another groaning halt in the Kansas night.

"Hello, there, neighbors." Frank James nodded to fireman and engineer. "Down on the floorplate, and think about your sins. We shan't be long."

The two went again to the floor of the cab, and Frank left them there to climb the coal car and supervise from its black cargo the loading into the Kansas wheat sacks, by Chadwell, Pitts, and Miller, of the total cargo of unsigned Denver banknotes found in the express car next behind.

With this task in progress, the loading ramp of the horse car at train's rear banged down once more, and Jesse came prancing down its cleated path riding J. W. Whicher's famed white Kentucky racehorse. Behind him, on a long lead rope, came the others of the posse's prized horses. He was no more than just up to the express car with the mounts when the door slid open, and his men, complete with stuffed wheat sacks, leaped out to saddle up on the horses of the Kansas City posse. They had to wait but a second only for Frank James to scramble down from the coal car and get safely aboard his mount, being held for him by brother, Jesse Woodson; then they were ready to ride out into history.

But the two brothers, with a true sense of that history, held in their mounts one last pinch of time.

"Well, Jess," said Frank, sober as a hanging judge, "you sure thought of something this time! Mail-order horse thieving! By jings, that's a buster, even for old Dingus!"

Jesse and his hard-faced men looked at one another.

Then all of them, with brother Frank, threw back long-locked heads and laughed crazily as loons on a sunset lake.

Then a common *"Heee-yahhHHH!"* shattered the night.

The wild Missouri guerrilla yell burst from all of them, and at the same time. But there was in it a note of danger shared and defeated, a tribute singularly from them to their driven youthful leader, who, in outlaw truth, always thought of something, always had a plan that worked.

With the yell, they spurred off, filling the night and the silent streets of Hatpin, Kansas, with overhead gunfire and the thunder of the hooves of the splendid remount horses shipped, rush order, to them through courtesy of J. W. Whicher and the main office of the Missouri & Western Railroad.

When they had gone, the legend of the Robin Hood of the Little Blue had grown another folklore larger, and $35,000 richer, for the simple want of a horse.

The Redeeming of
Fate Rachel

The rider, following the stage road west, came to the last rise before the town somewhere nearing eight o'clock. Warily, he turned his mount from the road. Shortly, hidden by the wither-high sage, he swung down from the horse and walked to a spot where the brush thinned to give an unobstructed view of the flat below. He squinted through the early darkness, studying the distant wink of the settlement's oil lamps.

Shaking his head, he stirred uneasily.

How many times outside how many towns had he gotten down in the sage to stand thus and stare through the dusty starlight while his mind weighed the excuse of sworn and salaried duty against the dark excitement of the hunt which no money could explain and no oath of office justify? He did not know. He could not remember.

They had called him bounty hunter, although he was not that.

A deputy United States marshal on special service, yes, that he had been. And the special part of the service meaning that the Federal Government paid him to work through its catalog file of warrants of first-degree murder marked "returned unserved," yes, that also was true. But that he had been the common scalp-hunting pariah, which the anonymity of his employment demanded he appear to be, was not true. Still the people, good and bad, of those other

85

times and other towns could not know this and so called him what they did.

It was because of this calling and because of his inability to defend himself against its charges that he had given up his marshal's shield and the long rides and lonely starlight waits which were the other badges of his thankless trade.

Yet now he wondered anew at the validity of his long-ago decision.

Ten years, he thought. A long, a very long time ago. But apparently not long enough. The habits of a man's past did not forsake him. It was only the years themselves that fled. The years that dimmed but could not destroy an acquired pattern of life and death. The years that slowed the hand but only sharpened the memory of its lost speed. Nothing else changed.

Until this moment he had believed the years of exile following his last job in this same settlement had cured him forever of the excitement sickness that formerly seized him with such a final mile's scanning, yet here he stood as tightly drawn as ever in the old dangerous days.

Rachel shook off the thought, but could not shake off its incubus. It was still sitting his shoulders when he checked his mount at town's edge to glance at the sign which had replaced the one he remembered.

Welcome to
MOBEETIE
Cultural Capital of
the Panhandle
Pop. 697

He crowfooted his eye corners in the wry grimace that was his trademark way of reflecting an inside, accepting grin to go with the outside, dubious headshake. He rode slowly on. What had the population been that other time? Fifty? Seventy-five, perhaps? A hundred on Saturday nights? And where had the cul-

ture been hiding then? The same place it most likely
was hiding now? In the bottom of a brown bottle at the
Cattleman's Bar, or the Boar's Nest Saloon? One thing
certain. Wherever it was, it wasn't hiding anymore. It
was standing up on its hind legs waving its paws to be
recognized.

Culture with a capital K. Mobeetie had changed.
She had come of age. No longer could she be called
by the affectionate bawdyism of Fate's day, "The Cowboy Outhouse of the Plains." She had class now. She
was a city. The cultural center of the entire, unadulter-
ated Staked Plains, and no less. It wasn't a few swift
years since Fate had been here. It was a whole lifetime. Fate felt sad about that. He spoke to his horse
and the animal picked up to a shuffle walk, moving
his rider more quickly past the tinpan blare of the
numberless saloon pianos, on down the street to the
darkened quarter of the few commercial houses flanking the entertainment district.

The maneuver was not in time.

Abreast the Pink Lady, obviously Mobeetie's answer to the prayers of the two-dollar trade, a blast of
gunfire kicked open the establishment's batwing doors
and a man, gun in hand, staggered backward into the
street. He was followed by two toughs returning his
fire. They cut him down squarely in front of Rachel's
horse, in mid-street, then shifted their Colts to cover
any play the passing horseman might have in mind.
But Rachel had been there before.

Checking his horse only enough to prevent tram-
pling the fallen gunman he touched his hat brim soberly to the two killers on the boardwalk, directed his
mount around the body, held him on a steady, slow
course down the street. The men from the Pink Lady
watched him a bit, then turned and went back to their
bourbon.

Down along the dark part of the main thoroughfare, Rachel pulled into the hitching rail in front of the
Anderson Express Company. Tying up, he stepped

quickly into the shadows of the roofed boardwalk. Nothing moved, or made noise in his vicinity. He put his hand to the office door latch.

Inside, a lone Rochester hand lamp burned on a wall base behind the door. Rachel, easing the dusted panels open, stepped through from the street. As he did, a figure moved out from the wall behind him. Another figure reached swiftly to blow out the wall lamp. Rachel set himself, but did not turn.

"I suppose," he said quietly, "that you have something in my back."

"Shotguns," answered one of the men. "Sawed-offs."

"It will do," said Rachel.

Now, from behind the shipping counter directly in front of him, a third man rose up and asked softly, "Rachel?"

The latter, unseen in the darkness, spread his arid grin.

"With one 'l,' " he said. "Who are you?"

"T. C. Barnes," answered the other. "Criminal Division, Anderson Express."

"You're the one sent for me."

"Yes." Barnes turned to his henchmen. "All right, you men, wait outside. Light the lamp as you leave."

The men did as told, departed, careful to adjust the drawn shade on the door in going out. Barnes turned back to Fate Rachel.

"It's been a term of years, Rachel," he said, "but we've got a real nasty one on our hands this time."

"What do you mean, 'we'?" asked Rachel. "You got a midget in your pocket, Mr. Barnes? I haven't worked a law job for a long time. I'm not about to start in again either."

"Circumstances, Rachel," said the other, "alter cases. Like I said, we're in trouble. You, me, the express company."

"And who else?" asked Rachel quietly.

Barnes eyed him. "You're pretty quick, aren't you?" he said.

"I used to be. Go ahead, Mr. Barnes. Me, you, the express company—who else?"

Barnes quit circling, closed in.

"Does the name Ransom Briscoe mean anything to you?" he asked.

"Should it?" shrugged Rachel.

"He seems to think so."

"Oh?"

"You put him in Yuma for ten years."

"Butcher Briscoe, yes!" Rachel's eyes narrowed belatedly. "I'd forgotten he had a human name. But good Lord, Mr. Barnes, that was—" He broke off, as the significance of it dawned on him, then finished softly, "—that was ten years ago."

Barnes nodded. "He served every day of the ten, Rachel. Got out last month, showed up here in Mobeetie last week."

"He would do that," said Rachel. "He was sentenced from here. This is where he stood trial, and where I brought him in, and where I had to give the testimony that convicted him. He had a wife here, too. Pretty little thing, and nice. I never forgot her, and she never forgave me." He paused, looking at the Anderson agent. "That was my last job, Mr. Barnes. You must know that. It was killing an Anderson clerk that put me on his track."

"Of course I know it, Rachel. It's why the company had me come out here to meet you. They felt they owed you that much."

"Let's get on with it," suggested Rachel. "I don't take to mystery stories."

"I'm not going to tell you one," said Barnes. "This is a murder yarn, out-and-out. Briscoe took this local office for the day's receipts on Tuesday last. Got maybe two hundred dollars. And left two messages with the clerk. One was that he meant to take Anderson Express for every nickel they had, west of Wichita, that he intended to set up a raiding operation out here in the Staked Plains that would make the James boys look like sneak thieves."

"Mr. Barnes," said Rachel irritably, "did you bring me all the way down here to Mobeetie to tell me Briscoe had a big mouth?"

"No, I brought you down here to give you the other message—the one he left for you."

"A message for me? From Rance Briscoe?"

"No less. He told the clerk to tell the bounty hunter he was going to get him if it took ten years and ten thousand dollars. The company figured he had to mean you, Rachel. You worked the job alone."

"I always worked my jobs alone, but it was decent of the Anderson folks to look me up and call me in. Briscoe's a bad lot. He might try it." Rachel scratched his chin with the side of his thumb, shook his head frowningly. "Now, the ten years I can figure. What's the ten thousand dollars supposed to mean, though? That throws me."

Barnes bobbed his head abruptly.

"Briscoe told the clerk that, too. He's put a price on your head, Rachel. Literally. He's offering ten thousand dollars for your ears—with your head between them."

Rachel returned the nod, embellished with his quirky, dry grin. "Well," he said, "that's ten times what I got paid for him."

"Yes, he mentioned that also."

"Oh? Well, one thing sure. It's a wise move on his part giving himself ten years to do the job. It's apt to take him that long to get up the price at the rate he's going."

"That's where you're wrong, Rachel. And it's why you ought to be interested in taking on this assignment—or at least the company thought you ought to be."

"*Assignment?* What assignment, Mr. Barnes?"

"To get back Anderson's money."

Rachel's warm gray eyes took on a puzzled cast.

"Didn't you just tell me he got only a couple of hundred in this Mobeetie haul, Mr. Barnes?"

"I did. But like Briscoe said, that was only the beginning."

Rachel spread his hands helplessly.

"I wish you would quit cat-and-mousing me, Mr. Barnes," he pleaded. "That is, unless you are just personally feeling mousy. I have ridden three hundred miles to find out what this thing is all about and so far you have been trying to pull me in with nothing but a wide circle of teasy bait drops. Now please lay off sprinkling the cheese, Mr. Barnes, and spring the trap."

The Anderson agent scowled, made uneasy by the other's diffident courtesy.

"All right, Rachel," he said, "here's the whole chunk. Briscoe and his bunch took the Texas and Pacific's Colorado Flyer at Red Rock station the day after he hit our office here in Mobeetie. Shot our messenger and cleaned out the express car, including our shipment of cash."

"Like what shipment of your cash, Mr. Barnes?"

"Like the Fort Bliss army payroll. Going from Denver down to El Paso. Rance Briscoe's got it now and the Army is howling."

"How hard would you say they were howling, Mr. Barnes?"

"You're not going to like 'how hard,' Rachel." The Anderson man paused, jaw outthrust. "Ten thousand dollars to the decimal point!" he snapped.

"Thank you, that's about hard enough," nodded Fate Rachel, and put thoughtful thumb to chin-side.

"I guess you can read the rest of the trail," said Barnes.

"Yes," said Rachel, "I reckon that's so. But how does she size to you?"

Barnes watched him, to make sure he was not smarting off with him. Seeing that he was not, he laid it out as he saw it, and as the company had instructed him to.

"It means," he said, "that every cheap and high-priced hungry gun in the territory will be out for you.

Every floater with a Colt, from here to Red River, will know that Rance Briscoe has come by the cash to back up his boast of buying your ears for ten thousand dollars. It means, exactly, that from the time you walk out of this office tonight, every armed stranger you pass on the street may be the one who has Briscoe's ten thousand already spent. Rachel, you're up against odds you can't buck alone. The company sent me here to tell you that Anderson Express will back you with every means at its disposal, if you are willing, and ready, to put on your gun again and go after this man."

"You mean, don't you," said Rachel, "if I will agree to go after the company's money?"

"You find the man, you'll find the money. He hasn't had time to fence it, and wouldn't dare pass it yet."

"That's so."

"Well, Rachel? It's your life and our money. Have we got a deal?"

Fate Rachel stood thinking it over. The years rolled back, and with them he could hear and taste again all the wickedness and hate that hunting men for money had earned him in those former times. At last he raised his eyes and said quietly to Barnes, "No thank you. I was there once. I didn't like it."

"We'll pay ten percent," said Barnes. "That's a thousand dollars on total recovery. A lot of money, Rachel. Especially, for saving your own life."

Rachel shook his head slowly.

"I want you to thank the company for warning me, Mr. Barnes. But I have earned my last dime as a 'dollar deputy.' I'll do my best against Rance Briscoe and his bunch, but I'll not take a dollar to go after his head."

"You're a fool, man. You won't have a chance."

"No, but I have a choice. And I made it ten years ago."

"There's nothing I can do to persuade you?"

"Nothing, Mr. Barnes. But there is something you could do to pleasure me. Is Mrs. Briscoe still living here?"

"Why do you ask that?" The Anderson agent pounced on the question with quick suspicion, but his companion only shrugged, soft-voiced.

"I thought you might have located her in your investigation," he said. "I'd like to look her up, if she's here in Mobeetie. Maybe she would listen after all these years. She was a fine girl, Mr. Barnes. I'd like to see her and try to set things straight."

Barnes suddenly felt sorry for the gray-haired rider before him. He felt, too, a little foolish for having made him the company offer, after seeing him. He had not himself known Fate Rachel. But that this slow-talking old fellow could be the legend of ten years ago, he found more than he could accept.

"Sure," he said, "Mrs. Briscoe's still in town, old-timer. She's working the Pink Lady."

His listener nodded. "I remember," he said, "that she sang in those days, too. It's how she met Briscoe."

"She's not singing anymore," said Barnes.

"Well, a voice will go with the years. That's only natural. Thank you, Mr. Barnes. The Pink Lady, you said?"

"First one back up the street. You can't miss it."

"I know. Met a fellow coming out oi ʰere tonight." Rachel touched his hat brim. "Thanks, again."

T. C. Barnes didn't answer him. He only stood and watched him go out into the street and untie his horse. Then he watched him go, leading the horse, walking up the middle of the street with that bent-kneed crouch and little rolling limp which never leaves the man who has worn the gun for a living, no matter the number of his years beyond the wearing. When Rachel had disappeared, Barnes blew out the wall lamp and muttered angrily to the smoky darkness, "Damn, it's hell to grow old!"

Rachel found it hard to think of Eileen Briscoe working in a place like the Pink Lady. But investigation established that she was, and was doing so at the rock-bottom level. She attempted to solicit Rachel at his table almost before he could get his chair under him. He only knew it was she by the remembered throaty sound of her voice, and when he touched his hat and said, "Evening, Mrs. Briscoe," she only stared at him blurrily and answered, "Well, you must be from somewhere far back in the better days, but I can't say how far back, nor how much better."

"Don't try," Rachel told her gently. "Just put me down for an old friend."

"You must be pretty old, all right. I haven't been Mrs. Briscoe for—for—" She let it trail off, staring into her glass, and Rachel finished it softly for her.

"For ten years," he said. "Isn't that it, Eileen?"

The woman rolled her head, trying to focus on him.

"Say," she managed, "who are you? You seem to know an awful lot about me, and maybe about my troubles, eh? That's it. Rance sent you. He's out now, I heard."

"Yes, he's out, but I'm not here from him. Excepting by a long trail around."

"Well, it can't be long enough for me. Not from Rance."

"Eileen—Mrs. Briscoe, ma'am—I got nothing to do with Ransom Briscoe. I'm only here to talk to you. I got but a little time, and I thought you might remember me and we could maybe even up the old days. You sure you don't know me? I was mighty close to your husband, once. I remember you."

She frowned, trying to steady her gaze long enough to trace his sunburned features. But the effort was beyond her, and Rachel let it remain so.

"We'll have another drink," he said, "and let things work along natural."

The woman weaved her head, accepting the offer. It was on the fifth round that the floodgates of memory broke loose, letting the long-dammed waters through. As she talked, Fate Rachel felt the old, iron-fingered squeeze start within him.

Briscoe had left his young wife six months pregnant when he went to Yuma. He had never replied to her letters, never admitted paternity, never sent any money. He had money, for members of his gang in Mobeetie spent big for two years after Rance had gone away. Eileen, her figure and courage returned after the baby girl was born, had started singing in the better places. But beauty and music were fragile items on the frontier. Before long she was dancing in the not-so-good places, then not even dancing in the places which were too low to have names, good or bad.

The reason for the fall was not moral, but economic. The baby, never well, had taken a nameless chronic ill and ten years of paying incessant medical bills had brought Eileen Briscoe to the level where Fate Rachel found her.

Just recently, a new doctor from St. Louis had passed through the Panhandle studying frontier medicine. He had seen the girl and given a name to her malady. A name and a hope. There was a treatment for the disease, and a clinic in Kansas City where the treatment was practiced regularly and successfully. Otherwise, the end was as certain as tomorrow's sunset. But Eileen Briscoe had sold herself as far as she could. There were no more customers and the small hoard of money hidden in the old dresser at her town-edge shack did not begin to approach the amount mentioned by the St. Louis specialist.

When the story reached this point, Rachel's companion put her head down on her arms and began to cry. He let her sob until she slowed of her own accord, then asked softly, "How much did this doctor say is needed, Mrs. Briscoe?"

Eileen Briscoe shrugged hopelessly, head down, voice low.

"A thousand dollars, to start treatment. It might as well be ten thousand—"

Fate Rachel's gray eyes narrowed. The iron fingers around his belly made a final closing. He got up quietly and put his hand on the woman's rounded shoulder.

"Yes, ma'am," he said, looking toward the door, and thinking, beyond it, up the street, to the darkened office of the Anderson Express Company. "It might as well be."

Back outside, however, he paid no heed to Anderson Express.

Eileen Briscoe, in her wanderings, had given Rachel one clue. A girl working the Satin Slipper, a winter-thin version of Tombstone's Bird Cage Theater, had boasted of seeing Rance Briscoe since the Red Rock robbery. To an old manhunter this meant two possibilities: Briscoe was holed up locally and not on the run; the girl, having seen him once, might see him again.

How, then, to bring the one possibility to bear immediately upon the other? That, too, had an old lawman's answer: to find the man, flush the woman.

Rachel tied his horse well down the street from the garishly lit Slipper. It was eight-thirty, the evening performance not yet begun. He had half an hour to plant his poison with Edna Darcy, Briscoe's boastful—maybe—paramour. Going toward the cut-glass doors of the theater, he grinned his inward grin. With his total capital vested in the five dollars clinking in the lonely roominess of the side pocket of his faded corduroy riding coat, a half hour was ample. In a place like the Slipper he would be lucky to last ten minutes with that kind of money.

The foyer bar was not yet crowded. Most of the house girls were unemployed and his request for Edna Darcy was replied to promptly. The latter proved to be young, quick-eyed, curvaceous. Rachel didn't like her and the feeling was returned. He bought two drinks and dropped his bait abruptly.

"I am looking for Rance Briscoe," he said, "and was told to see you."

"By who?" asked the girl.

"A friend of yours—and Rance's."

"That will buy you exactly nothing, mister. You had better hit the rusty-dusty. Your cows must be lonesome for you and I don't like the taste of your whiskey."

She poured the remains of her glass into the heavy silver cigar tray on the table, and started to rise. Rachel put a hand lightly to her powdered arm.

"Ma'am, listen, I've got to find Rance. It's about that money he's offering for that bounty hunter which put him away for all them years."

The girl paused, watching him.

"What the devil are you talking about?" she said. "You want me to call the boss?"

"No thank you," said Rachel. "If you don't know what I'm talking about, then there's no way for me to warn Rance. If I can't find him, I can't tell him."

Edna Darcy sat down again. "Tell him what?" she asked.

"I'd better go," said Rachel. "The boss is looking this way. I don't want any trouble."

The head houseman was indeed eyeing them, but the Darcy girl said, "Don't pay him any mind; he won't open his yap unless I throw him the high sign. What do you want told to Rance Briscoe?"

Rachel glanced nervously around. Lowering his voice, he said quickly, "The Andersons are after him."

"My God," said the girl, "don't you think he knows that? Where you been, mister?"

"Places," answered Rachel.

"Such as which?"

"The Mobeetie office—tonight."

"And?"

"They've hired a bounty hunter to get Rance."

"That will hardly surprise him. He's been bounty-hunted before."

"Yes, ma'am. It's why I figured he'd be interested to know who they hired to do the job this time. It's the same one did the dirty work ten years ago."

Edna Darcy's face shadowed over. "That," she said, "will surprise him."

"Not if we work fast, ma'am. Will you see he gets the word? It's powerful important."

"Yes, I'll see. Who'll I say sent it?"

Rachel shifted restlessly.

"I went to jail with him on that ten-year stretch," he said, not adding he had gone only as far as the prison gates with Briscoe. "Just tell him that. He'll know who it is."

"I'd rather have a name," insisted the girl.

"And I'd rather not give one. Aiding and abetting is worth five to fifteen years where the main charge is murder."

"Murder?"

"Yes, ma'am. That express messenger Rance winged in the Red Rock job, he died this afternoon. Word came in on the telegraph just as I was locking up the office."

"The Anderson office?"

Rachel again flicked a glance around the barroom, now filling with thirsty early birds. "I took a job down there, swamping out. Thought I might hear something that'd let me get in on that ten thousand Rance is offering around. Money comes tough for us old coots, Miss. Any part of that ten thous——"

The girl got up, interrupting him.

"Get out," she said, "and keep your mouth shut. I'll get your message to Rance. He'll pay you something for it."

"Yes, ma'am, I know he will," said Rachel, backing for the doors. "Providing you get it to him, he's bound to."

Outside, he found a dark spot, disappeared into it.

Edna Darcy left the Slipper within minutes. She went across the street to her hotel room, a second floor front. Rachel saw the room lamp light up, then passed an anxious five minutes watching the drawn shade for shadows. None showed. Untying his horse, he led him across the street and to the far corner of the hotel, where he knew a second floor, outside stairway led down to the rear of the building. The stairway was also empty. Now it was guess and gamble.

The hotel backed on Third Street, and on Hartman's Livery Barn. A man could guess that Edna Darcy did not mean to walk to Rance Briscoe's hideout. Or did she? Might Briscoe have the cold nerve to be laying up, right here in Mobeetie? Rachel, remembering the fish-eyed outlaw, decided he would not. Briscoe was murderous, but not imaginative. He would be out in the brush someplace.

Mounting up, Rachel rode around to Third. Holding in at the corner, he was in time to see a two-horse light surrey swing out of the livery and head off down Third. No light showed in the barn, none burned on Third Street. It was impossible to say whether the driver was a man or a woman. But the gamble was less this time. Rachel took it without the five-minute wait. When the surrey left the last shack huddled on Mobeetie's southern flank there was less than thirty seconds, and a hundred yards of murky starlight, separating it from its mounted shadow.

Five miles south on the main road, the driver swung off on the Wolf Creek Ranch road and Rachel knew that it was Edna Darcy and that she was going to meet Rance Briscoe in the last place the law would think to look for him—in the abandoned Anderson Express stage depot at Faber's Crossing.

The idea made a man uneasy.

Faber's Crossing was the place he had taken Rance ten years ago. There had been three killings made that night in the shoot-out with Rance, all listed to Fate Rachel's gun, and Anderson had closed the station fearing its bad name would spoil it as an overnight stop. It had stood a decade with no tenants other than field mice, pack rats, brown bats and gopher snakes. Now it held another, deadlier resident—or residents—if Rachel's guess were correct; and his uneasiness grew deeper with each fall of his horse's hooves in the disused dust of the Wolf Creek road.

When he came up to the place, trailing the surrey more closely now so that he would not miss the location of whatever guards might challenge its driver, memory, black and fearful, reared out of the darkness with the hipshot roof and leaning wall timbers of the station.

"My God," breathed Rachel, "what am I doing here again?"

He held up his mount at the edge of the station house clearing, wanting, suddenly, to turn him back into the brush, to give the horse his head and let him run as far and fast away from Faber's Crossing as his limbs might carry him. But he did not. He had tried escaping the past by putting his back to it. He had tried ten long weary years of it. Yet that other night still lay as dark and dusty and no different in his mind from this present one. His hesitation in the sage outside Mobeetie had not been a false one. The years changed nothing but the hunger for the hunt. The thing which had to be done, which could not be faced away from, that didn't change. Rance Briscoe had waited in that darkened stage depot ten years ago; he waited in it still.

Rachel slid out from its worn black holster the obsolescent Cap-and-Ball .44 Remington. It felt like the handshake of an old friend, one once loved above all others but absent for too long. It felt strange, awkward, stiff and a little embarrassed. He put it back in the holster, shaking his head.

Across the clearing only one trace of light shown from the station house; a tiny, faint streak paint-brushing the sage out behind the relay-stock corrals. It fell, Rachel knew, from the kitchen window. It had to. There were no other windows in the rear wall of the rotting building. Edna Darcy guided her team to the beacon, halted the surrey just beyond it, in the weed-grown corral. No guards challenged her. No signs of life

Somewhere mustangs still run free.
Zane Grey will lead you there.

He's more mountain lion than mustang. With hellfire eyes. A mane like black flame. And a back that's never known a rope or rider.

The Indians call him Panquitch. And the old chiefs say that when you see him, the blood dances in your veins.

Zane Grey will lead you to Panquitch in <u>Wild Horse Mesa</u>, the story of two desperate men who fought to the death for the right to possess the King of Wild Horses.

If this is the kind of rousing adventure you enjoy, let us send you—for just $1—<u>Wild Horse Mesa</u> plus three other action-packed Zane Grey novels:

<u>Riders of the Purple Sage</u>, probably the most popular of all Westerns. A mysterious rider and the girl he loves gamble their lives in the winning of the West.

<u>The Thundering Herd</u>. A cowboy riding to

(continued on other side)

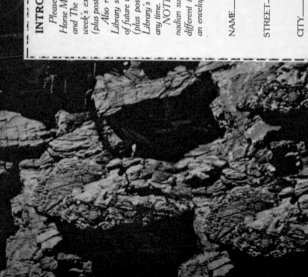

arose within the station. When she disappeared behind the corner of the rear wall, Rachel shadowed forward across the clearing, slid around the corner and
up to the near frame of the lone rear window. He was
in time to see nothing. The Darcy girl had vanished,
and he had to assume she had already gone inside.
That could mean the kitchen door was unbolted upon
her arrival, and was unbolted still.

Rachel felt for the walnut handle of the old Remington. It gave him no reassurance. He set his jaw,
craned to see what he might through the two-inch aper-
ture of lamplight where the horse blanket hung on the
inside failed of meeting the warped framing of the
window. The effort yielded frustratingly to a decade's
collection of spiderwebs, dead flies and Staked Plains
dust. The door, then. Perhaps the ear might succeed
where the eye had not. Again, frustration. He could
hear the hum of voices but could not separate them
either as to nearness, or number. One was a woman's
voice, that was all he knew.

Good Lord! had the parallel of the past come
down to this fineness, this last chanceful irony? Was he
going to have to kick in the door and blind-jump a
roomful of blurred voices exactly as he had done
ten years ago. Would the guns do all the talking once
more? Giving neither side the time to surrender, to
parley, to make any kind of sense at all? He made his
mind quit marching the fearful circle. It was no good
milling around the truth. The situation had come down
to where it must; he was here, the wanted man was
there. Only a door stood between him and his past.

Leave it, Rachel, leave it! the stillness around
him shouted. Ride out, ride out! No one knows you
came here, no one will know you have gone. Turn
away, turn away....

The crack of the door latch splitting out from its
rusted socket beneath the drive of his boot broke into the stale-aired kitchen with the sudden, rapping
sharpness of a rifleshot. Rachel, following it in, threw
his first round at the lamp. Some segment of the old

skill favored him. The heavy .44 bullet caught the
base of the glass chimney, bursting out the light as
though with a deft, blown breath, and breaking free
none of the oil in the reservoir beneath the chimney,
until the wick was lifeless of fire. Then, in the point-
blank gloom of the plunge into darkness, the overly
loud *drip, drip, drip* of the leaking fluid, spreading
over the tabletop from the ruptured reservoir to fall
upon the greasy floor beneath, was the only sound
punctuating the blind dark of the Faber's Crossing
station house.

"Briscoe," said Rachel, from his position prone
before the boarded-up door leading to the front of the
abandoned building, "get the lady out of here."

There were no answering bursts of gunfire attracted
by his voice, nor had he expected any. Total darkness
confused the senses. A man is put out of element when
he literally, and suddenly, cannot see. "Get the light,"
was not by accident the first law of the lawless—or of
the lawful, who pursued them. Plunging, blinding darkness had disarmed more desperate gunmen than all
the daylight drops on record.

"Just the lady, Briscoe."

If a man kept his word-strings short, and could
force his play before all eyes grew accustomed to
the pitch dark, he had some chance. Even when he
had seen what Rachel had seen in the half second before his bullet crashed out the light.

There had been four of them, the same as the
other night so long gone. Three riffraff hirelings, probably from the Red Rock job, and Briscoe. Briscoe
seated at the table, the trio of gunmen bent behind
him, listening to Edna Darcy. The dancehall girl talking swiftly. The four men watching her as wolves watch
a buffalo calf when the snow is deep.

The singular identicality of place and number
compounded the whipsawing of memories that went
on, now, in Rachel's mind. But the problem remaining
was no longer one of decisions; it was one of commit-

ments already made, against those yet to be made. And no reply, either of voice or revolver, came from across the room to direct Rachel in the making. He waited, counting the seconds of silence like drops of life's blood, knowing they could become that if Briscoe and his men had the intellect, and the intestines, to outwait him, to hold motionless where they were until nature inevitably adjusted their confused vision. But Briscoe had a problem in this regard, a handicap beyond his choosing. He had Edna Darcy over there. And Edna might not want to wait for ten shades of black to become seven of gray.

"*Run, lady!*" hissed Rachel, cupping his hands to throw the sound to his left, falsely.

The sibilant warning was the trigger. There was a bumping scuffle, a curse, a rustle of satin. The rear door banged open, framed the dancehall dress and surrey-blown blond curls, hinged rattlingly shut on the return throw of the tension-spring which alone held it closed with the latch-socket destroyed.

"You son of a bitch," said Rance Briscoe, into the echoing stillness. And that was all. From then, Rachel heard only a lip-rustle of cross-room whispering, quickly stilled.

After what seemed like fifteen minutes and was perhaps ten seconds, he caught a bump to his left. Then a scrape of rough cloth to his right. They were coming to him, working around the kitchen walls, both ways from the table, to converge on the shuttered door into the front, most likely. It was a good plan. It was second nature for an outnumbered man to put his back to a wall. Briscoe and his pack had figured that move. Now if they kept coming with their counter to it, they had him.

Rachel shook off the chill of the thought. He set his teeth to hold back his suspended breathing. In the intense quiet, the steady dripping of the coal oil from the broken lamp on the table was the moment's only sound. But, suddenly, to Rachel, its insistent thinness had the sweetness of a cavalry bugle calling the charge from over the hill. That damned lamp! Maybe, just maybe—

He pulled himself together, tensing for the leap. Fixing his target from memory, and from the oil's steady, small splash, he leaped out and away from the wall, rolled across the room, felt his back strike a table leg on the third roll, and froze dead still, on the contact.

The stink of the oil was in his nose, hand-close. As he crouched, motionless, he felt the splash of the next drip hit the back of his left hand. Feeling forward, he came to the wet slick on the floor. It went as prayed-for from there. He got the match from his vest pocket with the left hand, sent it on a long scrape and following-through drop into the center of the pooled oil. There was a hiss and flutter, a spurt of tiny, sulfuric fire. Then the oil caught and flared, orange and smoky, and the guns from cross-room thundered into its greasy bloom, even as it roiled upward. They splintered nothing but the grimy planking of the floor behind. Rachel, a full roll to the right of his tossed match, and clear of both fire and table, shot from the floor.

The range was no more than twenty feet, his targets set up like gallery ducks by the leap of the fire's light against the wall upon which they crouched. He dropped the first two with a round each. His third shot was a miss and he needed a fourth to anchor the third of Briscoe's gunmen. Swinging on Briscoe himself with the last round, he was too late. The outlaw chief had sprung through the rear door and was gone running through the starlight across the tumbleweeded stock corral. At the door, Rachel took a brace against its frame, brought the long barrel of the Remington in line, squeezed off the sixth shot with no sight picture save the instincts of ten years gone, guiding his unhurried aim.

He heard the sound of the bullet strike. It was like the slap of a wet bar rag upon dense, sour wood.

Rance Briscoe didn't stumble, didn't fall. He was driven forward, face-flat, into the sunbaked adobe. And he lay there in a way that Fate Rachel had seen many times. A way that needed no walk-up to confirm the quality of eternal stillness shrouding the huddled posture.

At the house it was different. Two of the men, Kagel and Stillwell, proved lightly wounded. Both were local cowboys, young, ignorant, drawn into the Red Rock affair when wiser men had refused it. Arbecker, the third man, was an old hand, and tough. But he had taken his .44 slug high in the hip, a crippling if not dangerous wound, and it must appear his days along the owlhoot trail were ended, given the best of recoveries.

The gang had a buckboard hidden out in the corral hay barn, toward which Rance had been running, and in the jumping light of the now-burning station house Rachel made a little speech to its remaining members, concerning some possible use of this vehicle. His essential suggestion was that if the two young cowboys could get their aging outlaw mate into the buckboard and be gone across Faber's Crossing inside of the next deep breath, he would be inclined to forget he had met any of them. Providing, of course, that, prior to departure, the Red Rock loot might be accounted for, give or take say fourteen dollars and fifty cents.

This offer produced five seconds of hard-frowned, sober consideration, to which Rachel added encouragingly.

"Arbecker," he said, "you are no yearling and this is no strange pasture to you. You have told me that it was Rance who shot the Anderson messenger and since this agrees with the company's report I am ready to accept your claims. But you are well aware what 'accessory after' will bring you in a murder case and if you wish to earn that ten thousand of Anderson's at the rate of five hundred a year, why you have only to keep your mouth shut. For my part I will take

no further action against you, save to place you in so-
cial contact with T. C. Barnes of the Anderson Express people, and that's a sacred promise."

The wounded outlaw eyed him, greed yielding
finally to pain.

"I believe you would do it," he said between
gritted teeth, "and I think I will take your word for it,
as you seem to me a man who would not sell watered
whiskey. Boys, bring out the box and help me to the
buggy."

It was seven minutes before midnight when Fate
Rachel rode up to the Longhorn Hotel in Mobeetie
with the body of Ransom Briscoe sacked across the
latter's led-horse. It was five minutes later that he
roused T. C. Barnes from sound slumber to trade him
the outlaw's remains for an Anderson Express Company sight draft, made out in blank, for $1,000. When
the wall clock in the lobby began counting off the
hour, Rachel was counting out the last of the company's $10,000 upon Barnes' rumpled bed, and Barnes
was still in his long-handled drawers yelling for a
quill pen and sanding pot to sign over the bounty
money.

With the sight draft undried in his vest pocket,
Rachel departed the Longhorn. Out front, the crowd
of curious night crawlers attracted from the Pink
Lady to analyze the burden hung across Rance Briscoe's horse, parted politely, even admiringly, to let his
slayer through.

"That's him," he heard a man say. "That's Fate
Rachel, right there!" It didn't dim the patent respect
in the first man's tone when his companion replied,
"That old geezer? You're drunk. He couldn't bounty-
hunt a bobcat."

"What the hell," demanded the first man, "has
being drunk got to do with it? You want to talk to
somebody sober, go down to the jail and talk to that
Darcy girl."

"And what the hell," inquired his companion, "has she got to do with it?"

"She was in with Briscoe's bunch. Come a-driving hell for San Antone into town about half an hour gone. Wanted to turn herself in. State's evidence. Wanted the sheriff to get up a posse and go out and bury poor old Rachel, decent. She blabbed the whole thing. Said she never seen such guts. One old man kicking in a door and jumping four of the top guns in the Panhandle? And him with nothing but an old wood-handled .44 Cap-and-Ball? Huh! And you with the gall to stand there and—"

The words, and the crowd around Briscoe's horse, faded out for Rachel. True to the temper of street gatherings, this one was more interested in resolving its own arguments of ignorance than in gaining information bounded by the facts. They let Rachel ride out with neither hail nor farewell, so busy in describing to one another precisely the manner in which he shot down the four top guns of the Texas Panhandle, that none thought to inquire of him if he might have a word to say for himself in the matter.

For the record, however, he did not.

If two itinerant young cowhands and one rheumatic old train robber, along with Rance Briscoe, made up the four most feared gunfighters on the Staked Plains, that was no more than fair. For he knew, by the evidence of his own ears in guiding his old horse away from the din in front of the Longhorn Hotel, that before he put the last light of Mobeetie behind him, the history makers milling the dirt of Main Street would have the number of outlaws built to regimental strength and the artillery with which Fate Rachel destroyed them reduced to a .41 Short Colt derringer, or a single-shot caplock pistol, Model 1812.

Moreover, he was not interested in what Mobeetie made of the killing of Rance Briscoe. It was what he, Rachel, now made from it which counted.

He found Eileen Briscoe's shack on the north

edge of the settlement. It was gray-board, unpainted. The two windows were broken out, patched with butcher paper and tacks. Over the door, on a trellis which must have been the only one in Mobeetie, grew a rambler rose.

Rachel got down from his horse, but did not need to knock. The woman came out, stood confronting him, a pale, pretty youngster of ten peering uncertainly from the doorway behind her.

"Who is it, Ma?" asked the child and Eileen Briscoe said, "Hush, honey—it's a friend who knew your father."

Rachel took her hands and put in them the Anderson draft.

"What is it?" she said.

"A sight draft, Mrs. Briscoe, ma'am. On Anderson Express, for a thousand dollars."

"A thousand dollars—"

"Yes, ma'am. All you need do is fill in your name where the blank is, and they will pay you the money. It's for Rance, ma'am."

The woman was sober now, long sober. She looked up at Rachel and said tonelessly, "They got him."

"Yes," said Rachel.

"You got him," she said. And, "Yes," said Fate Rachel again.

She stood a moment. He could almost see each year pass across the emptiness of her eyes. Then she shook her head.

"I can't take it," she said. "It's yours."

"No, ma'am," said Rachel, inclining his head toward the nightgowned youngster, "it's hers."

She studied him, the lines of thought smoothing at last.

"It's like you," she said. "I remember you now. The trial. The sentencing. All of it. Do you think a thousand dollars—"

"A thousand dollars won't do anything for you nor me, ma'am," Rachel cut her off gently. "But it will do a lot for her." He kept his voice down, so that the child would not hear. "You remember what you told me about that clinic in Kansas City?"

"Yes, oh yes." The woman spoke quickly, then looked down at the draft in her hand. "A thousand dollars. In one night. Dear God, dear God—"

Rachel nodded, wrinkled his eye corners.

"I never did work cheap, Mrs. Briscoe," he said. "Sentiment doesn't pay in my business." He paused, warming the last words with his inside grin. "But sometimes express companies do."

He turned for his horse, putting foot to stirrup and swinging up. Eileen Briscoe stepped haltingly forward. She started to speak but he leaned down quickly.

"The Anderson people will take care of your bill in Kansas City—anything past this advance."

Eileen Briscoe looked down at the Anderson draft once more, the tears beginning to run now. She dropped her gaze, lips compressed, gestured helplessly with the draft.

"But this—it's still yours—I can't—"

She had started forward impulsively, but Rachel heeled the horse a sidestep away. She halted and he checked his mount, looking back and down at her and at the little girl who had come out of the house to stand beside her in the puddled dust of the street. His words came very softly, very seriously.

"I'm happy, if you are, ma'am. It comes out even the way I figure it. A thousand dollars to end one life and begin another. You can't beat a trade like that in my line of work."

He checked the nervous horse for the final time, tipping his hat to the woman and child, voice rising happily.

"Fate Rachel, ma'am. A little old, a little tired, and an awful lot lucky."

He wheeled the horse, put him on a high lope. Eileen Briscoe and the girl stood watching after him. Both took a wordless step forward, waving hesitantly. In the uncertain sweep of the starlight they thought they saw him turn in the saddle and wave back to them. It was the way they told it later and a good way to tell it in any case. But it was not the true way.

Fate Rachel did not return their wave. When he swung his horse away from Mobeetie that long-ago night, he had done more than buy a new life for Eileen Briscoe and her daughter—he had sold an old life for himself. He never looked back on Mobeetie, never rode that way again.

King Fisher's Road

I came into Kearney on the afternoon stage. It was four hours late, pretty bad even for the American Mail Company. When I got down in front of the division office it was ten minutes of six P.M. Even so, no one had gone home yet. American Mail paid for twelve hours work and got it.

I stood a moment, unwrapping a fresh cigar and wondering anew why they had sent for me. The assignment was to open a new stage route between San Antonio and Uvalde, Texas, that I knew. But opening new routes was not exactly the way in which I earned my company keep, and so my curiosity mounted.

Going into the office I nodded at two clerks I knew but they kept their eyes to their accounts. Aha, I thought, I've been let out at last. The poor fellows are embarrassed by what they know and what I am about to find out. Well, no man lasts forever. The hand is quicker than the eye, they say, and in my business it had better be. Apparently, though, some diligent employee had reported to the division super that I was coming down with a hard case of slowing up. How this rumor had taken wing interested me. To my knowledge I hadn't turned down any private invitation to compete, nor come out second in any public performance of my work. This should have reassured me, but it did not. The truth was that of a given cold morning or after too many hours in the saddle I was a whisper less quick than an eye wink these latter days. But who had found me out, and how? That was the matter of interest.

Giving the cowardly clerks a good eyeing, I went on past their desks and stopped at the one to the rear of the office. This one bore a sign which read, "EVERETT D. STONE, SUPERINTENDENT," an accurate statement, if superfluous. Anyone would know Stone was a superintendent. He was too fat for a working man, and not worried enough. Presently he was frowning, though, and I took it he was not happy with the report he was studying. That seemed reasonable. It was a thick report and had a telegram pinned to it, and telegrams are always trouble. I stood by a polite bit, then scuffed my boots.

"Hello," I said, "somebody here send for a road opener?"

Stone looked up sort of flustered. He put the report quickly under some other papers, taking off his glasses and then acting real surprised to see me there.

"Harry, boy! Harry Roebuck!" he said, getting up and placing me a chair. "Sit down, sit down——"

I gave him a pretty well wrung-out nod, took the seat and said, "Well, Mr. Stone, who turned me in?"

He just looked at me, beaming.

"Harry, you old coyote," he said, "how have you been?"

"I've been right fine," I said, "but I got an idea I'm not going to stay that way."

He gave me the eye and said, "Um, yes, let's see here now," and began ruffling through some old waybills on his desk. "Cuss it all, I had that file right in front of me."

I gave him the eye back and reached over and pulled the report out from under the other papers.

"Yes, sir," I said. "Could this possibly be it, Mr. Stone?"

He took the report, looking it over as though it had just come off the key.

"Why so it is! I tell you, Harry, my eyesight is going bad."

"Mine isn't," I told him. "Mind reading me that telegram you got pinned on top? It looks to bear the same date as the one you sent me."

He gave me one more look and surrendered.

"First let me go back a ways," he said. "Do you remember Bunker Johnson?"

"Why don't you ask me if I remember my mother? You know I remember Bunk. He broke me in on this job." I watched him close now. "Don't tell me," I said, "that anything has happened to old Bunk."

Stone put up his hands.

"Now wait, get the whole story. We called you in here to go down to Texas and supervise the opening of a new stage route into Uvalde. Am I right?"

"As summer rain. And that brings up another point. Why me?"

"That," nodded Stone, "brings us right back to Bunk Johnson. We put him on the job and he couldn't handle it."

"Bunk couldn't handle a route opening? Must be some route. He's one of the best men you've got."

"He was one of the best," Stone said, handing over the telegram. "Read this."

I held the telegram up to the sunset light. It read:
JOHNSON KILLED GUNFIGHT J. K. FISHER UVALDE THIS DATE. SIGNED. WESTCOTT.

I gave it back to Stone.

"Who's Westcott?" I asked.

"Our Uvalde office manager."

"That leaves us with J. K. Fisher."

"Yes. Ever hear of him, Harry?"

"Not till now. Should I have?"

Stone nodded grimly, voice tight.

"Try 'King Fisher,' " he said.

"Him," I answered, "I've heard of. Go ahead."

Stone laid it out for me then. Fisher had announced to all Texas that he was closing the Uvalde road to through traffic. Specifically he had warned American Mail they were not going to run their new stage line over it. Moreover, he had run the Uvalde manager out of town and back to San Antonio. He had then planted a sign squarely in the middle of the road proclaiming it was his road and that the rest of the world could take the other. When the company sent Bunk Johnson, their senior shotgun guard, over from the Dallas office to make certain the first stage went through to Uvalde on schedule, Fisher ambushed the stage at his sign in the road, forced Bunk, an older man no longer in his prime as a gunman, to draw, then shot him off the seat box of the stage and left him dying in the dirt of the Uvalde road. It was here that they had sent for Harry Roebuck and the question now was, would Roebuck take the job or wouldn't he? Roebuck being me, and me seeing no place to hide in the division office, I threw in.

I still had a question or two of my own, however.

"I don't get it," I frowned. "Why would Fisher want that road closed? What's he got against American Mail? It don't make sense."

Stone wagged his head, held up his hands again.

"It makes sense, Harry," he said. "Hard, dirty sense. By now, most folks know the law has a habit of following American Mail west. We move into a town and trouble moves out. Fisher knows that, too, and trouble is his business. He's a hell-raiser and a rustler and is making money with his left hand faster than his right can spend it. Uvalde's his town and unless we get that new run through, it's going to stay his town. If he can buffalo American Mail, who's going to stop him?"

"Well, for one thing, what's holding up the Texas Rangers?"

"They're not on our payroll, Harry. You are."

"That's a handy way of looking at it—for the Texas Rangers," I said. "But it suits me. I'll take the job. When do I leave?"

Fool questions never go long begging for blunt answers and this one was no more than decently out of my mouth than a train whistled sharply down at the depot. Stone pulled out his watch.

"That's the 6:05 for San Antone," he said. "How soon you want to leave?"

I wasn't going to let him run any cold bluffs on me. I pulled out my own watch.

"6:01," I said. "Good a time as any to go to Texas and kill a man."

Stone looked at me a little hard.

"How's that, Harry?" he said.

"It's what you want done isn't it, Mr. Stone?" I answered him.

"Now, Harry, I didn't say that!"

"No, we never do *say it,* Mr. Stone. But somehow it always manages to come out that way, doesn't it?"

I started for the door but Stone caught up to me.

"I know it's a rough job, Harry," he said. "You don't have to take it."

"No," I said, "and I don't have to take the company's money, either, but I've developed some soft habits doing so all these years, and eating is one of the worst."

"Now see here, Harry," he came back at me, "there's no call for you to take such a hard-nose attitude. American Mail will always have some kind of a job for you."

"Thank you," I said, "but some kind of a job is not my kind of a job." The train tooted again just then and I started out the door once more.

"Harry," said Stone anxiously, "be careful!"

"Thank you," I repeated, "I never got hurt running for a train yet," and that is the way we left it.

It was seven hundred miles from the division office to San Antonio. The 6:05 was a makeup train of two mail cars, one chair car and thirty-three cattle car empties to be dropped at Fort Worth. Naturally we did not establish any new line records. I had plenty of time to think, which I didn't need at all. I had known when I left the office why American Mail had sent for me, and what my job was—or rather what it was meant to be—to go down to Texas and kill King Fisher, one of the two fastest guns alive. I didn't blame the company for the order, as a man with a reputation like King's doesn't leave either the law, or legitimate business folks, much of any other approach. But I had a hunch about young King Fisher and I intended to play it through. Providing, that is, I could get somebody to play it with me. In that direction my first move was almost straight across the street from the depot in San Antonio, and I made it as soon as I lighted down there the next evening.

Angling through the dust away from the depot, I squinted through the twilight to make sure my friends were still doing business in Bexar County and sure enough they were. The oil lamp hung from the front roof eave had just been lit and its rays showed me the sign hadn't changed a dot or a comma. "HDQTRS. TEXAS RANGERS, CO. A," it read, which was a good thing, for I required—required?—I had to have—the approval of my hunch by the Rangers before trying it on King Fisher. Also I might need their active backing, and they were pretty fair country gunfighters or, for that matter, city gutter-fighters, and what I had in mind for King was a sort of combination of John Wesley Hardin and the Marquis of Queensbury set to Texas rules.

Luckily, I caught Captain Randolph in a sinking spell and he not only approved my idea for dealing with the one-man war in Uvalde County but said that any further aid the Rangers could furnish me, I had only to name it. They had tried several of their own hunches on King Fisher and his Uvalde crowd without what you might call a crowning success anywhere along the line. My underhanded approach sounded just right to them and they graciously gave me the green light to go ahead and run its track into Uvalde—if I could.

My first need was for a good night's sleep, which I got for a dollar and a half at the Unicorn Hotel. I had quite a few visitors during the night but it takes more than a couple of hundred playful bites to keep a really tired man awake. Besides, everybody has to make his living the best way he can in this life, and I never did grudge an honest bedbug his pint of my blood.

Sunrise next morning I was hitting along the main road west out of San Antonio in a two-horse rig rented from the Alamo Livery & Prairie Hay Company, across from the firehouse and down the street from the Ranger headquarters building. That's the old firehouse, on the corner of the square, not the one they have now.

It was a fine morning, my team full of ginger and even me feeling like I might live. My purpose, of course, was not to study the Texas daybreak but to feel out the party of the second part. When you go up against a gunfighter of King Fisher's reputation you have got to call it a war. And in a war the first thing you do is scout the enemy lines. For me, I had to see that reported sign of King Fisher's with my own eyes and, if possible, get a close-up look at the famous young man who had put it there, before deciding precisely how to open my campaign to get American Mail's first stage into Uvalde on time and as advertised.

Presently, I struck a county road coming in from the side. The turn-off sign read, "UVALDE, 55 MI.," and I set myself for the long drive. About four that afternoon, coming around a sharp bend made blind by heavy mesquite, oak and catclaw thorn trees, I very nearly had to burn off the hide on my team's hocks, hauling them up. The rig slid sideways, decided not to tip over, settled down in a cloud of red Texas real estate. I dug the grit out of my eyes and shook my head three to five times, but it would not go away. There it stood planted right square in the middle of the wagon ruts of the Uvalde road, and what it said was as to-the-point as a sat-on pin.

THIS IS KING FISHER'S ROAD
TAKE THE OTHER

I got down from the rig, still shaking my head, and walked over for a closer study of the sign. Looking at it, I had to grin.

There it was sure enough, the sign which was to become a legend, along with the wild youngster who put it there. How could you help grinning at that kind of brass? Planting a split-board sign in the middle of a public thoroughfare and expecting folks to take it seriously? It was one too many for an old hand like me, and I stepped up to work it loose and throw it aside, still chuckling over the pure gall it had taken to put it there. But that was what fooled so many people about King Fisher. And what made him different. Deadly different. He did have that lighthearted sense of humor and playful good clean fun.

I had no more than put my hands to the sign, than a string of gunshots set in from immediately up-road. The first one took off my hat and knocked it skittering through the air. The following ones kept it going on the same jumpy course. I froze right where I was, hands still on the sign. But I did move my eyes enough to see who was working the artillery.

What I saw would have made a man break his gin bottle.

He was a young fellow, twenty-odd. Tall, dark-skinned, soot-black hair, Mexican handlebar mustache, eyes like obsidian chips, and dressed as no gunman of reputation before him, or since.

Starting at the top he wore a Chihuahua sombrero, snow-white, with a gold Aztec snake for a hatband. Next came a gold-embroidered soft buckskin jacket, a red silk waist-sash and—it's hard to believe even retelling it—chaps made out of Bengal tiger skins! After the chaps, the fact his boots were grass green leather with yellow dragons sewed in eight rows of pale petunia stitching couldn't shine. Neither could his spurs being hung with little silver bells which actually chimed when he walked. Nothing could hope to touch those cat-hair pants, not even the brace of ivory-handled Colts with which he was chasing my hat. But the way he was using those Colts was two other things again. He didn't miss that hat with a one of the twelve shots he threw at it, and he fired right- and left-handed, alternately, from horseback! He jumped that hat around like it was a tin can and him firing a .22 pumpkin roller from the shoulder. And he was only getting started.

When the hat hit the ground following his last shot, the gunman got down off his horse and walked slowly past me. Reaching the fallen hat, he reloaded one shell into his right-hand gun and pointed the gun at the hat. Then, turning away as though he couldn't bear to watch himself do it, he shot that poor wounded hat. Having put it out of its misery, he removed his own sombrero and held it to his chest while he bowed his head in respect. Then he turned to me and said with genuine commisery, "It's done for, poor thing. I'll give it a proper burying for you, mister."

Well, I looked him over and answered back: "Thank you. I reckon you would do as much for me, too, providing I asked for it."

"Let's say, providing you keep on asking for it, Mr. Roebuck," he said with a nice smile.

I looked at him sideways.

"You seem pretty well acquainted with me, friend," I said. "Who are you?"

The young fellow stepped back and looked down at himself as though to see if maybe he had forgotten to put on his pants, or something. But seeing the tiger skin chaps, red silk bellyband and all the rest of it was in place, he glanced back up at me sort of hurt like and said in a most gentle and courteous voice, "Now, Mr. Roebuck that wasn't too kindly of you. Take another careful look and see if you can't do better. Squint hard, now, it's bound to come to you."

I nodded, more to myself than to him.

I knew who he was all right and he knew that I

did. There just weren't that many gunfighters wearing
tiger chaps and white Mexican sombreros running loose
in West Texas that spring. I was looking at the one and
only, the original and no substitute—Mr. J. K. Fisher,
of Uvalde.

The latter, waiting politely, said at last.

"Well, Mr. Roebuck?"

"Well, Mr. Fisher," I countered.

He shrugged.

"I'd say it was your move. What would you say?"

"I'd agree."

"What do you aim to do with it?"

"Go buy me a new hat."

He liked that. He broke into his sudden, sunny
smile.

"You know, Mr. Roebuck, it's too bad you're
working for American Mail. I got an idea we could
get along right fine riding for the same side. What
you think?"

"I got that idea, too, King," I told him carefully.
"Otherwise, I wouldn't have taken on this job of opening up your road for the company."

Now the smile turned frostbit, chilling the voice
along with it.

"Nobody's opening up my road, Mr. Roebuck. Not
you, not American Mail, not nobody." He frowned
in honest dismay, pointing to his sign. "Can't you
read?"

"Sure," I said quickly. "But can you?"

That worried him. He knew I wasn't getting smart
with him, and his frown deepened.

"What you mean?" he said.

For answer I gave him the paper which I had
had the Rangers draw up for me.

"Open it up, King," I urged him, "and read it."

He hesitated, wanting to look inside and see what
it said. He sensed it was something out of the ordinary, something to do with him and with why I was
there for American Mail. But in the end his natural

outlaw suspicion was too strong for him. He shoved the paper back at me, shaking his head.

"You read it," he said. "On your way back to San Antone. You'll have lots of time for you're getting started right now."

"Don't be a fool, Fisher," I said, taking the paper. "At least read it—see what it says."

"Mr. Roebuck," he replied, "you get back in that rig and you wheel it around and you light out and don't you slow down till you're shut of Uvalde County, hear?"

"That your final offer, King?"

"It is unless you want to wind up where that other American Mail fellow did."

"You mean Bunker Johnson?"

"Whatever his name was."

"Whatever his name was, eh?" He had said it offhandedly and now caught the anger in my slow repeat of his words. At once his attitude changed.

"Listen, Mr. Roebuck," he said, "there wasn't time for getting any names. I asked this fellow to turn around and go back easy and nice as you can ask a man to do anything. He drew on me, left me no choice."

I shook my head, still seething inside.

"No choice, King?" I asked. "You sure you wanted a choice? I just tried to give you one all wrote up in black and white." I tapped the paper in my hand. "You wouldn't even look at it. No, you didn't want my choice and I don't think you wanted Bunk Johnson's. Now you listen to me, boy, and you listen good. You're going to get another kind of a choice now—from me personally. I'm ordering that stage you shot Bunk Johnson off of sent back through to Uvalde. When she comes, she'll be bringing you that other choice, *sabe?*"

"No *sabe*," he said. "Try it again."

"I'll be on that stage," I told him, "right where Bunk Johnson was."

"Then you'll wind up in the dirt right where he did."

"That's the chance I'm taking, King. The one you're taking is something else again."

"Such as?"

"Such as the difference between me and Bunk Johnson."

I had turned and headed for the rig with the statement, but he called softly after me.

"What difference is that, Mr. Roebuck?"

I wheeled on him, flashing the draw. The old Colt bucked and roared to the thunder of five shots blending. King Fisher's white hat jumped off his head and kept right on jumping through the air behind him, exactly as had mine earlier. As it landed in a chaparral thicket, I holstered the .44 Special and said just as quietly as I could.

"That difference, Mr. Fisher. Good day, sir."

I gave him a nod as short as a bobcat's tail and climbed into the rig. Backing the horses, I swung them about, heading them for San Antonio. King Fisher had to jump to avoid being run down. The last I saw of him he was standing in the dust peering off after me and shaking his head as though to say what a damned shame it was American Mail didn't know when it was licked.

Personally, I sort of agreed with him.

That night I spent in Castroville, a cowtown halfway between San Antonio and Uvalde. My idea was to spare myself the extra miles on the stage out of San Antonio next morning, while at the same time hoping to pick up some interim information on the enemy in the Castroville cantinas. I caught a mail rider going east and gave him a note for Captain Randolph and one for Charley Mertens in our San Antonio office requesting that he roll the Uvalde stage as planned, seeing that it picked me up here in Castroville not later than high noon. That done, I waited for midnight, time for the native telegraph to start clicking in from

Uvalde and for local tongues to get sloshy enough to repeat what came off the key from King Fisher's town.

I had my news by one A.M.

Word was that another damnfool American Mail agent had collared King and challenged him on his own terms and trade—as a gunfighter. Over in Uvalde the populace was waiting and wagering on the outcome. Or rather waiting and looking for wagers on the outcome. For American Mail money was mighty scarce. King was swaggering the main stem of his hometown good-naturedly offering to lay ten for one on himself and getting no takers. The synthesis of opinion in Uvalde was that if the Texas Rangers couldn't pin back King Fisher's ears no mealy-nose American Mail detective was going to do it. As for King, he was telling his fellow Uvaldans that if they wanted to see how fast a four-horse stagecoach could get turned around in the middle of a thirty-foot county road, they need only show up out by his sign late next afternoon. Last I heard, going to bed, was that Uvalde was planning to take King up on his invitation, wholesale. It figured to be the biggest turnout in West Texas since Captain Jack Coffee Hays whipped the Mexicans at Salado.

Next morning the stage rolled in Castroville at 11:36 A.M. After a twenty-minute rest to water the teams, I took over on the box, relieving the regular driver. I noticed that on my way out of town several of the locals took off their hats and held them to their left breasts as I passed by. It gave me a nice feeling to know I wasn't without friends, even though a stranger.

I wasn't fooling myself any about King Fisher, however. His hand wasn't going to be holding a hat. But where I wasn't fooling myself about him, I was hoping I had fooled him about me. I had led him to think he had me in the same corner he had old Bunk Johnson, making me come at him with a gun in my hand. Yet I had no intention of playing the game to those rules. A man doesn't get old in this business giving away advantages to young gunfighters. I didn't mean to give one ounce of edge of King Fisher. All's fair in love and war, I figured, and what young King and I had to settle between us wasn't precisely a love affair. And I didn't let my conscience slow me up any, either. I wasn't five minutes off regular schedule—four P.M.—rounding that mesquite bend just shy of King's sign.

Well, I don't think Grant got a bigger cheer for taking Vicksburg than I did for taking that last turn on two wheels. That crowd was happier to see me than Sitting Bull was to see Custer, and for the same reasons. Still a man had to admit it was a thrill seeing that many good folks collected in one piece so far out in the sagebrush, and in such a high, fine humor, too.

The atmosphere at that road sign of King Fisher's was that of a small-time Manassas. As the citizens of our national Capital turned out to watch the boys in blue rout Johnny Reb at the Battle of Bull Run, so the voting populace of Uvalde had come along to watch King Fisher and the American Mail detective shoot it out. I could tell with one look, coming around that bend, that I was being given less chance than Lee at Cemetery Ridge. That piebald collection of saddle horses, buggies, buckboards, surreys, Studebakers and Conestogas coagulated there in the boondocks was 110 percent in favor of their man. When they sighted me down the road and let out that yell, I don't think you could have sold a chance on American Mail for six hundred dollars, Union.

And King didn't keep them waiting.

Mounting up immediately, he swung his flashy paint into a high lope, skidded him up, short, ten feet the Uvalde side of his sign. On my side of the sign, maybe fifty feet—no, closer to seventy—I was doing the same with my four-horse hitch and big old highside Abbott & Downing coach. It got that quiet you couldn't hear a baby cry nor an old man hawk to spit. I mean that multitude didn't let out a peep.

In the stillness, King slid from his saddle, stepped clear of his horse. I wrapped my lines, set the brake, eased down off the driver's box, moved out to one side of the coach. There we were, the two champions, one of the law and the other of disorder, come to a halt facing each other at a distance of maybe sixty feet— just a deliberate shade outside good gunfighting range. The crowd sucked in and took a tighter hold on its breath. All eyes were on King Fisher and he knew it. He took one step toward me and spoke up frosty.

"All right, Mr. Roebuck, let's start the walk-up. You make it as close as you want. Cut loose when you're ready."

He started toward me again but I held up both hands real quick.

"Hold it, King," I said. "That's close enough."

He grinned and made a little bow.

"Age before youth and beauty, Mr. Roebuck. Make your move."

I returned the grin as best I could.

"I'm going to, King," I told him, "but not the way you think."

His grin was well gone now.

"Pull your gun, Mr. Roebuck—"

I shook my head, still holding up my hands.

"The only thing I'm going to pull, King, is the buckle on my gun belt. You shoot me while I'm doing that and you got a whole townful of readymade witnesses right behind you."

"Yeah," he said, "but you're forgetting one thing, Mr. Roebuck. They're friendly witnesses."

"All right," I answered him, "let's try it this way: you cut down on me while I'm dropping my buscadero rig and you'll get your own belt punched six extra holes before your gun clears leather. You don't believe it, *you* take a look behind *me*. Maybe you can't read but you can damn sure count. So count."

The crowd got pin-still as King looked past me to the stagecoach. I saw his eyes go wide, and knew why.

The old Abbott & Downing had sprouted rifle-snouts. She was bristling steel barrels like a stirred-up quill pig. From beneath the canvas luggage cover of the roof decking two hard-looking riflemen held their Winchesters on a line with King Fisher's belt buckle. From the two forward and two rear window curtains of each side, below, peered four more earnest marksmen, their carbines pinned to the same target. Their total number was six, their reputations certain, their identity undeniable. They were the gentlemen in the white hats—the Texas Rangers.

King Fisher gave them, and me, a look of black disgust. He showed no fear of the Rangers but did include an expression of great disappointment in Harry Roebuck.

"It's a pretty lowdown trick, Mr. Roebuck," he said. "But what does it prove?"

"It proves you've got a lot to learn about life, King," I told him. "And, personally, I think you're man enough to learn your first lesson right here."

"What have you got to teach me, Mr. Roebuck? How to be a liar like you?"

"I didn't lie to you, boy," I said. "But maybe you did to me."

"Now what you mean by that?"

"I said I'd come back alone on the driver's box of that stage, just like Bunk Johnson came. I did it."

"Yeah, with six Rangers hid out behind your back!"

"Well, King, it looks like you brought along a few friends too."

"It isn't the same. You know it isn't. You lied to me, Mr. Roebuck."

I looked him in the eye, answering quietly.

"Well, boy, if I didn't keep my word, let's see if you can keep yours."

I unbuckled my gun belt and let it slide to the ground. The crowd from Uvalde pulled in behind King, the Rangers got out of the stage and moved up behind me. I armed out of my coat, started unbuttoning my shirt.

"You said," I went on, "that if I came back on that driver's box where Bunk Johnson was, you would put me right where you put him, in the dirt of this road."

I dropped my shirt and my voice with it.

"Let's see you do it, King. Like a man, without your guns."

He studied me through the longest five seconds on record, then slipped off his gun belt, slid his vaquero shirt off over his head and put up his hands. Soundlessly, under that hot Texas sun, we began circling.

What followed was the wildest bare-knuckle fight ever staged south of Chicago, with the six referees wearing white hats and Winchesters and the audience all armed and ready to cut loose with anything from a .22 derringer to a sawed-off shotgun if it didn't like the decision. But it would be unkind to detail that battle. King Fisher didn't have a chance. I beat him very nearly blind and when it was all over he was down in the dirt and all done. I was about as bad off but I was still on my feet. The cheering of the crowd had fallen off as though somebody had stuck its collective head in a bucket of swamp water. The Rangers moved silently in on King Fisher and the folks from his hometown moved silently away from him. Within five minutes the last of them was started back toward Uvalde. Groggily, King watched them go, leaving him alone with his enemies, a chastened, humbled man. When two of the Rangers had helped him to his feet, he turned to me.

"Well, Mr. Roebuck," he acknowledged unhappily, "it looks as though you were right. Your word is better than mine. What is the next stage of the ambush? Back to San Antone with the Rangers?"

I shook my head soberly.

"No, King, the Rangers didn't come along to arrest you. They were just here to see we had a fair fight and to make sure, to their own satisfaction, that you couldn't read. I told them you acted like you couldn't, but I reckon they'd feel better about it if you showed them your ownself. Here."

I handed him the same paper I had tried to get him to read before, and this time he took it. After a puzzled look at all of us, he unfolded it and began frowning his way through what it said. Pretty quick, he looked back up.

"Why, I don't believe it," he said. "This here is a deputy sheriff's appointment for Uvalde County in my name. It's writ right there, 'J. K. Fisher,' plain as fresh paint."

"That's right, King." I smiled. "She's all yours, courtesy of the Texas Rangers. You see, they agreed with me that you'd make a better live deputy than a dead outlaw. They got Governor Marvin to go along with them on my idea and he added one of his own. There's a full executive amnesty for the state of Texas goes with that star Captain Randolph, yonder, is fishing out of his vest pocket."

I bobbed my head toward the Ranger captain standing off to our left. King looked over at him and Randolph stepped toward him holding out the emblem. King kind of straightened up.

"I guess that makes it my move, don't it?" he said.

"I'd say it did," I replied. "What you aim to do with it?"

He looked at me dead serious and said, "Same thing you did when I asked you that question, Mr. Roebuck."

I returned his look, puzzled.

"How's that, King?" I said.

"Go get me a new hat." He grinned. "Care to come along?"

"Oh, I dunno. What kind you going to get?" I played it sober-sided now but it didn't slow him a wink.

"Well, something appropriate to my new standing in the community, I should think," he said. He moved to Randolph and took the star from him, pinning it carelessly upside down on his Mexican shirt, which he had gotten back into while we talked. Then, easing back over to me, he went on as though nothing had interrupted his statement. "Whatever kind of a hat they're recommending for wet-eared deputy sheriffs in West Texas this spring."

I had to hand him back his grin now, and something else as well. Reaching down, I got his gun belt out of the road and reached it over to him.

"Hang it on, Sheriff," I said. "I got an American Mail Company passenger run needs guarding into Uvalde."

King belted on his gun and, while I was getting into my shirt, picked mine up from the dirt and handed it to me with a bow and a sweep of his arm toward the coach.

"After you, sir—"

Straightening up he put his hand over his heart.

"The welfare of American Mail is the civic responsibility of every decent law-abiding resident of Uvalde County. I am deeply affected by this opportunity to make sure the sons of bitches understand it."

He watched me pass him by, headed for the stage, then gave his gun belt a determined hitch and started after me. The Rangers caught up his horse, tied him to the luggage boot, climbed aboard and waved the "all set" sign. I swung up to the box, followed by King Fisher. Reaching under the seat, King pulled out the regular guard's shotgun, barred it across his knees.

"All right," he said, "let's go."

I whistled up the teams. Slapping them smartly with the lines, I kicked off the brake and yelled, "Hee-yahh! Hee-yahh!" They hit into their collars and the stage began to roll. The minute it did, King made an excited motion toward the road in front of us and hollered out, "Hold on!"

I slammed the brakes back on and hauled up the teams. King jumped down and ran off up the road. Pretty soon he was back lugging his uprooted sign. Climbing back up with me, he stowed it under the roof-deck tarp, picked the shotgun up again and nodded to me.

"You never can tell, Mr. Roebuck. I might want to go back in business for myself someday."

I gave him the eye, shook up the teams, got the coach to rolling again. Half an hour later she was parked in front of American Mail's new office in Uvalde and the adventure of King Fisher's road was closed.

As for King, he did go back in business for himself some years later, and was killed in an ambush with Ben Thompson in the Vaudeville, a theater-saloon in San Antonio, in March of 1884.

They say King Fisher never had a chance, but I know better. I gave him one and it was a good one. Yet he didn't end any different from all the other wild guns before and after him. When the bullet with his name on it came along, he was there.

The Trap

C anady felt the horse beginning to go rough beneath him. He had been expecting it. On this rocky going no mount could make it for long when he was already ridden out in coming to it. "Easy, easy," he said to the laboring animal. "It's only a posse." The horse seemed to understand the tone of the words, for it slowed and went better and steadier for a ways. "We'll rest on the rise ahead," Canady said. "I can see back a few miles and you can catch some wind and we'll go on. We'll make it."

He knew they wouldn't. He knew it before they came to the rise and he got down and walked out on the overhanging spur of gray-black basalt that gave view down the canyon behind them for ten miles. It wasn't a canyon, really, but a narrowing valley. The canyon proper lay before them. Canady grinned and wiped his streaming face. It was hot, and going to get hotter. "Hoss," he said, "they're pushing. They mean to take us. They must know the country ahead. They don't ride like there's any hurry." The horse, now, did not respond with its ears and a turning of its soft eyes, as it had before. It stood, head-down, blowing out through its distended nostrils. Canady came back and squatted down and put his hand below the nose of the horse, where the moisture of its pained breathing would strike his palm. "Damn," he said softly. "Blood."

He got his field glasses from the saddle pocket and examined the pursuers through them. "Eight," he

said aloud, "and six ropes. I wonder how come it is
that they always fetch so many ropes? Never saw a
posse yet didn't feel they'd each of them ought to have
a rope."

His fingers went to his sunburned neck. They felt
it tenderly, and he grinned again. "Son of a gun," he
said, "it could happen."

Canady's grins were not the grimaces of a fool,
or of an unfeeling man. They were the grins of a gam-
bler. And of an outlaw. And a thief. Canady knew
where he was and where he had been and, most apparently, where he was going. It did not frighten him.
He would grin when they put the loop over his head.
That was his kind. He wouldn't curse or revile, and he
wouldn't pray. Not out loud, anyway.

"Hoss," he said, "what do you think?"

The animal, slightly recovered, moved its ears
and whickered gruntingly. Canady nodded, turning his
back to the approaching posse and glassing the country
ahead. "Me too," he agreed. "A grunt and a whicker
is all she's worth. We haven't got no place to go."
He tensed, as he said it, the glasses freezing on an
opening in the rearing base rock of the closing valley.
It was to their right. A good horse, fresh and sound,
could take a man up to that gap in the cliff. The spill
of detritus and ages-old fan of boulders and stunted
pine that lay below its lip would permit of perilous
mounted passage. There was water up there, too, for
Canady could see the small white ribbon of the stream
splashing down a rainbow falls to mist up upon the
lower rocks in a spume of red and yellow and tur-
quoise green lights, splendid with beauty in the early
sun. "I take it back," he said. "Maybe we do have a
place to go. Pretty, too, and handy to town. You can't
beat that."

Directly ahead was a level sunlit flat, dotted with
tall pines and scrub juniper and house-sized boulders.
The clear stream from the high hole in the right-side
valley wall watered the flat, growing good mountain
hay upon its sandy red loam and making a ride across

it a thing to pleasure the heart of any Western man.

"Come on," said Canady to his horse. "You canter me across the flat and I'll climb the fan afoot leaving you to pack up nothing but the saddle and the grub sack. You game? Least we can do is make those birds scratch for their breakfast. And who knows? Our luck might change. We might get up there and into that hole-in-the-wall before they come up to the rise, here, and spot us. If we can do that, there's a chance they'll ride on by, up the valley, and we can double back tonight and make it free."

He was talking to Canady, now, not to the horse. It was the way of men much alone and when they needed to do some figuring. They would do it out loud, the way Canady was doing. It sounded better that way, more convincing, and more as though it might really come off. Canady even swung into the saddle believing his own advice, telling himself what he wanted to know, then accepting it as a very good chance indeed. Again, it was his way. A man didn't live by the gun and the good fast horse without acquiring a working philosophy with lots of elastic in it.

"Move out," he repeated to the horse. "It's your part to get us across the flat in time."

The little mustang humped its back and shook itself like a wet dog. Running sweat, and caked, as well, flew from its streaked hide. It's gathering of itself in response to the rider's words was a visible thing. The horse was like the man. It wouldn't quit short of the last second, or step, or shot. They were of a kind with the country around them. It was all the edge they had ever needed.

Canady panted. He wiped the perspiration from his eyes and started upward again. Behind him, the little horse came on, unled, the reins looped over the horn so as not to trail and be stepped on. He followed the man like a dog, panting with him, struggling where he struggled, sliding where he slid, and lunging on as he did, after each setback.

They had made nearly the top of the fan of fallen rock below and leading into the opening of the side canyon. In another four or five minutes they would be clear of the climb. They would be off the slide and safely into the notch in the high wall of the valley. They would be out of sight of the posse, and the posse still had not come into view of them on the rise back across the pine flat.

"Easy, hoss," gasped Canady. "We're going to make it."

But Canady was wrong. Thirty yards from the top, the mustang put its slender foreleg into a rock crevice and drew back quickly. The movement set the slide moving and caught the leg and crushed it like a matchstick below the knee. When the horse had freed itself and was standing hunched and trembling behind Canady, the shattered leg hung sickeningly aswing and free of the ground, and Canady cursed with tears in his eyes. It was not the luck of it that brought his angry words, but the shame of it. It was his pity and his feeling for a gallant companion that had given its all and almost found it enough.

The hesitation, the wait there near the top of the slide, near the safety of the hole-in-the-wall, was the natural thing for a Western man. His horse was hurt. It was hopelessly hurt. He would have to leave it, but not like that. Not standing there on three legs hunched up in the middle with pain and fright. Not standing there watching him with those liquid brown eyes. No, he couldn't leave his horse like that.

But how else? He couldn't shoot the mustang, for the noise would key the posse to his location. Had he had a knife he could cut its throat. Or had he an ax he could have crushed its skull above the eye-socket and put the poor devil down painlessly. With a rock he might be able to stun the brave little brute, but he could not be sure of killing it cleanly. The same held true for the butt of his Colt or the steel-shod heel of his Winchester. He could stun the horse, likely put it to its knees, but not, still, be able to go on knowing it would not recover and try to get up again and go on, and so suffer as no horse-riding man could think to let his mount suffer. But, damn it, this was *his* life he was arguing with himself about. It wasn't the damned horse's life. If he didn't do something and do it quick, the posse would be over the rise and he and the horse could go to hell together. Well, he would use the Colt butt. He knew he could hit the exhausted animal hard enough with it to put it down for the necessary time for himself to get on into the hole-in-the-wall and for the posse to ride by and on up the valley. That was all the time he needed, or at least it was all he could ask for. He pulled the Colt and started back to the horse sliding and stumbling in his hurry to get to the trembling beast and knock it down. But when he got up to its side, when he looked into those dark eyes, he couldn't do it. He had to be sure. "The hell with the posse," he said to the little horse, and spun the Colt in the air and caught it by the handle and put it behind the ragged ear and pulled the trigger. The smoke from the shot was still curling upward, and the little pony just going slowly down, when the first of the pursuing riders came up over the rise across the flat and yelled excitedly back to his comrades that the game was in sight, and on foot.

Canady went up the little stream. Behind him, where it fed the rainbow falls leaping outward into the main valley, the possemen were just topping the detritus fan and closing in on "the hole." Back there Canady had made a decision. It was not to stay and fight from the entrance cleft of the hole, where the little rivulet went out of the side canyon. He did not know what lay on up the side canyon, and feared there might be a way by which the possemen, familiar with this territory, could ride a circle and come in behind him. He could not risk that, he believed, and must go on up the creek as far as he could, hoping it would be

far enough to find a place where he could put his
back to the wall and fight without their being able to
get behind him.

Now, going along, the way becoming steeper
and narrower and the creek bank little more than wide
enough to pass a good horse and rider, he saw ahead of
him a basalt dike, or cross dam of rock, which cut
across the narrowing floor of the side canyon. Here
the stream took another plunge, this of about thirty
feet. Above the dike, Canady could see the boles of
pine trees and hence knew that the ground above the
dike lay fairly level. The cross-laying of rock apparently served as a barrier against which the winter ero-
sions of snow, ice and thaw had worked with the
spring floodings of the creek to bring down and build
up a tiny flat.

Canady's gray eyes lit up. His brown face relaxed
and he said aloud, "By God, maybe this is it," and
went on with renewed strength and some hope of keeping his life a little longer. Up there, above that rock
cross-bank, a man with a good carbine and plenty of
shells could hold down most eight-man posses for several afternoons. Well, two or three, anyway. Or one.
For certain, until nightfall. Twelve, fifteen hours, say.
It was better than nothing.

His luck held. There was a good angling trail
going up that thirty-foot vertical face of rock. It was a
game trail, and somewhat of a cow trail, too. He made
out the droppings of elk, blacktail deer, range steers
and, then, suddenly and strangely, a fairly fresh piling
of horse sign. This latter find sent a chill through him.
He was on his knees in the instant of the sighting,
but then he straightened, grinning. It was all right.
The pony was unshod. Moreover, he suspected, from
the hard round prints that it left, that it never had
been shod and was one of a bunch of broomtails—
wild mustangs—that came into this rocky depth for
the water that flowed so green and cool in the stream.

Clearing the top of the stone dam, Canady's grin
widened. The flat above lay precisely as he had imag-

ined it did. He laughed softly, as a man will who is alone. Now, then, it would be a little different from the way those hungry lawmen had planned it. This was perfect. At the apex of the triangle of the flat he saw the thick stand of sycamore and cottonwood, aspen, laurel and willow, and he knew that the water headed there. A moment later, he made out the source of the stream, a large artesian spring gushing from the native rock under great pressure. The spring was set above the grove some few feet, its stream falling rapidly to plunge into the foliage. Likely it pooled up there under the trees and at the foot of the down-plunge. That's what lured in the wild horses and the other game and the cattle, too, what few of the latter were hardy enough to come this far into the mountains for feed. All a man would need to do, now, was hole up in those boulders that girded the spring, up there above the trees, and he could command with his Winchester the whole of the small, open flat between the spring grove and the stone cross-dam that Canady had just clambered up. Taking a deep breath, the fugitive started across the flat, toward the spring and its hole-up boulders. It was not until he had climbed safely into this haven at the canyon head and laid down pantingly to look back on his trail and get ready for the possemen, that he saw where he had come.

Below him in the trees the spring pooled up exactly as he had expected it would. Also the rim of the pool showed the centuries of wear of the hoofed animals coming to its banks for water. But there was something else—two other things—that he had not expected to see there, and his grin faded and his gray eyes grew taut and tired and empty.

The first thing was the wild horse. It had not gone up out of the little side canyon as Canady had hoped, showing him the way to follow its tracks and escape over the rim where no mounted man might follow. It was still in the grove of trees that sheltered the spring-pool waterhole, and it wasn't still there because of its thirst. Beyond the trees, back where Can-

ady had come from, and so skillfully blended and
built into the natural cover of the canyon that even
his range-wise eyes had missed them, were the two
woven brush and pole wings of the second thing Canady had not dreamed to find there. Those were the
manmade wings of a mustang corral down there.
Canady had stumbled into a wild horse trap. And he
was caught there, with this unfortunate lone mustang
that now cowered in the trees and could not get out of
the trap any more than could he, and for the same
reason—the posse and the box canyon.

"Steady on," Canady called down softly to the ter-
rified horse. "We'll think of something."

Two hours after high noon the sun was gone from
the canyon. Canady could see its light splashing the
far side of the main valley still, but in the side canyon
all was soft shade, and hot. Canady drank enough
water to keep himself from drying out, yet not enough
to log him. He noted that the wild mustang did the
same thing. It knew, as Canady knew, that to be ready
to fight or fly called for an empty belly. "Smart," said
Canady, "smart as hell." The horse heard him and
looked up. "Coo-ee, coo-ee," Canady called to him
reassuringly. "Don't fret; I'll figure something for us."
But it was a lie and he knew it was a lie.

He had gone down, right after he first lay up in
the spring boulders and saw the trap and the wild
broomtail in it, and closed off the narrow gate of
the funnel-winged corral with his lariat. He had done
that in a hurry, before the posse had worked up into
the canyon and taken its position along the top of the
cross-dam. His one thought had been that the broomtail was a horse, wild or not, and that so long as a man
had a horse he wasn't out of it in that country. And
he had wanted to keep hidden from the posse the fact
that he did have a horse up there in that headwaters
timber. The mustang had played with him in that last
part of it, lying up shy and quiet as a deer in the trees
and brush, not wanting any more than Canady wanted

for the men to know that it was there. "It" in this case was a scrubby little stallion, probably too small and old to hold a band of mares. The little horse had not only the fixtures but the temperament of the mongrel stud animal. Watching him lie still in the spring brush and keep his eyes following every move of the men below him, as well as of the single man above him, Canady knew that he and the trapped horse were friends. The only problem was proving it to the horse.

Sometimes these old scrub studs had been ridden long ago and would remember man's smell and voice. He tried a dozen times to talk the mustang up toward his end of the spring pool. But the animal gave no sign that the sight, scent or sound of mankind was familiar to him, or welcome. He bared his teeth silently and pinned his ears and squatted in the haunches ready to kick like a pack mule on a cold morning. He did this every time Canady said more than three or four words to him, or accompanied his talk with any movement that might mean he was coming down to see the horse, if the horse would not come up to see him.

What possible good the horse could do him, even if, by some miracle Canady might gentle him down and put his saddle and bridle on him, Canady didn't know. Then, even in thinking that far, he laughed and shrugged. His saddle and bridle were down there on that rock slide below the hole-in-the-wall. He'd had no time and no reason to take them off his dead mount. So if he went out of there astride that broomtail it would be bareback, and that was about as good a bet as that the crafty old stallion would sprout wings and fly up out of the canyon. A bridle, of sorts, he could rig from splitting and unraveling a short length of his lariat. It would be sort of a breaking hackamore arrangement and might do to give simple directions of right and left and whoa-up. But even if he rigged this Sioux headstall and got it on the shaggy little horse, then what? That was, even if the rascal wanted to be good, or had been ridden in the past, and remembered it of a sudden? Nothing. Not a damned thing. Canady

couldn't ride out of that canyon if he had the best
saddle mount in Montana waiting and eager to make
the try with him. It was all crazy, thinking of that wild
stud. But just finding any horse up there was bound to
start a man's mind going. Especially when he had just
shot his own mount and was fixing to put his back to
the best rock he could find and go down with lead
flying. But it was crazy all the same. All Canady could
do was what the old broomtail stud could do—fight
the rope to the last breath he had in him, then kill
himself, if he could, before the others did it for him.

The afternoon wore on. The heat in the deep-
walled little canyon was enormous. The deerflies
swarmed at the spring pool and bit like mad cats.
They nearly drove Canady wild, but he fought them
with hand and mind and swathed neckband and,
when evening came, they lifted up out of the canyon
on the first stir of the night wind. In the early part of
the waiting there had been some desultory talk between the posse and Canady, talk of Canady coming
out peacefully and getting a fair trial, but the fugitive
had not bothered to take that offer seriously. He knew
the trial he would get. The posse had its own witnesses
with it. They would bring up these two or three men
who had "seen" the shooting and say to them, "Is
that him?" and the men would say, "Yes, that's him,"
and the trial would be over. Witnesses! thought Canady. God, how he hated them. It wasn't that he minded
being identified if he was the man. In his business no
feeling was held against the witness who *had* seen
something. It was those devils, like the ones with the
posse, who had *not* seen the job and yet who were
always ready to raise their right hands and be sworn,
who were the ones Canady hated. There had not been
any witnesses to what passed between him and that
teller. All the other bank people had been on the floor
behind the cage, and there had been no customers in
the bank, or out in front of it. The shooting had happened and Canady had made it to his horse in back of
the bank, and made it away down the alley and into

the sagebrush south of town before he had passed a
living soul. Then, it was two farm wagons, both carrying kids and driven by women, that he had ridden
by well out of Gray's Landing. How those good folks
—and they were the only real witnesses, save the
cashier and the other teller on the bank floor—how
they could identify him as anything other than a horseman not of that area, Canady did not know. As for the
three shots that had killed the teller, and they must
have killed him or the posse would not have pushed
so hard, those shots had been fired *after* both barrels
of the .36 caliber derringer that the teller brought up
out of the cash drawer had been triggered and put
their slugs, one in Canady's chest, and one in the ceil-
ing of the Second National Bank of Gray's Landing,
Montana. But the only witness to that fact was dead.
Canady had reacted as all men with guns in their
hands react to other men with guns in their hands. He
had fired by instinct, by pure conditioned reflex of long
experience, when that first .36 bullet went into the
pectoral muscles of his left chest.

Armed robbery? Certainly. Twenty years in the
Territorial Prison? Of course. A man expected that.
But to be run down like a mad dog and cornered and
starved out and then strung up on a naked cottonwood
like a damned Indian drunk or a common horse thief
was not right or fair. Murder? Could you call it
murder when the other man was a professional in his
business and he could see that you were a professional
in yours? When you told him he would be killed if he
tried anything funny? Then, when on top of the fair
warning, you gave him the first shot? Could you call it
murder, then, if you shot in answer to his try at killing
you? Self-defense was the actual verdict, but of course
an armed robber could not plead self-defense. But he
was not guilty of murder, or even of assault with a
deadly weapon, or even of intent to commit murder,
or of a damned thing, really, but to sack that cash
drawer and clear out of Gray's Landing just as fast
and peaceably as he and the old horse might manage.

Canady grinned, even as he exonerated himself.

It was no good. He knew it was no good. A man had to be honest with himself. If he was in another business he wouldn't need a gun to conduct his trade. Needing and using a gun, he was always in the peril of being forced to use it. The teller was an honest man. Frank Canady was a crook. The teller was a dead honest man and Canady was a live dishonest man. Canady was a killer.

"No!" he yelled down to the posse. "I won't do it; I shot second; I didn't mean to harm that fellow. He pulled on me and shot first. But he's dead, ain't he? Sure he is. And you say to me to come on down peaceable and you'll see I get a fair trial? With a dead teller back there on the floor of the Second National. That's rich. Really rich."

The possemen were startled. It had been two hours since the fugitive had made a sound. Previously he had refused to come down and they had thought he meant it. Now, did they detect a change? Was it that he wanted to reconsider and was only protecting his ego by the defiant outburst.

"That's right, you heard us right," the leader of the posse called up to him. "You come down here and we'll guarantee to take you back to Gray's Landing and get you to either Cheyenne or Miles City, wherever the court is sitting, by train and under armed guard. You'll get the trial we promised, and the protection beforehand." He waited a significant moment, then demanded, "What do you say? There's no use any more people getting hurt."

Canady's gray eyes grew tired again.

"That's so," he called back. "It includes me, too. I don't want to see anybody else get it, either. 'Specially me. No thanks, Mr. Posseman. I'll stay up here. I don't fancy that you brung along all them ropes just to tie me up for the ride back to Gray's Landing."

There was a silence from below the cross-dam of rock in the upper throat of the canyon that lasted perhaps two, perhaps three stretching minutes. Then the posseman called back. "All right," he said, "you'll have it your way. When it's full dark we're going to come for you, and you know what that will mean. There are eight of us, all good shots, and you won't have the chance of a rat in an oatbin. We've got bull's-eye lanterns to light you out. We will set them up behind boulders where you can't snipe them, and yet where they will throw light up there around you like it was bright moonlight. We mean to stomp you out. There will be no trial and no talk of a trial. You're dead right now."

Canady sank back behind his breastwork of basalt and gray-green granite. He hawked the cottony spittle from his throat and spat grimacingly down toward the mustang stud. The animal had been crouching and listening to the exchange of voices intelligently like some big gaunt sandy-maned dog. Seeing him, and noting his apparent interest, Canady managed a trace of his quiet grin.

"What do *you* say, amigo?" he asked.

The horse looked up at him. It was the first time in all the long hours that Canady had tried gentle-talking to him that the animal had made a direct and not spooked response to the man's voice. Now he stomped a splayed and rock-split forehoof and whick-ered softly and gruntingly in his throat, precisely as Canady's old horse had done.

"All right," said Canady, for some reason feeling mightily warmed by the mustang's action, "so we've each got one friend in the world. That isn't too bad. As long as you have a friend you have a chance. Rest easy; let me think. We'll still make it, you and me...."

It was dusk when the old steer came down the cliff trail. He was a ladino, one of those mossy-horned old rascals that had successfully hidden out from the gathers of a dozen years. He was old and crafty and cautious as any wild animal, but he had to have water and he was coming down to the spring pool to get it.

He certainly saw the men of the posse, and winded
their mounts, but they did not see him and he knew
that they did not. His yellow buckskin hide with the
dark "cruz" or cross-stripe on the shoulders, and the
dark brown legs and feet, blended perfectly into the
weathered face of the cliff, and he made no more sound
coming down that hidden trail than a mountain doe
might have made. But he had failed to see Canady or
to separate his scent, or the scent of the mustang stud,
from the other horse and man scents coming from below. He came on, carefully, silently, yet quickly down
the wall of the canyon from the rim above and Canady, seeing him, was suddenly lifted in mind and
heart. He had been right in the first place! There *was*
a trail up out of that blind box of a side canyon. A
track up that dizzy sheer cliff, up there, that would pass
a desperate man, or a catlike wild mustang, but not a
mounted man or a man going afoot leading his tamed
and trained saddle mount. "Come on, come on," he
heard himself whispering to the old outlaw steer.
"Come on down here and let me see how you do it.
Let me see how and where you get off that damned
wall and down here where we are."

He grinned when he said that, when he said "we,"
meaning himself and the wild stud, without thinking
about it. It was funny how a man took to anything
for a friend when he had run out of the real McCoy
and was in his last corner. He supposed that if a side-
winder crawled along at the final minute and that
was all he had to talk to, a man would find some excuse
to think kindly of the snake tribe. Well, anyway, he
was thinking with deep kindness about the animal
kingdom just then. Especially the horse and cow part
of it. And extraspecially about the latter half. "Come
on, keep coming on, don't slip, for God's sake," he
said to the gaunt dun steer. "Easy, easy. Let me see
you do it, just don't fall or spook or get a bad smell
and change your mind. That's it, that's it. Easy,
easy. . . ."

He talked the steer down that cliff trail as though

his life depended on it, and it did. And the steer made it. He made it in a way that caused Canady to suck in his breath and shake his head in wonderment. He made it in a way that even caused Canady to think for a moment about there being something to the idea of a divine providence, for it was the sort of thing no man could have figured out by himself, the weird, crazy, wonderful kind of a last-second reprieve that no force but God Almighty could have sent to a man in Canady's place. It was a miracle.

The dun steer performed it with an easy quickness that defied belief, too. He came to that place on his side of the canyon where it seemed to Canady that the trail must end. The man could see the sheer face of the rock dropping sixty feet to the creek bed. A giant outcropping of granite hid the exact end of the right-side trail, but Canady could see, and with absolute certainty, that the trail did not continue downward past that outcrop that hid its actual terminus. But as he watched the steer disappear behind the outcrop and as he wondered what would happen next, he saw the lean yellow body launch itself in a graceful leap from behind the outer edge of the outcrop, and sail outward through the thin air of the canyon's dark throat. It appeared as though the leap would smash the ribby brute into the rearing face of the opposite, left-hand canyon wall, which lay no more than fifteen or twenty feet from the right-side wall. But again the steer disappeared, this time seemingly into the very face of the opposing cliff.

There was a tricky turn in the rock wall of the canyon's left side at just that point, however, and while Canady could see the creek's raggedly broken bottom, he could not see where the steer hit into the wall. All he was sure of for the moment was that the animal had made his landing somewhere other than in the creek bottom. Difficult as it might be to accept, that old outlaw steer had somehow made it from one side of the wall to the other. But, even so, then what? Where was he now? The questions were soon answered when the

missing steer appeared to walk right out of the waterfall that came down from Canady's elevated vantage
to strike into and begin following the brief section of
creek bed into the pool grove. While Canady gaped,
the animal stole swiftly to the pool, drank sparingly,
returned and disappeared again behind the curtain of
misty water cascading down from the spring above.

So that was it. As simple and as remarkable as
that. A trail ran from behind the waterfall up the
left-hand wall. At a point opposite the right-side trail's
end, it, too, terminated. But it was obvious that there
was room enough for a running jump and opposite
safe landing, to and from either wall, with both take-
off and landing spots completely masked from the
lower canyon.

Gauging the distance of the jump, Canady knew
that he could make it. With his boots off and laced
about his neck, or better, thrown over with his Colt
and the saddlebags with the bank money, the Winchester being slung on his back, alone, he could make
that distance through the air. But, then, what of
that? He made the jump safely and went on up the
right-side cliff trail behind the ladino steer and gained
the rim; then what? He would still be afoot in a hostile land in midsummer's blazing heat without food,
water, or a mount. That was the rub. Even if he made
the jump and the cliff climb beyond it and got to the
rim, he would have to have a horse. Otherwise, the
possemen, within an hour or two of dark, having come
for him and found him gone, would go back out and
climb out of the main valley and cut for his sign on
both rims of the side canyon, and they would still get
him. They would get him, easy, with them mounted
and he afoot.

No, he had to take that broomy studhorse with
him.

Somehow, he had to get that mustang to go with
him up the cliff. If he could do that, could get the little
horse to make the jump with him on its back—it
would have to be that way for he could never trust the

brute to follow him or to wait for him if he allowed it to jump first—if he could make that gap in the canyon on the back of that little wild horse, then stay with him, hand-leading him up the cliff trail, then, oh then, by the dear good Lord, he would make it. He and the horse would make it together. Just as he had promised the raunchy little devil. Up on the rim, he would remount the tough wiry mustang and together they would race away and Canady would have his life and the broomtail stud would have his freedom and the Gray's Landing posse would have their ropes unstretched and their vengeance unadministered and left to God where it belonged.

The thought of the Almighty came very strong to Canady in that moment of desperate hope. He turned his face upward to peer out of the narrow slit of late twilight far above him where the walls of the canyon seemed almost to touch at the top and where, far, far up there, he could now see the yellow steer climbing the last few steps of the steep trail and humping himself over the rim and losing himself to canyon's view. Canady nodded and said to the dusk-hushed stillness about him: "If you'll let me make it, too, Lord, me and that little hoss down yonder, I will try to set things as right as I can. I'll take this money, Lord, the bank don't need it and I won't want it any more after this night, and I will give this money to the widow of that poor teller. I will figure some way to do it, Lord, that she don't know where it came from. And I'll turn loose this little wild hoss, if you will let me gentle him enough to get on him and push him to that jump, up yonder. I'm going to try it, Lord. I'm going down there to the pool and try putting my loop on him right now. You reckon you could help me? I surely hope so, as I think you wouldn't send that ladino steer down here to show a man the way out, and then not help him to make it. Nor likewise do I think you would put that little old mustang studhorse down there in that trap by the pool unless you wanted him used. It looks to me, Lord, as if you truly wanted to pull me

out of this here trap, and if that's the way it is, why
thank You and I'll do my best. . . ."

In the little light remaining, Canady went down
from his rocks by the spring to try for the trapped
wild horse. He took his rope from the trap gate and
closed the gate, instead, with brush and poles, hoping
it would turn the stud should he break past him when
he came at him with the lariat.

The actual catching went, as such things perverse-
ly will, with a strange easiness. Oh, the little horse
fought the loop when he felt it settle on him, but he
did not do so viciously. The very fact that he permitted Canady to come close enough to dab the loop on
him to begin with was peculiarly simple. It made the
matter suspicious to Canady and he thought the little
stud was merely stalling on him, was trying to tempt
him in close where he could use his teeth and hooves
on him. He knew the small mustangs would do this.
They would fight like panthers in close, using their
teeth like carnivorous animals, and their feet with all
the savagery of elk or moose fighting off wolves. But
this was not the case with the tattered broomtail in the
mustang trap. When Canady got up near enough to
him, he saw the reason why, or thought that he did.
The telltale white marks of the cinch and saddle, the
places where white hair had grown in to replace the
original claybank sorrel hairs, showed clearly in the
darkening twilight. Canady's first thought that this horse
had been handled before was now assured. And it
certainly explained the change in the animal the moment the man snugged the loop high up on his neck,
under the jaw, in a way that showed the horse he
meant to hold him hard and fast, and to handle him
again as he had been handled years before. Memory
is a strong force. The stud made Canady throw him
on the ground, using the loose end of the rope to
make a figure-8 snake and roll it around the front legs
to bring the little pony down, but once he had been
thrown and permitted to stand up again, it was all over.

This man had gentled many horses. He had spent his
life with them. Their smell had become his smell. The
very sound of his voice had a horse sound in it. The
mustang had heard it the first word of the day. He
had sensed his kinship with this particular man, then,
and he sensed his mastery of the horsekind, now. He
submitted to Canady and stood quietly, if still trembling, while the man stroked him and sweet-whispered
to him and got him to ease and to stand without shaking, and without dread or apprehension.

Then Canady cut and wove the makeshift breaking halter, the Plains Indian's simple rope rein and
bridle arrangement, continuing to talk all the while to
the small mustang. When, in half an hour more, it was
full dark and the split-ear hackamore-bridle and its
short reining rope were finished and put upon the
horse, the animal was to all practical purposes reduced to a usable saddle horse. It was a piece of the
greatest luck, Canady knew, that he had been able to
catch and work the little brute. But it was not so entirely luck that it had no sense or possibility to it, and
his success only made the fugitive believe that his
hunch of higher help was a true one, and this thought,
in turn, strengthened him and made his spirits rise.

"Come on," he murmured to the little horse, "it's
time we got shut of here. Come along, *coo-ee, coo-ee,*
little hoss. That's good, that's real good. Easy,
easy. . . ."

They went in behind the creek falls, as the yellow ladino steer had done. The mustang pulled back
a bit at the water but once it had hit him he steadied
down and followed Canady's urging pull on the lariat
as well and as obediently as any horse would have
done in similar straits. Beyond the sheet of the falls, the
left-hand trail went sharply but safely upward and
around the trunklike bulge of the canyon's wall which
had hidden it from Canady's view at the spring.
Around the turn was the expected straight run at the
leap-over. It was better, even, than Canady hoped.
There was some actual soil in its track and, here and

there, some clumps of tough wire grass to give footing
and power for the jump.

"Steady, now," said Canady, and eased up onto
the crouching mustang. The little mount flinched and
deepened his crouch, but he did not break. Canady
sighed gratefully and nodded upward to that power
which clearly was helping him now. He took his grip
on the rope rein and put the pressure of his bowed
knees to the mustang's ribs. Beneath him, he felt the
little horse squat and gather himself. Then he touched
him, just touched him, with his left bootheel. The wild
stud uncoiled his tensed muscles, shot down the run-
way of the trail, came up to the jump-across as though
he had been trained to it since colthood. Canady felt
his heart soar with the mighty upward spring in the
small brute's wiry limbs. He laughed with the sheer
joy of it. He couldn't help it. He had never in his life
felt a triumph such as this one; this sailing over that
hell's pit of blackness down there beneath him; this
gliding spring, this arching, floating burst of power
that was carrying him high above those deadly rock
fangs so far below, and was carrying him, too, up and
away from those blood-hungry possemen and their
winking, glaring, prying bull's-eye lanterns, which he
could just see now, from an eye-corner, coming into
view down-canyon of his deserted place at the spring
above the pool and the peaceful grove of mountain
ash and alder and willow there at the head of Rainbow
Creek in Blind Canyon, sixty and more miles from
the Second National Bank and that fool of a dead
teller in Gray's Landing, Montana. Oh, what a won-
drous, heady thing was life! And, oh! what a beholden
and humble man was Frank Canady for this gift, this
chance, this answer to his fumbling prayer. He would
never forget it. Never, never, never.

They came down very hard at the far end of the
jump. The concussion of the horse hitting the ground
rattled Canady's teeth and cracked his jaws together
as loud as a pistol shot. He saw lights behind his eyes
and heard wild and strange sounds, but only for a

second or two. Then all was clear again and he and the little horse were going together up the right-side cliff trail, Canady leading the way, the little horse following faithful as a pet dog behind him. It seemed no more than a minute before they were where it had taken the yellow steer half an hour to climb, and it seemed only a breath later that they had topped out on the rim and were free.

Canady cried then. The tears came to his eyes and he could not help himself. He didn't think that the little mustang would care, though, and he was right. When he put his arms about the shaggy, warm neck and hugged the skinny old stud, the mustang only whickered deep in his throat and leaned into Frank Canady and rested his homely jughead over the man's shoulder. They were of a kind. They belonged to each other, and with each other, and that was true; for that was the way that the possemen found them when they came probing carefully up the bed of the creek in its brief run from the deserted pool grove to the foot of the spring's waterfall. The horse had fallen with the man beneath him, and neither had known a flash or a spark or a hint of thought, in the instant their lives had been crushed out among the granite snags of the creek bed below the jumping place of the yellow ladino steer.

The Hunting of Tom Horn

Sometimes a man has to lie to save his own neck, and sometimes to save somebody else's. I had to lie once to save another man's life, and I don't know to this day whether I did right or wrong.

It was on the old Jim Birch stage road about halfway between Lordsburg and Tucson. I was Tucson-bound, coming back from having trailed a bunch of rustled stock for the Association over into New Mexico. In those days we could do that, the cattlemen's associations in both territories being glad to see a cow thief caught, no matter whether by an Arizona detective, or a New Mexican one. I will say, though, strictly as an item of professional pride, that we boys from the Arizona side had a little better record for arrests and convictions. Maybe that's why I hadn't gotten too much cooperation from the Lordsburg sheriff, just now, and why I was riding back to Tucson empty-handed. Anyway, I was over a week late in getting back, and in no need whatever of further delay. But on a lonely stage line in Arizona Territory, trouble was always as close as the next bend in the road.

In this case, what lay around that next bend was a lynching bee, and when my pony snorted and put on the brakes and that hard-tailed bunch of range riders posed around the kid on the piebald gelding eased off on the rope around his neck and looked my way, mister, you could have heard a drop of sweat hit that roadside dust.

It was trouble, all right, the worst kind. Only question was, was it my trouble, or just the other fellow's?

I didn't know yet. But I got down off my horse nice and quiet and went walking toward the lynchers real easy. You see, the way I'm built, I couldn't help myself; I had to find out. I suppose that's the streak of cussedness that made me a stock detective. Anyway, it was the streak that put me to walking up on those flint-faced cowboys, when I ought to have been hightailing it away from them as fast as old Shoofly could carry me. Which was somewhat.

But I was never known for good sense, only for inferior judgment. I picked out the foreman and braced him.

"What seems to be the difficulty?" I asked.

He jerked a thumb over his shoulder, his reply notably unloquacious. "Take a look for yourself," he advised.

I stepped around his horse and complied.

It was a tied-down, two-year-old beef, thrown alongside a small fire. The running, or single-iron, was propped in the flames, still heating. The evidence, though simple, was ample: a brand blotter had been interrupted at his trade. I turned back to the foreman.

"You know a single-iron when you see one, mister?" he inquired, giving me a look as hard as gun-hammer steel. "This particular one fits just perfect under this boy's stirrup fender. That satisfy you?"

I tried to trade tough looks with him.

"Not quite," I said. "You can't hang a man just for changing a brand. Not these days. It's eighteen-eighty, mister."

"*I* can hang him," he answered back, not flicking a lid. "I'm E. K. Sanders, managing foreman, Mescalero Land & Cattle Company. Now, how about you?"

"How about me?" I said, eying him back. "I'll tell

you about me, Mr. Sanders. I'm against hanging a man without full and fair trial, for *any* reason."

This Mescalero Company foreman was a big man, running a big, notoriously hard-case cattle outfit. He wasn't of the breed to buy any offhand interference.

"Mister," he said, "you open your mouth once more, we'll run you up alongside this hot-iron artist. We been after him six months, and we mean to swing him. *Now,* how about *you?*"

"Do you even know who he is?" I stalled.

"Don't know, don't care. The kid was caught burning a Mescalero cow. We didn't wait for no formal introduction."

It was time for the lie. I had set it up. Now I had to carry it off like the cold-deck bluff it was.

"Well, I do know him," I said. "What's more, I want him, and I mean to take him."

The foreman nodded past me to two of the cowboys behind me. They moved up, flanking me, hands on their holsters.

"And who might you be?" he asked, real quiet.

"Charlie Shonto," I answered, just as quiet.

"From Gila Bend?"

"There's another Charlie Shonto?"

"Don't get smart," he said, "you're flanked. Your fast gun don't mean a thing to my boys. Moreover, we ain't sent for no help from the Arizona Cattlemen's Association. Time comes we can't catch our own cow thieves, we'll let you know."

I shook my head.

"You don't listen good, Mr. Sanders," I said. "This boy has been on our list since last July. That's a year ago, come next month. We're tired of chasing him."

"So?"

"So, he's our boy, and I'm taking him into Tucson. I got to earn my keep, Mr. Sanders, same as you and your boys, here." I eased one step to the side, half turning to get both him and the two hands in pulling view. The other riders were out of it and sitting quiet. "Now, I do hope you don't mean to make me earn it unpleasant," I finished up. "I prefer working friendly."

Sanders gave me a long looking over. Then he waved carefully to his hard-case flankers. He wasn't going to fight the Association—an outfit that had an unmatched reputation in the Southwest—but all the same he felt compelled to go on record, personally.

"All right, Shonto." He nodded. "But you know range law and you know you had no call to mix in here. We had this kid dead to rights."

It was my turn to nod. I took it on the acid side.

"You pretty near had him dead," I agreed, "but not to rights. Not to *his* rights, anyhow." I gave him three seconds to think about it, then went on. "Yes, I know range law, Mr. Sanders, and I know regular law, too. So I'll tell you, right out, what I mean to do. I'm turning this boy over to Sheriff Gates in Tucson. You want to come in and press cow-stealing charges against him, that will be the place to do it—not out here on the range, with you and your men as judge and jury." I threw him another pause, then nailed him down. "The day of the rope is done, Mr. Sanders. You know it, I know it. And we both know I'm only doing what's right and legal." I bent my crouch a little more toward the two gunhands. "Now, you men get the noose off the boy and cut his hands loose. Hop it!"

They hesitated, looking to Sanders for their yes or no. He gave them another yes, and they cut the rustler free.

"All right, kid," I said, "rein your horse over here."

He did so, and Sanders watched him bitterly.

"You're only putting off the inevitable, Shonto," he told me. "The kid was born to hang. He'll make it without your help, *or* mine." I nodded to that, agreeing with the general idea, then started off with the boy. Sanders raised his voice. "And, Shonto," he warned, "you'd better have him in that Tucson jail when we come after him!" I held up my horse, nettled by his tone.

"He'll be there," I said, flat-out, "safe and sound."

"He'll still hang," he persisted tartly. "Range law or regular, he'll end on a rope. Remember I said it."

"I'll remember," I promised. "See you in Tucson, Mr. Sanders."

He held me a minute with that hard look of his, then nodded and said very soft, almost to himself.

"It's a long ways, yet, Mr. Shonto. With that boy you may just never make it."

We were lucky at Cow Creek Station. The weekly stage from Lordsburg was there, hung up with a wheel-change. All I had to do was wait around until after supper, and ride on into Tucson with my prisoner in style. It was a prospect pleasing in more varieties than getting that kid rustler back of bars. I had been sitting on Shoofly the better part of two weeks and was good and touchy in the tailbone. Those old Concord seats were going to feel like feather beds. Overcome by the prospect, I offered to take the kid for a walk to sort of let him get the ache out of his own backside before we sat down to eat.

It was deep dusk, when we set out down the road below the station. I was preoccupied somewhat. I hadn't been able to get out of my mind the foreman's warning about the boy. There was something about it, and the kid, himself, that I kept thinking I ought to remember. I had seen him, or his face, somewhere before, I was certain. But I couldn't remember where for the life of me—and that fact was very nearly the death of me.

He was a big kid, curly-headed, handsome, good-natured as a hound pup. And smiling, always smiling. Polite, too. Polite as a preacher talking to the devil. Like right then, for instance, as we strolled along under a three-quarter moon, just smelling the sweet sage and hot sand cooling off after the daytime swelter.

"Mr. Shonto," he grinned sheepishly, "I wonder if it would trouble you too entirely much, sir, if I was to ask you—well, naw, you wouldn't—excuse me, sir."

"Well, come on, boy," I said. "Don't lead me to the altar like that and then leave me standing there. Speak up, I ain't the sheriff."

"Well, sir, I was just thinking if you would have the trust in me to turn my hands loose for just one good stretch. I'd give you my bounden word, sir."

"You would, eh?" I eyed him good. "All right, I'll just take your word, then. For one stretch."

I undid him—took off the cuffs—and he flexed his hands, worked his shoulder muscles and the like.

"Oh, my," he said, "that certainly is some grand, Mr. Shonto. Thank you ever so kindly, sir."

He put his hands up and took the stretch, long and luxurious. Then lowered his reach and put out his hands toward me, shy-smiling like I'd commuted his sentence, or something. Unthinking, I went to put the cuffs back on him and he struck at me so fast I didn't know what had happened until I'd landed on my back in the dirt, and he'd grabbed my gun off me whilst I was shaking my head to get the cobwebs out of it.

"Indian wrestling trick," he said. "Learnt it from the San Carlos tribe, over to Fort Apache. Sorry, Mr. Shonto, but I only give you my word for one stretch. Now, ain't that so?"

I made it back to my feet, still groggy.

"You seem to be doing the talking, boy," I replied. "Just keep going."

He smiled, bright-faced enough to shame the moon.

"Yes sir, thank you, sir. Just what I intend doing, soon as we can get back to the station stock corral and pick up my pony. And please move steady and nice, Mr. Shonto. You know how I feel my debt to you."

I had started to edge away from him, to get a set at jumping him. Now, I nodded and gave it up.

"Yes, it seems I do, boy," I said, feeling the crick in my back where he had thrown me. "You don't need to fear for me turning on you."

"I reckon that's so, sir," he grinned. "Let's go."

I got his pony out of the corral for him, him directing me from behind the hayshed corner, my own Colt covering me every step of the way. He swung up on the paint back of the shed, stuck my revolver in his belt, told me goodbye and God bless me till I could find more rewarding work.

"Hold on, boy," I said. "I don't believe I caught your name."

"Don't believe you did, either, Mr. Shonto. Didn't toss it."

"Would you mind, son? A man sort of likes to know who his friends are."

"You mean his enemies, don't you, Mr. Shonto?"

"You know what I mean, kid. I'm bound to come after you. I give my word in the Association's name that I'd turn you over to Sheriff Gates in Tucson. I'll do it, too, boy. One way or the other."

He shook his head, the smile still 100 percent uncut good will.

"Some other summer, maybe; not this one, Mr. Shonto—" He started his pony away, then held him up. Obviously, another impulse of charity had seized him. He yielded to it with charming grace. "However, sir," he said, "in case you want to send me a picture postal of that Tucson jail, just mail it to General Delivery, Arizona Territory, care of Tom Horn. So long, Mr. Shonto."

This time when he turned the paint and flashed his happy smile, he was gone. All I could do was stand there scratching my thick head and talking to myself in terms of tenderness never meant for mother's ears—his, or mine.

Tom Horn! One of the most fantastic badmen the Southwest ever spawned. He didn't look a day over eighteen years old and already had a reputation for cold nerve second to nobody's in the outlaw business.

I had seen his smiling likeness on enough wanted flyers to paper a six-room house; and I would rather have gone blindfold into a gopher hole after a rattlesnake than to take out, alone, after that boy. But I had told a deliberate lie to save his life, and I had used the name of the Arizona Cattlemen's Association into the bargain. The fact it was a poor bargain didn't change a thing. It was still up to nobody but Mrs. Shonto's simple-minded boy, Charlie, to make good on its stated terms.

I would have that kid back in Tucson for that Mescalero Land & Cattle Company rustling trial, if it was the last ride-down ever I set foot into stirrup for.

The country down below was desolate, brooding, empty; full only of the glare of desert sun and big silence—Apache country. I was bellied down on a high rock scanning it through a pair of field glasses. My nerves were balled up like a clenched fist.

Tom Horn had headed straight into that stillness down there, figuring I wouldn't follow. Odds were, he could have won his bet. That was bad country any time, and especially bad just then.

Broken Mouth, called Boca Rota by the local Indians, and, by any name, the poorest friend the white man ever had in Arizona, was making a last move to keep Apacheria for the Apaches. He and his mixed band of New Mexico Mescaleros and local "Cherry Cows," Chiricahuas, had been on the raid since early spring. The old chief had served notice on the U.S. Army at Fort Yavapai that any soldier, or civilian, caught in his hunting preserve would be given the full welcome. In Apache talk that meant they would entertain a man all night, then—well, you could put it this way, that man's first sunrise with Broken Mouth and his red wolf pack would be his last. Still, I had to face the fun.

Tom Horn was down there, somewhere. That left me no choice. In my business a man has got to be ready to live by his word, or die by it.

It was late that afternoon when I saw the old dreaded Apache sign, black smoke rolling upward from some burning settler's home or barn. The track line I'd been running on Tom Horn led toward the smoke, and I spurred over the near rise in the wagon road he'd been following, to see if I might be in time to help the poor devils. I wasn't. I no more than topped the rise, then I hauled old Shoofly in.

Coming toward me, up the far side of the rise, was an old farm wagon loaded down with cheap furniture, torn mattresses, chicken crates, all the pitiful remnants of an Indian burn-out, including two red-eyed little kids. On the seat with the kids, was a dismounted cavalry trooper, doing the driving. Behind the wagon rode seven other troopers, and, in front of it, came their sergeant. When he saw me, the sergeant threw up his hand and called the halt, and I rode down for the talk.

"You're a little late, mister," he opened. "And so were we."

I nodded, tight-mouthed.

"I can see that. Apaches, eh?"

"Some folks call them that."

"Yeah, I know what you mean." I looked past the sergeant, to the two kids. "Poor little things. I reckon their folks were both—"

"Yeah," said the sergeant, "they were."

"Which Apaches?" I asked. "Do you know for sure?"

"Bronco Mescalero. Some Cherry Cows mixed in. Broken Mouth's bunch. You ever hear of him?"

"Somewhat."

"Well, then, you've heard enough to turn around and follow us back to the fort."

"That depends, sergeant. You haven't by any chance seen a tall, curly-headed boy riding a red sorrel paint, have you?"

"Might be we have. Why so?"

"He's a wanted man."

"You a bounty hunter?"

"Nope. Stock detective for the Cattlemen's Association."

"Oh? Well, yes, we seen your boy. Not thirty minutes down the road." He jerked his thumb over his shoulder, toward the smoke, and I turned my horse.

"Thanks, sergeant. Good luck to you."

"Yeah. Sorry I can't say the same to you."

A little puzzled, I held up. "How's that, sergeant?"

"Just that I hope you never catch the kid," he said. "He's the one saved these two little ones, here. Rode into the Apache surround, head-on. Broke through it, got into the house, held them off till we hove in sight. Then he lit out like we'd caught him sucking eggs."

"That's like him." I nodded. "Which way did he take?"

"A way I'd advise you not to follow, mister detective; smack-dab in the tracks of them Apaches."

"It's a poor way," I agreed, "but I'm bound to go it."

He shook his head scowlingly, turned his horse to signal the forward-ho to his men.

"Oh, sergeant," I added. "You're a soldier. You ever took on an order you'd rather get horsewhipped than to go through with?"

"Sure. What you getting at?"

"I'm only doing a job of work. It don't pleasure me at times. You buy that?"

"Yeah, I reckon. I dunno. So long, detective." He started to signal his men again, then melted a little. "Happen you get back with your hair in one piece, detective," he grudged, "might be you could still use some help to hold it together. If so, remember Fort Yavapai lies yonder, six miles down the road. They won't chase you past the front gates—I don't think."

"Thanks for the kind thought, sergeant." I grinned. "It'll likely keep me awake all night."

"It better," he answered, with no grin, and yelled at his troopers to move it out. They went over the rise, none of them looking back, and I was left alone with that job which didn't always pleasure me. I clucked to old Shoofly and we got on with it.

Along about sundown, I got too close to Tom Horn. I jumped him out of a dry wash just shy of some badland hills. Neither of us wanted to shoot, and so it settled into a horse race.

It soon became apparent to Tom that I had the better horse. He had to do something to lose me, and he did. He led me square through the middle of the Apache camp, and left me there to do my own explaining. In a physical way, it was simple. He had spotted the camp from a high point, and I hadn't. He was able to dash his horse right over their supper fire, so sudden did he come on them, and to get on away into the thickening twilight before they realized they'd just missed a certain chance to grab themselves a white man. Thus aroused, they were ready for me, and didn't miss their second chance. Old Shoofly ran right into them, but those devils feared no horse and could handle any that was ever foaled, running full tilt or standing. They had him halter-hung and sat on his haunches, and me knocked off his back, in about fifteen seconds. I was lying on the ground alongside their scattered fire, while the beat of Tom Horn's horse's hoofs was still drumming away into the desert dusk. When my head quit swimming and I could sit up and take a look, I found the ugliest one Indian in southeast Arizona bending over me. We didn't need any introductions.

"White man know me," he mumbled through his disfigured lips. It was a statement, not a question, but I felt bound to answer it, no matter.

"Yes," I said, "I know you. You're Boca Rota, the Mescalero chief. The one that's declared war on all the whites."

"Yes," he grunted, acid-bitter. "Me Broken Mouth." He pointed to the terrible scars and purple burn welts that twisted his face. "You know how me get sick mouth? Yes, from white man." He sat down by me, while, behind us, the other Indians rebuilt the fire. His face, though hideously marked, was not a cruel face. Hard, yes. And bitter as bear gall about something. But not outright vicious and mean, as a man would have expected from his reputation. Now, while I listened, Broken Mouth told me his brief story. And the bitterness and the flint-steel look of him fell into place.

"White man own store, right here, Apache Wells," he began. He pointed to the remains of the old adobe ruin in which his band had camped. I looked around. There were the still-standing walls of two buildings, some nearly complete, some weathered down to three or four feet high. A few cottonwood trees grew near the hand-dug white man's well, which the nomad Apache kept cleaned out for their own use, and which gave the place its evil name. I shivered and nodded. He returned the nod, resumed his tale. "White man store owner he say me steal from store. Me say I no steal. No Apache steal anything from white man when he give word he no do it, I tell him. But he say me lie. He say he teach me no lie any more. His friends hold me by arms. He take branding iron for cow, and heat in stove. Then he burn my mouth like you see. He say, 'There, you no lie no more, you no steal.' But white man wrong. I come back, steal one more time."

He paused to point again. My eyes, following his direction, came to a halt on a weathered wooden head-board surrounded by sagging, sun-warped pickets, just beyond the store.

"I have *my* friends hold *him*. Take out tongue, far back in throat. Then me tell him, 'There, now we even. You no lie no more either.' Next day soldiers come down when see buzzards in sky. Find him dead, all blood run out his body. Soldier Chief he say, '*Dah-eh-sah*,' death to Broken Mouth. Broken Mouth answer, '*Zas-te!*' kill Soldier Chief. So long time war now. No peace for Apache people until last soldier gone."

With this pause, he pointed to me, tapping me on the chest.

"Last soldier no go, until last white man gone. So me say *zas-te!* all white man, then we have peace again."

He sat silent after that, and finally I asked him the big one, using all the control I could.

"Does that mean you're going to kill me, chief?"

"No can help it." He shrugged. "Apache law. Me no hate you. You look like brave man. Words good, eye steady. But Mescalero law say you die."

"All right. When?"

"When sun come, first light of day in morning."

"How about meanwhile, chief?"

"No, you no worry about meanwhile. We no hurt you. We treat you good. Put you against wall when sun come up, just like soldier do Apache warrior. You die honorable. Quick. Many bullets through head and belly. All right?"

As he saw it, this was high courtesy. I answered to it the best way I knew how.

"Yes, certainly. Thank you, chief. I salute you."

I looked around again, stalling in desperation, hoping for some miracle to develop, trying, the while, to tough it out, to "talk light" of my coming execution.

"You got any particular wall in mind, chief?" I asked, backing it with what I supposed was a tip-off grin.

But the Apache sense of humor wasn't this well developed, it seemed. Broken Mouth took me literally. He also took his sweet Mescalero time in the process of so doing, examining the available selection without prejudice, and mighty carefully. Finally, he nodded through the darkness, now fully down, toward a piece of standing wall with a gaping doorway in it.

"We use that one," he said.

Unconsciously, my eyes hung on the spot, while his didn't. And a good thing, too. I only saw the face peering around the edge of that doorframe for a

split-tail second. But the firelight bouncing past the
Apaches squatting around broiling their supper meat
had lit up the happy grin and quick bob of curly
brown hair just long enough.

That was Tom Horn over back of that doorway
wall.

It was an hour later, the moon not yet up but
coming any minute. Broken Mouth and I sat along the
wall where he was planning to have me shot, he on one
side of the empty doorway, I on the other. I was
trussed up like a Thanksgiving turkey, he was almost
asleep under his black felt hat. On the ground in front
of us, scattered in blanketed lumps on the bare dirt,
slept the other Apaches. One of them sat hunched upright, dozing on guard at the fire. Of the Horn kid,
there had been no further sign and, by now, I had
given up hope of his making a play to break me free.

I had no sooner nodded to myself in mute
agreement with this dismal opinion, however, when I
saw a white hand slide out past the doorframe, curl itself in my direction and throw me a sassy finger wave,
before pulling back out of sight.

I straightened up both myself and my opinion.

Tom Horn was one of the greatest Indian scouts
who ever lived. The Apaches admitted it, as well as
the whites. To begin with, he apparently had circled
back and snuck in to enjoy himself watching me
squirm. But he had stayed a little too long for his
own peculiar set of morals. Tom was against capital
punishment in any form. You might say he was pro-
fessionally opposed to it. When he heard what he
had led me into, that old Boca Rota was meaning to
cut me down come daybreak, it just wasn't in his character to set by and wait for sunup; or moonrise, either, for that matter.

As I watched, the hand came out of the doorway again.

This time, it crept around Broken Mouth's side
of the frame. Gentle and deft as a cardsharp palming

a spare ace, it lifted the chief's hat off his head and laid it on the ground beside him. Then it disappeared to return with a chunk of adobe brick in it. It raised the brick up and brought it down on Boca Rota's skull. Then it put down the brick, picked up the hat, put it back on the chief's head. With the old devil unconscious, the rest of Tom Horn slid out that doorway and stood sizing up the other Apaches out by the fire. Looking over at me, he nodded and touched the brim of his hat, sober as a circuit judge. Next thing, he floated out through the ground-sleepers and came up behind the one at the fire. Easing out his revolver, he took hold both edges of the guard's hatbrim, jammed the hat clean down over his ears, caved in the back of it, nice and quiet, with his pistol barrel. *Then,* he grinned over at me, and had the gall to tap himself on the forehead with the tip of one forefinger to indicate the overall braininess of the total operation.

When he drifted back to begin slashing me loose, he frowned at the tightness of my bonds, speaking under his breath.

"This here sort of thing is bad for the circulation, Mr. Shonto. A man your age has got to be more careful how he gets tied up."

I handed him a walleyed look and a likewise whisper.

"I'll be a damned sight more careful who I save from the rope, hereafter, I'll promise you that, boy," I told him.

"Shucks, now, Mr. Shonto," he said reprovingly, "if you hadn't of saved me, who'd be untying you now?"

"Well, that's one way of looking at it," I answered, standing up and working my limbs to get the numbness out of them. "But let's don't quibble it. We can continue auguring your noble unselfishness closer to Fort Yavapai. You any objections to that course?"

He bowed, sweeping off his hat.

"*Después de usted, patrón,*" he said in Spanish. "After you. Age before beauty."

"Thank you," I said, "for nothing."

The rest went pretty good. We got over to the Apache picket line without any fuss being put up by the ponies. We cut them loose and hazed them out into the night with wild yells and arm waves, then ran through the rocks to where Tom had our two saddled horses stashed and waiting. We went aboard them and got long gone from there, as the first angry yelps of the horse-chasing hostiles began to burn the night behind us.

It was the second morning, real early. Tom and I were laid up in some high rocks, looking over the back trail. We were feeling edgy. The kid shook his head.

"Damn," he said, "I wish we had them field glasses of yours, Mr. Shonto."

"I'd rather have your eyes, boy," I told him. "They saved us from getting jumped twice yesterday. How about this morning? You figure we've lost them for good? Maybe they've quit and went home. Who knows?"

"I do, Mr. Shonto," he said. "They never quit and they ain't got no homes. How far we from the fort, you figure?"

"Eight miles maybe. But I don't like the looks of that meadow just ahead. Too many rocks, and too big ones."

He nodded, agreeing.

"It's that way, or none, though. Either we go through that meadow, or ride half a day around it. And we ain't got a half day, Mr. Shonto. Look down yonder."

I looked. Far down, looking like sow-bug dots crawling the trail we had just come up, were a dozen Apache.

"You're right, boy," I said. "It's more like half an hour. Let's use it."

Twenty minutes later we were into the first of the meadow rocks. Another few pony steps and we stopped dead. Ahead of us on a ridge closing off the far side of the meadow sat another dozen Apache. We were bottled.

"If you will excuse me, Mr. Shonto," grinned Tom Horn, "I think I will be riding along."

"Just a minute, boy," I said. "You by any chance going on toward Fort Yavapai?"

"Well," he scratched his jaw, "hadn't thought of it, but now you mention it, why not?"

"Why not, indeed?" I gritted, and jumped my horse, with his, into a hammering gallop toward the Indians ahead. We got up pretty close to them and might have broken through, just on brass alone, when of a sudden I took one through the meat of my right leg and was knocked clean out of the saddle. Horn saw me go, and slid his horse to his hocks, turning him to come back for me. He made an Indian-style pick-up of me, and we got going again, double-mounted, just as the Apaches came over the ridge behind us, to join those we'd tried to butt through in front.

Now, I'd have thought the cork was in, tight. But not Tom Horn.

"Hang on, Mr. Shonto!" he yelled. "Here we go, double or nothing!"

He was grinning as usual, the threat of death by Apache rifle lead no more impressive to him than that by Mescalero Land & Cattle Company hemp rope. But his high-spirited shout was wasted. Five jumps and his horse took a smoothbore musket ball through the shoulders. He went down hard, us getting free of him on the fall, but forting up behind him the next minute, Tom putting a Colt bullet through his head to quiet his thrashing, while I looked to my hurt leg and our general position.

The leg wasn't bad, only bad enough so that I couldn't run on it. Our setup was not so lucky, but we did have some reasonably good rocks to back us. We also had another little chance. Old Shoofly was grazing off about fifty paces, with good rocks and brush cover between him and us. I pointed him out to Horn.

"I reckon I can put up enough smoke to hold

them off long enough for you to get to him," I said. "Good luck, Tom." It was the first and last time I called him by name, and I saw him react to it. "Fort's not far. I can stick it here, till you get back. Now beat it, kid. One hero's enough in the family."

I'd thought he was going to refuse, but he only grinned.

"All right, Mr. Shonto. A boy's bound to respect the wishes of older folks. Hold the thought—I'll be right back!" Which he was. He didn't head for the fort, at all, but only spurred Shoofly right back to our rocks, slid off of him with his big grin, and announced, "Like I said, Mr. Shonto, double or nothing."

Well, after that I could believe anything, and very nearly had to. That crazy kid talked me into another run at those Indians, claiming if I could put him up alongside of one of them, he would guarantee to knock him off his mustang and we'd ride out in style, each with our own horse. He did it, too. And we managed to get a lead on them, I suppose by the out-and-out shock of us having the guts to try anything so empty-headed. It was only a few pony lengths to begin with, but Horn had picked a good scrub and we soon opened it up to where they quit forcing, and firing. Other than lobbing an occasional rifle shot to keep us honest, and loping along about a half mile back, they seemed to have lost real heart for closing in. Especially, after the kid got two of them, and me, one, in the early hard running. They made a second go at us when we rounded the last butte and saw Fort Yavapai a mile off across the juniper flats, but we lasted them out. I think that next to seeing Tom Horn's hand reach out that doorway and crown Broken Mouth, the next best sight of my life was watching that army sergeant friend of mine yelling down off the catwalk for the gate detail to, "Swing 'em, you bastards—riders coming in!"

Inside, I couldn't get out of the saddle and had

to be helped down. Horn was there to do it with the
troopers siding him. They got me onto the ground just
as the sergeant puffed up.

"I just remembered your invitation," I told him.
"Sorry we're a little late."

"Better late than never, which you almost was,"
he answered. Then, frowning it, "I see you brought
the kid back."

I looked at Horn, smiling a little wearylike.

"You got that wrong-side-to, sergeant," I said.
"The kid brought me back." Horn ducked his head at
this, and put on that shy grin of his. I moved over to
him and laid my arm on him for support. "I mean what
I just said, boy," I told him. "You saved my life." I
straightened a little and caught his eye. "But I mean
what I said before, too. Nothing can change that. Soon
as I'm fit to sit leather, you're going to Tucson. I give
my word to put you in that jail, kid, and you're going
to be put in it. You hear?"

He'd been looking a mite worried, but now bright-
ened.

"Oh, that!" he said, relieved. "Shucks, now, Mr.
Shonto, don't you fret none about that. I understand
your situation, sir." Here, he reached a hand to my
shoulder, sincere as a Methodist minister. "Moreover,
Mr. Shonto, sir, I agree with it wholeheartedly."

"What's that, boy?" I said, surprised.

"A man's got to stand by his word, that's what,
sir!"

I studied him a minute, barely able to suppress
my astonishment at this about-face. But he didn't crack
one inch.

"Well," I finally said, "if that's the case, you
won't mind giving me your word that you won't try
anything on the way back to Tucson. How about that,
boy? You game?"

"As a gouty rooster," he swore at once. "You've
got my word, Mr. Shonto, and this time I mean it.
You can trust me all the way."

I looked at him good and hard, then nodded.

"All right, remember that, kid. I'll be depending on you." I turned to the troopers. "Come on, boys," I said. "You better get me inside. I'm a shade used up."

We rode up the center of Old Tucson, heading in at the hitchrack in front of the mud-walled jail. We'd come the last five miles on Shoofly, Horn's Apache mustang having suddenly gone lame as a kicked dog. I'd thought maybe it was some trick of the kid's to get me in front of him, mounted double, but he hadn't said boo, and was still grinning and saying "yes, sir" to every word, when we got down. I threw the reins over the rail and we marched in, me still watching him sharp as a hawk.

Jim Gates got up from his desk when he came through the door. He knew me, of course, but I could see the kid was a stranger to him. He just had that kind of a sweet face. No matter how many times you saw it on a wanted flyer, you couldn't remember it for a bad one.

"Sheriff," I said, "this here is Tom Horn. I'm turning him in on a cow-stealing complaint by the Mescalero outfit. They'll be in to press charges, if they haven't already."

"They have, Charlie." He nodded, then sized up the kid. "Tom Horn, eh?" he said. "Son of a bitch, he sure don't look it, does he?"

"Oh, I ain't really, sheriff," claimed Horn, with his head-ducking grin. "You see, acherally, I was took at an early age by the Pima Apache, and never heard of Tom Horn till this here Association man come along and—"

I put a hand to his arm, and cut him short.

"Save it for the jury, son," I advised him. "The sheriff's got a dozen pictures of you right in his top drawer." I turned to Gates. "Jim," I said, "no matter this kid has got a poor start, he deserves better. He saved my life at a time—two times—when he could have got clean away, by himself. But he stuck, and then gave his word to come in to Tucson and surrender peaceful, and he's done it. I'm asking you to remember all that when his trial comes up."

Gates took hold of young Horn.

"All right, Charlie," he agreed. "I'll see he gets a total fair trial." He started over to the cell block with the prisoner. At the door into the block the sheriff held up to fuss picking the key out of his ring, and I called to Horn, "So long, boy, and good luck to you." He just looked at me in an odd, sidelong sort of a way, shook his head slightly, and said not a word. "What's the matter with you, kid?" I asked. "Don't you believe in saying goodbye?" Then, he grinned, but still wagged his head in that funny way, and said, real soft.

"Not till it's time, Mr. Shonto. Not till it's time—" Then, just as soft but to the sheriff. "Let's go, Mr. Gates, sir. I don't want to keep you from your work."

Jim and me traded looks, then he took the kid on into the cell block and I said, "See you down the road, Jim," and walked back out in the street to see about some breakfast and a hot-towel shave. The hash house was half a block down, so naturally I went to ride it. I took a minute, maybe two, to tighten Shoofly's cinch, check my bedroll and the like, just as a matter of habit. Then I took hold his reins to mount up. That's when the voice hit me from behind.

"Wait along a bit, Mr. Shonto," it said.

Well, I knew that voice by now, and I made my turn slow and careful. It was Tom Horn, of course, just standing and grinning in the jailhouse door and jangling the Sheriff's keyring in his left hand, while his right balanced the office sawed-off in my general direction. As I stayed quiet, eyeing the shotgun, he called back over his shoulder cheerful as a jaybird.

"Now don't you fret in there, Mr. Gates. You told me yourself that it was your best cell."

He moved out onto the boardwalk, scanning the

empty street before tossing the keyring into the dirt under the hitch rail. Then he sauntered up to me, ducking his head.

"Sorry, Mr. Shonto, but I need *our* horse."

"Boy," I charged him reproachfully, "you give me your word." He nodded soberly, then lit up his 100-carat grin.

"I sure did, Mr. Shonto," he admitted, "but I didn't make no similar promises to that sheriff, did I, now?"

He looked at me pure as a choirboy. I couldn't help myself. I'd been taken again, and I hoped I was man enough to appreciate it. I stepped away from old Shoofly.

"Boy," I said, "he's all yours."

He got on the horse, keeping the shotgun my way. I put a hand on his near thigh, easy and light.

"And, boy," I added, "there's something I said in yonder, which I'll repeat out here, scattergun or no scattergun. Good luck to you."

I was sober with it, and it got to him. He looked down an awkward minute, then, impulsive as usual, reached down his hand.

"Mr. Shonto, sir," he said, "if you don't mind—"

He wasn't grinning anymore, and I took his hand. We exchanged a quick, hard grip. Then I stepped back away from Shoofly and Horn was back to his quirky grin just as fast as he'd turned serious the minute before.

"Well, here goes nothing," he said, with the final, sunbright smile. *"Hee-yahhh!"*

With the yell, he spurred the old horse away from the rail and off down the Tucson main stem on the cowboy run, fanning him with his hat on every jump. I stood and watched him go, following him down all the long gallop which took him out of Old Tucson and into his dark future in far-off Laramie County, Wyoming.

They can say what they want about Tom Horn, and it is true that he did wind up at the end of a rope.

But that was twenty years later, and for my part I will always think of Tom Horn as a boy with a grin crackly enough to warm your hands by on a cold day —yes, and more pure nerve to go with it than a train robber with a toy pistol.

I don't know for sure to this day whether I did right or wrong to save Tom Horn's life that time down in Arizona Territory, but I will tell you one thing.

I got a pretty good idea.

Sundown Smith

It was utterly still upon the mountainside, as befitted a Sierra sunrise. Beside the lovely little mountain stream in a forest glade seemingly as remote as the moon from human evil, stood a ragged, one-man tent. Before the tent the coals of last night's campfire drifted a lazy wisp of scented pine smoke. The scolding of bluejays and the cheery small talk of the rushing creeklet provided the only important sounds.

Presently the tent flaps stirred and a man came out.

He stood yawning and stretching and scratching, clearly a man in no hurry to rush on toward his destiny. He was dressed in his customary nightclothes—which were also his dayclothes—a combination of worn, but very clean, blue jeans, and threadbare long-handled underwear. His faded gray flannel shirt he bore in the crook of his left arm; his run-over workboots he carried dangling in his right hand. The manner in which he accomplished his yawning and stretching and scratching while still retaining possession of these items was not a thing—not an art—lightly come by. It had taken years of patient practice.

Directly, the man had satisfied the morning's demand to ease the body ache of ground-sleeping and the minor epidermal disturbances set up by pine needles, small rocks, sand fleas and the other habitués of his mountain couch.

Taking pause, he contemplated his campsite. He

was, in the act, surveying the new day, and his entire
worldly wealth with it.

He did not see much. A weary, wise old saddle-
horse. An ax with a broken haft stuck in a cedar stump.
A battered black coffeepot beside the fire. A shard of
shaving mirror hung on a branchlet of a nearby pine.
A mug, a brush, a bar of soap and a granite washpan
seated upon a stump beside the pine. Little things, of
little value.

Back at the tent flaps the man pursed his lips,
shook his graying head in a dolefully philosophic way
at what he saw.

Everything that met his eye was much like him-
self: a little old, a little worn, a little worthless. Yes, he
told himself musingly, he was a poor man. A very poor
man, and, in the ordinary sense, homeless. Yet he knew
that, somehow, he was rich. And, somehow, more at
home in the world than most.

He nodded to himself with the thought, then
looked over toward the fire. It was not twenty feet
away, still the decision to cross over to it was not to
be made hastily. After a suitable bit he nodded again
and set out upon the journey. Arrived at the fire, he
reached to pick up the coffeepot and set it upon the
hook above the coals. But the moment that he bent
forward, the old horse whickered petulantly.

The man stopped and looked off at the old horse.
His glance, if testy, was alight also with some inner
warmth, for this was a very old, a very dear friend.

"Mordecai," he announced severely, "how many
times I got to tell you not to talk to me till I've had my
morning coffee?"

The question put, and going unanswered by Mordecai, he huffed on about the business of putting the
coffee to boil—measuring and grinding the precious
handful of beans—pouring the cold creek water—setting the pot on the hook over the coals—throwing
onto the coals the exactly three chunks of bone-dry
cedar required to roll the water, just so, wasting neither
the man's time—which was worth nothing—nor the

forest's firewood—which existed in an abundance of supply sufficient to stoke all the coffee fires of his lifetime ten million times compounded.

As he worked, he talked continually to himself in a lively two-sided conversation; this in the manner of the Western man who is much alone and who, perforce, enjoys his own company, or none at all. The man did not mind this for it reduced argument to the minimum and guaranteed victory in any debate to the party of the first part.

At the moment he was discussing Mordecai's future.

"Dawgone horse," he grumped. "Acts like he'd been took off his maw two weeks ago, 'stead of twelve years. I'm gonna get me another pony soon's I find work." He paused, glaring off, or trying to glare off, at Mordecai.

"You cain't stop and spin decent no more. You cain't cut, nor change leads without stumbling. You cain't head a critter worth a Indian-head nickel, and you cain't catch up to nothing over three months old, and you—"

He broke off, stomping his foot and whistling sharply.

"You hear me?" he demanded grumpily.

Mordecai heard him and whickered politely in reply.

"Dawgone right you do!" said the man. "And I mean what I say, too. I'm a'going to do it. Someday—"

"Someday" meant another ten or twelve years from then, or twenty. The old horse knew it, if the man did not. He had heard the identical threat more times, already, than there were pine needles on the floor of the little mountain glade. He whickered once more, the sound coming as closely as a dumb brute might come, to saying, "huh!" and then subsided wisely.

At the fire, the man gave him a ferocious look and returned his attention to the coffeepot.

A wisping stringer of aromatic steam was issuing from the ancient vessel, now, and the man removed the

lid to inspect the cause thereof. Poking a tentative forefinger down into the pot, he winced and withdrew the
member in considerable haste, flipping it and putting it
tenderly to his lips to demonstrate that, as usual, he
had burned himself in the line of duty.

But he was a man of some character, not to be
deterred by the mundane frustrations of life.

Straightening from the fire, he moved over to the
pine tree which bore the shard of shaving mirror. He
peered into the glass, examining the quality of his five-
day beard. In the marvelous mountain stillness the
sound of his callused fingers scraping over the wiry
stubble was clearly audible. The man grimaced and
shook his head at what he saw in the mirror.

He was looking at the reflection of advancing middle years and was not encouraged thereby. But the
mirror showed more than that. It showed the crowsfeet
at the eye corners deeply cut from the many years of
smiling more often than weeping when the river failed
to wash his way. It showed a tenderness of mouth and
eye which knew no age, a love of the world and all
within it, which could no more grow old than the rocks
of the mountain around him. Yet all that the man saw
was Sundown Smith, graying cowhand, itinerant ranch
worker, saddle tramp, drifter, failure; a creature of the
long-viewed, lonely places; a man without friends, family, or known next-of-kin.

Still, there was a certain light behind that aging
eye.

Sundown tilted his jaw. He angled it here and
there, judging the condition and harvesting readiness of
his beard with the eye of a wilderness expert.

"I dunno, I dunno—" he said to the face in the
mirror. "A man should truly ought to keep hisself
slick-jawed in case of company."

He picked up the old-fashioned straight-edged
razor, which lay upon the stump among the other
shaving tools. He held it out from him, eying it askance
and at arm's length, as though it might bite him, if
provoked. Then, warily bringing it closer, he ran a

testing thumb over its honed bevel. At once, he cried
out sharply, wincing and sucking his thumb and shaking it to show, undeniably, that he had cut himself.

The performance was as predictable and invari-
able as that of burning himself to see if the coffee was
hot. Sundown Smith was an inept man. A man who, in
his entire life, had never learned a solitary thing—
except how to be happy.

He now cocked a rueful eye at the injured thumb,
then looked back at his reflection in the mirror. His
grin, when it came, was as optimistic as the morning
sun.

"Naw, shucks," he decided, touching the beard
again and shaking his head. "I won't do it. I ain't
'specting no callers. Leastways, not this year." He re-
folded the razor, returned it to the stump, adding in
explanation to the man in the mirror. "Besides, I got to
pack up and move on this morning." He nodded to
both his selves and stumped off toward the fire, mum-
bling to the original. "Yes, sir, got to be moving along.
But I'll just have my coffee before I think about it. As
for reaping that there stubblefield, I can shave any
time. Maybe next February. Say, March at the earliest.
Yes, sir, April, anyway. Or May. . . ."

In such deceiving ways are ordered the lives of
us all. Sundown Smith had just made a decision which
could cost him his life. He did not know that, of course,
and believed that he had handled the situation with
great firmness and determination—qualities he admired
vastly and knew very well that he did not possess.

Returned to the fire, he pulled up a convenient
rock and seated himself. He poured a cup of the as-
phaltic brew from the tarred pot and sampled it cau-
tiously. With an effort he swallowed the preliminary
taste, his reaction indicating that it had the zest of
liquid carbolic. Yet, with the brew once down, he
widened his pale blue eyes and exclaimed to the mountainside, "Wonderful!"

When he took a second, exploratory sip, however,
he shook his head critically. "Might need just a touch

of sweetening," he allowed, doubtfully, and reached
into one of his many pockets—he had donned the
tattered shirt now—and brought forth an ancient
leather poke of the variety used to carry nuggets and
gold dust.

Peering around to make sure he was not observed,
he loosened the drawstrings and extracted one lump of
cane sugar.

The moment he did this, the old horse whickered
aggressively from his picket pin on the grassy creek
bank. Sundown glared over at him resentfully. Closing
the poke, he restored it to its hiding place and com-
plained his way over to the old horse. His mien was
one of outright menace, but once at Mordecai's side, he
again searched the clearing to make certain there were
no spies about, then growlingly fed the sugar to the
bony gelding.

Starting back to the fire, he stopped, wheeled
around and said defiantly to the horse, "One of these
days I'm going to find out what it tastes like with
sugar in it! You see if I don't! Dawgone horse—"

At the fire, he seated himself, upon the ground
this time, his back to a friendly, windfallen log. Reaching, he retrieved his coffee cup from the rock upon
which he had left it. As he started it toward his lips a
mountain jay scolded him with sudden sauciness from
above.

Sundown scowled up at the jay and scolded him
right back in a whistle-perfect imitation of the bird's
rusty-throated comment. Then, winking broadly at the
offender, he turned back to his coffee. Retasting it, he
smiled as though it were the veritable nectar of the
gods. He leaned back against the log, raised the cup on
high, drank steadily.

All was right in the small, lonely world of Sundown Smith.

The little campsite beside the talkative stream was
now as nature had made it. It was a rule of Sundown's

existence that man was not created to improve upon the other works of the Lord. When he left a place, he tried to see that no stone lay differently from the way it had when he had come upon that place. It was, perhaps, his way of acknowledging, without presuming upon the relationship, that there was a Creator and that he, Sundown Smith, was mightily beholden to Him for such gifts of sunshine, pine smell, bluejay argumentation and creek-water small talk, which made of Sundown's life the blessing he considered it to be.

But now Sundown was tightening the last strap upon the ill-shaped bedroll behind Mordecai's saddle. Then, standing back to scan the campsite, he nodded, finally satisfied he had left no scar upon the sweet land.

For some reason he sighed. He always felt a little sad when he left a place which he knew he would never see again. It was like saying farewell to an old friend even though he had known that friend a mere brief night.

But it was time to go. Where, or why, Sundown Smith did not know. It was just time. Time, maybe, to look for that job that never got found. Time to seek out a new set of bluejays with which to argue. Time to climb a new mountain. To see a new sunrise. To hear a new stream laugh in some different, lonely place. It was just time to travel on.

Sundown waved his hand to the little glade and turned to mount up. As he did so, he stood, poised, one foot in the near-side stirrup, head cocked, listening intently.

Far and faint and thin with distance, he heard the baying of a pack of hounds. It was not a musical baying but a fierce and savage and an eager sound, and it made Sundown fearful. The least shadow of a frown crossed his face.

Leaving the old horse, he went up on a rocky ridge, nearby, which overlooked the entire slope of the mountain. It was the first time that morning he had

moved faster than a contemplative amble, or muttering
stomp, and it was evident he sensed some impending
trouble.

His instincts had not betrayed him: he was about
to learn that the question "to shave, or not to shave,"
could be a deadly one.

The previous night, down in the valley mining
community of Carbide Wells, an unknown killer had
struck at an isolated ranchhouse outside the main settlement. He had gotten away into the hills without being identified, save that he was a "kind of rough-look-
ing, trampy man; a stranger with a 'stubbly' beard"—
and that dangerous identification had been made by a
small boy at the ranch.

The nature of the killer's crime had no bearing
upon Sundown Smith's story, and, moreover, decent
words could not be found to describe it for anyone's
story. Suffice to say that when the townfolk and rough
miners of Carbide Wells found the young widow Bromley, they voted the killer the rope—*whoever* he was,
and *wherever* they should find him.

Now, having reached the rocky bridge, Sundown
crouched poised atop it, peering down upon the slope
below. The sight which met his anxious gaze fulfilled
the fears put up in him by the angry baying of the
hounds. Far down along the rocky shoulder of the
mountain, a mounted posse was moving upward, single
file. Ahead of this grim string of manhunters, held in
leash by a man on foot, three cross-bred Airedale-and-
bloodhound trail dogs bawled fiercely, as they followed
upon the track of their demented quarry.

That was the manner in which Sundown Smith
became aware of the presence of evil upon his mountainside; with the sighting of three vicious cross-bred
hounds and a hanging posse five minutes behind the
human brute who would come to have, in later years
of mountain lore, a name remembered to this day on
the eastern slope of the Sierra—the Beast of Carbide
Wells. And it was the manner in which, seconds later,
Sundown came to learn that there was nothing but

himself, and his wise, weary old horse, standing between that shadow of human evil and certain death at the end of the posse's rope.

As Sundown now straightened from his frightened look below and would turn to go back to Mordecai and remove both the old horse and himself from this climbing danger, a noiseless figure rose up from out the rocks behind him and felled Sundown with a single blow from the gnarled tree-limb club which he bore in his hairy fist.

Sundown fell heavily and his assailant seized from his frayed belt-holster the old cap-and-ball Colt's Revolver, which had been Sundown's camp mate for perhaps longer than even old Mordecai. He turned its muzzle upon Sundown, as the latter now rolled over and made groggy effort to sit up. Succeeding in the effort, he squinted painfully up into the face of the man bending over him with the rusted gun.

When Sundown saw him, he knew that his first fearful feeling at hearing the hounds crying upon the mountainside had been a true premonition.

The face above him was the face of a madman. It peered at him from the form of a Neanderthal brute who cowered and crouched and snarled like the hunted beast he was. There was no similarity between the Beast and Sundown Smith save that both were born of woman. But, wait. There was one small sameness about them. No, two small samenesses. Both wore poor and rough and ragged clothing, and both wore a five-day bristle of heavy, graying beard. It was a singular similarity. And, swiftly, a lethal one.

"Get up!" ordered the Beast, jamming the Colt's muzzle into Sundown's temple. "Make one sound and I'll blow your head off." His voice was a rasping, throat-deep growl, and he certainly meant his command literally. But Sundown was compelled to advise him otherwise, out of all honesty.

"Not with that old cannon, you won't, mister." He grinned painfully. "Shucks, firing pin's been broke most fifteen year. I use her for hammering tent-pegs."

Instantly, the Beast slashed Sundown across the forehead with the long barrel of the weapon. The blow smashed him down onto the rock of the ledge.

"It will kill you all the same," snarled the fugitive. "You had better believe it!"

Sundown nodded his head with difficulty.

"I believe it, mister," he said. Then, with a jerk of the thumb which indicated the slope below, he added.

"They after you?"

The other's lips writhed in what was intended to be smile, but came out a silent snarl. "They *were* after me," he said. Then, savagely. "Get out of them clothes! Boots and all! We're gonna switch duds, complete."

Sundown's blue eyes widened apprehensively.

"Now wait just a minute, fella," he protested. "That posse don't know me from Adam's off-ox!"

"Don't worry," leered his companion. "They don't know me either."

Sundown at first nodded, as though that were an information of some relief. Then, belatedly, he realized what had gotten past him. "That's what I meant!" he gasped. "If they don't know you and they don't know me, and they was to catch up to me in your clothes, they might—"

"Percisely," said his threatener. "Not only they might, I'm betting my life they will. Now you get out of them clothes. Boots, first!" He broke off, cackling in a wild sort of demon's laugh which put the goose bumps up Sundown's spine from chine to clavicle bone. "Them hounds don't know me, personal, no more than the posse does. It's these here old workboots they're trailing—" As he talked, he was toeing off his low-heeled brogans and kicking them toward Sundown Smith. "They'll foller whoever's in them!"

He interrupted himself for another of the demoniacal laughs, then let Sundown in on the secret of the joke.

"I never did want to die with my boots on," he chortled, "so I'll just let you do it for me!"

As instantly as the crazy laugh had broken, it

stopped. Sundown had been standing still, listening to the demented fugitive, forgetting to continue with the disrobing which the latter had ordered. Like a bolt, the long revolver barrel struck again. It caught Sundown across the bridge of the nose, driving him to his knees on the rock ledge and spinning the forested world about him. When he could hear again, it was to recognize the snarl of the Beast in his ringing ears. The words were, *"Hop to it, you hear me? I'll lay your skull wide open next time!"* and Sundown nodded that he understood, and began pulling and tugging to get his boots off, so that he might exchange them for his life—and the foul footgear of the killer.

The two men stood by Sundown's wise old horse, down at the abandoned campsite. They had now completed the transfer of clothing and the time, for both of them, was growing short. Upon the mountainside, beyond, the baying of the hounds was hoarsely near, and the voice of their handler could be heard shouting them on.

Staring off toward the renewed clamor of his pursuers the Beast growled like a cornered animal, then swung up on Sundown's old horse. He pulled Sundown's old Model '73 Winchester from the saddle scabbard and snarled down at its owner, "You use this for driving tent-pegs, too?"

Sundown put up his hands as though to ward off a possible shot, and answered hurriedly. "Oh, no— that's my camp meat gun. Be careful. She works."

"She better work!" rasped the Beast, and levered the Winchester in a sharp, hard way which showed that he knew the gun and how to use it for something deadlier than getting in camp meat. He stood in his stirrups, twisting to look off in the direction of the mountain slope.

"Listen to them hongry-bellied devils a'bawling for their breakfast," he muttered. "Ain't that sweet music to a man's ears? Especially, when he's got a good horse under him and a center-shooting gun in his hand?" He laughed the weird laugh again, then snapped at Sundown, "Get going. Walk toward them yonder trees. And walk nice and deep and straight. Stomp hard. Leave them hounds a sharp-edged set of prints to sniff out. March!"

Sundown threw up his hands, appealing to the other's human mercy.

"Listen, mister. This is cold-blood murder. That posse won't give me two seconds to explain. They won't even let me open my mouth." He paused, then concluded fearfully. "Mister, they won't give me a chance!"

The brutish rider leaned down, hissing the words at him.

"They won't give *you* a chance? Listen, you no-good saddle-bum, I killed a woman down there last night. She played the lady with me and I killed her for it. She called me an animal, you hear? *Me!* An *animal!* Well, she won't call nobody an animal now—not ever. . . ."

He paused, a fiercely angry expression passing over his face. There was a sudden sort of fear in it, too, as though he had just remembered something about his crime. Something he had forgotten, and which was dangerous to him. He shook his head, talking now to himself.

"Nor that kid neither; the dirty, sniveling, little sneak!" He tailed it off, then went on. "Not by the time I get back down there, he won't. I'd ought to have got him before. I knowed there was something I forgot. If only them three cowboys hadn't of rode in on me just when they did. But the kid won't tell. Oh, no, he won't tell. He'll be just like his maw. Nice and quiet and with that funny, vacant-eyed look—" He uttered the cracked laugh once more, sat in the saddle staring off emptily. Recovering with a jerk, he whirled back to Sundown Smith.

"They won't give *you* a chance," he repeated hoarsely. "Mister, what chance you think they'd give *me?*"

Sundown looked up at him with quiet dignity, answering with a courage that neither of them recognized.

"Mister," he said, "what chance you think they ought to give you?"

The Beast kicked the old horse into Sundown and drove the steelshod butt of the rifle down into the cup of his shoulder, caving him to the ground.

"Now you get up, mister," he told Sundown in a dead level growl, "and you walk like you was told to walk."

This time Sundown obeyed him. He crossed the open ground of the glade, his enemy herding him from horseback, and behind. At the timbered edge of the clearing the latter hauled up the old horse and snarled down at Sundown, "That's far enough."

He hesitated, twisting in the saddle, again, to listen to an excited burst of yelping from the dogs. Then he turned back to Sundown Smith.

"Good luck, 'killer,' " he told him, uttering the crazy laugh in appreciation of his own grisly joke. "You oughtn't to have no trouble with that posse. Just tell them who you are. They'll understand." Then, wanderingly, and with the vacant look in his eyes once more. "We're all just strangers passing on the long, long trail. So long, 'stranger.' "

He broke forth into his wild laughter for the last time, and rode out, driving the old horse into the timber. They had disappeared in a matter of seconds.

Sundown stood stock-still for a long, held breath, staring after them. Then he wheeled and ran back toward the rocky ledge. There, he fell upon his stomach and peered over, tense and fearful of his pursuers as the true killer had been before him. What he saw below turned his saddle-tanned face pale as a clean-washed bedsheet, brought the beat of his frightened heart high and suffocating into his throat.

The hounds and the posse were nearly upon him. They were, in chilling fact, coursing the very ledge beneath the one where Sundown crouched—not thirty feet from his whitened face. They had one more switch-back of the trail to negotiate and they would be upon the ledge with him.

Now the prospect of death was very near, and very clear, to Sundown Smith. Also the prospect of life.

On foot, unarmed, a man who had never raised either hand or voice in anger against a fellow man, he had, somehow, to run down and seize the real murderer for the Carbide posse, before the Carbide posse ran down and seized him for the real murderer. The odds against him were eleven to one—the number of men in the posse—plus three savage, cross-bred hounds and thirty feet of hemp rope.

Sundown wheeled blindly to flee, instinct his only guide.

He began sliding and slipping down the rocks to-ward his former campsite, and toward the cheery little mountain streamlet which formed its frothy skirt. At water's edge, he plunged in to his knees, and began stumbling and fighting his way up the green-foaming current. He made it to an upper bend of the small raceway, got around the bend and up and over a four-foot falls above it. There, he held up to regain his breath, looking back and downward upon his late camp, as he panted desperately, and thought, in the same vein, of some way in which he might extend his momentary advantage over the hounds and their hard-eyed masters.

As he watched, the dogs came bawling into the clearing below. At mid-clearing they went into a mill, straightened out, ran Sundown's track to the stream-bank, milled again where he had entered the water. Their handler pulled them off the scent and returned, with them, to mid-clearing. The posse now came up on the gallop. Swinging down from their lathered mounts, its members went into gesturing discussion with the houndman. The delay, Sundown knew, would be brief.

He was now at the bend of another stream than the icy small one in which he presently crouched.

He had been lucky, had gotten a start on the dogs, had borrowed ten minutes on his life's saving account. He could, possibly, get away now if he thought only of himself. But in his entire life, Sundown Smith had never thought only of himself. And the habits of a lifetime do not alter, even in the face of death.

Sundown's mind was not on the hounds or the possemen. It was on the words of the Beast—the words he had snarled about that little boy left on the lonely ranch somewhere down in the valley—a very young, very innocent, very much alive little boy who would now be the only witness in the world who could identify the *real* killer. It was suddenly in the desperately reaching mind of Sundown Smith that the brute who had brought down the mother, would not hesitate to stalk the son; as, indeed, he had threatened to do.

The criminal will always return to the scene of the crime, was the thought which now framed itself in Sundown's mind. Well, Sundown did not know about that. But he did know about something else. He had spent a lifetime in the wild and he knew this: *that an animal will frequently return to its last night's kill*— and the man who had taken his old horse, Mordecai, and left him afoot in his murderer's filthy rags, was not a man but an animal.

Sundown's face mirrored the terror that thought brought up in him. He reached, again, to seize the pine root which would pull him out of the stream. Once upon the rocky bank, above, he resumed his flight, following the faint trail along the stream's edge. Soon he was out of the heavy timber, into a more open, boulder-dotted country on the very flank of the mountain that loomed above Carbide Valley. As he reached this exposed terrain, the baying of the hounds was renewed with a bursting clamor. Sundown knew what the change in the baying meant. They had found his exit-point above the waterfall and their handler, sensing the nearness of chase's end, had unleashed them.

With the speed of life urgency, but not panic, he wheeled and ran once more. He knew where he was

going, now, and he ran with a strength he had not pos-
sessed before. He was running for two lives, now, and
somehow that idea lent him the will to outdistance the
dogs to the objective that could mean the second, far
more important, of those two lives.

He remembered, from the previous day's journey
around this same mountain flank, an old logging flume
standing stark and rickety upon the crest above the
trail. From its vantage above the trail, it plunged down
the mountain's side straightaway toward the valley so
far below. If a man could reach that flume ahead of
the hounds, and if it still ran with water, and if he still
had the strength to climb up its underpinnings and
plunge into its precipitous race—

The three questions drove Sundown onward. They
drove him well. He did beat the hounds to the flume,
he did clamber up its sun-bleached timbers, he did
find water in its weathered flume and he did summon
the will to leap into that water and to be whirled away
down the mountainside.

The hounds had come so close they had torn a
strip of cloth from his trouser leg. The posse had galloped up so swiftly that they had seen him poised to
plunge into the flume, and had fired at him from horseback, one of the ricocheting bullets striking him across
the bunched muscles of his right shoulder and staggering him almost off the high dizziness of the flume's
trestle.

He was thus marked for the killing, should they
ever come up to him, but Sundown did not care about
that. He cared only about the one other question which
still remained unanswered in his race to reach the valley: who would come first to the secluded ranch
house outside Carbide Wells?

Would it be Sundown Smith, or the Beast who
struck by night?

The sun went, twilight came, lingered briefly and
was gone. Full dark fell and still Sundown had not
come to the ranchhouse. But as the moon rose far out

across the misting fields of the long valley, he saw, close at hand, and hidden until now by some bouldered brush lands lying before him, the lamplight of a cheery kitchen window winking at him with warm hope. Gathering his tired limbs, he set out on the last of the hours-long trail.

The Rochester lamp on the red-checked tablecloth in the kitchen of the Bromley ranchhouse guttered to a sudden draft stirring through the room. Both the small boy and the old woman seated over their supper in the kitchen, glanced up at the one window. But the window was closed, and so was the one door into the room from the front of the house, and the one door out of it to the back of the house; and Bobbie Bromley and his Aunt Martha Sonnenberg nodded to each other and matched pale smiles and bent again to their eating.

Outside the house, along the kitchen wall, a shadow rose up from the high grass and brown weeds ten feet past the window, toward the front porch of the house. The shadow moved along the wall, to the window, and stopped. Then it moved again, and its maker slid in beneath the window and stood up beside it to peer in side-glancingly and swift.

It was Sundown Smith.

When he looked in, his first thought was to sigh and to smile, for the boy was all right, and he was in time. But the second thought came in on the heels of the first, and he glanced nervously toward the front porch.

Was he in time?

He had just sneaked past that front porch and seen, there, the shotgun guard posted by the posse. The guard had been propped up against the closed and bolted front door, tilted in his chair as though naturally dozed off at his post of duty. But now it seemed to Sundown that he had never seen a man sit so still—a breathing man—and, of a sudden, the chilling thought re-took him: *was he in time?*

He had feared to stop and alert that guard. The man, in the startlement of being awakened, and seeing

him so roughly clad and unshaven, might fire before
he asked any questions, or before Sundown could answer him any. The sawed-off 10-gauge L. C. Smith in
his lap had loomed awfully blunt and deadly-looking to
Sundown, and he had not dared to move over the rail
and announce himself, at the time. Now, that second
chilling thought was telling him that perhaps he was
not in time, that perhaps it was now too late to awaken
the guard. A man had to know, however. He could not
simply stand there beneath that window waiting for the
killer to make himself known—if he *was* there ahead
of Sundown.

The drifter shrank closer to the wall, returned
again to the tall weeds, crawled swiftly to the front
porch rail and over it to approach the guard on tiptoe
and to touch him lightly on the shoulder and whisper
aloud, "It's a friend—please don't move or make a
sound."

The guard obeyed Sundown. He neither moved
nor made a sound. And it was then Sundown noticed
something. The shotgun which had been in the guard's
lap only moments before was no longer there. The
shotgun was gone. And around the guard's neck, as
Sundown leaned fearfully forward to see, was a short
piece of broken halter rope, tied and rove in a perfect
imitation of a tiny hangman's noose.

The guard was dead. Sundown did not touch him
and did not need to. A man senses these things when he
has lived long alone among the wild creatures, learning
their ways, acquiring their instincts. The guard was
dead and the small boy and the old woman were alone
in the Bromley ranchhouse.

Alone, except for Sundown Smith.

Sundown was at yet another bend of the stream.

He could flee, now, and save himself. The posse
man's horse stood saddled and ready in the outer yard.
Life lay only that short distance away, and life was still
sweet to Sundown Smith. But he looked at the shadow
of the horse under the cottonwoods in the outer yard,
and shook his head.

There had been something in the little boy's face, a look of loneliness and longing, all too familiar to Sundown Smith. Sundown knew how it felt to be alone—and lonely.

He shook his head again, and turned and went back over the porch rail and toward the kitchen window and toward seven-year-old Bobbie Bromley. Sundown was terribly afraid but would not turn away now. He understood the terminal quality of his decision. It was Sundown Smith against the Beast of Carbide Wells.

The kitchen window glass shattered with an inward, nerve-wrenching crash. The boy gasped and the old woman cried out. By then Sundown was through the window, had leaped to the table, seized and blown out the smoking lamp. The inrush of total blackness was blinked away by all three in the handful of seconds which followed. In this stillness, Sundown's soft voice pleaded with the two at the table. "Boy," he said, "and you, lady, you must believe me. I am your friend. There is not time, now, to tell you who I am—but the other one, the one you may think I am—is outside the house. He is yonder, there, in the night, somewheres, and he has come back down off the mountain to kill the boy—"

He stopped, and he could hear their breathing, close and tense in the thinning darkness of the room.

"But, mister—"

"No, boy, don't talk. Listen."

Sundown stopped, again, taking his own advice and listening for a sound outside the house. He heard only silence, and the stir of the wind wandering up the valley.

"Lady, are you kin of the boy?"

"No, not bloodkin. He ain't any of that left."

"It makes him and me even," said Sundown softly. "Boy, do you think I killed your mother?"

"You look like the man—your clothes and all— but you don't sound like him."

"Believe your ears, boy. Will you do that for old

Sundown? Lady, will you believe in me? And tell the
boy to listen? A woman knows. A woman's not like a
man. She feels. She senses things. I mean past her eyes
and ears. You know what I mean, lady? You believe
me?"

"Yes," said Aunt Martha Sonnenberg. "I believe
you. We will do as he says, Bobbie. If that man who
killed your poor dear mother is out there—"

Outside the broken window a dry weed scraped
against the cracked sideboards of the house's wall.
There was no wind moving at the moment, and Sundown finished quietly for her, "That man *is* out there,
lady. Come on. Into the parlor. Go first, boy. Take my
hand. Here, lady, you take my other one."

They went soundlessly, Bobbie leading the way,
feeling the excitement and fear of the deadly game rise
up within him. Sundown held up, listening at the door
into the kitchen. Then he came away, quickly, and
whispered to Aunt Martha. "He is out there in the
kitchen. Just came through the broken window. Now,
there is that horse of the shotgun guard's out under
them cottonwoods. Can you ride?"

"Of course I can ride!"

Sundown eased open the front door, took her by
the arm, forcing her out upon the porch.

"Then, lady," he said, "you get on that horse and
you ride for Carbide Wells and you pray every jump of
the way!"

Aunt Martha Sonnenberg was sixty-seven years
old. She had been in that valley when the Paiutes were
bad and when a woman took orders from her menfolk
without talking back. "Lord bless you, cowboy!" she
murmured. "I'll be back with help soon's the horse will
let me." She was gone than, scurrying across the dust
of the moonlit yard like an old hen running from a
hawk shadow. She got the horse free, and made it up
onto him and got him safely away in a snorting gallop.

But it had all taken time, and made noise, and
now the door into the kitchen slammed open and
banged back against the parlor wall, and Sundown

could hear the brute breathing in the blackness. He had not let go of Bobbie Bromley's hand the whole while, and now he squeezed it hard. Bobbie squeezed back, firm and quick, and Sundown thanked the Lord above that the boy had gumption and innards enough to go around.

Sundown felt in the dark for the chair back near his left hand. Finding it, he changed the set of his feet, let go of the boy, swept up the chair and hurled it across the room toward the breathing of the Beast.

It was the luck of the innocent, then. The chair struck thuddingly and, as it did, Sundown seized up the boy and ran out the front door and dove, with him, over the porch rail into the tangled, windblown weeds. Behind him, he heard the Beast growl deep in his throat. He put his hand over Bobbie's mouth and whispered, "Lie quiet, boy. I don't think he seen us go over the rail. The chair must of took him, full-on, and that's God's luck, as ever was."

Presently, they saw the silhouette of the killer come out and move around the porch. Then it disappeared back into the house and they saw the flare of the match spurt up in the kitchen, as the Beast found and lit the lamp. His figure, black and hulking against the lamplight, the guard's shotgun dangling from one long arm, the deepset eyes shining like a varmint's in the yellow glare of the coal oil put the shivers to the bone in Bobbie Bromley's thin body.

Sundown tightened his arm about him and said, "Boy, we cain't stay here, now. He means to come out and tromp us out with the light and the scattergun. He knows I ain't got no weapon. And less'n we can find one—"

He stopped, listening hard again.

A new sound—or, rather, an old one—had come to his straining ears. Just up the valley, near the rock-girt rise over which he had come to drop down on the Bromley ranchhouse, the baying of hounds in full tongue burst into sudden, startling clamor. Sundown shivered now. The odds in the game were going up.

Now he had not alone the deadly stealth of the killer against him, but the lethal creep of the clock, as well. For if the posse should come up soon, with the men finding the murdered shotgun guard and the dogs finding him, Sundown Smith, then he would still hang. And hang so swiftly he would be given not even the chance to state his true name, let alone the nature of his defense, or state of innocence.

"Mister Sundown—" The boy had been thinking, and now whispered tensely to the old cowboy holding him. "You said something about us finding a weapon. I know where there's a turrible weapon. I seen Paw use it onct, when I was little, to near kill a proddy range bull that had wandered into the yard and cornered Maw 'twixt the barn and the house."

"Boy," said Sundown Smith, "what are you talking about?"

The killer was moving through the house again, now, coming from the kitchen, through the parlor, with the lamp and the shotgun.

"The old hayfork," answered the boy, watching the killer, with Sundown, and keeping his voice down to a field-mouse rustle. "It's in the barn, where Paw left it. He broke it on the bull and bought hisself a new one next trip to town. Maw sold the new one when we auctioned off the equipment after Paw was took."

"You sure it's there where your Paw left it? You seen it lately, boy?" muttered Sundown.

"No, I ain't certain. But I know where he left it."

"Can you find it, you reckon?"

The boy was still watching the house. The killer had come out on the porch now and was standing holding up the lamp, throwing its light this way and that.

"I reckon I'd better *try*," he said to Sundown, and Sundown nodded and felt a lump come up in his throat. He patted the boy on the shoulder and whispered back, "Me, too," and reached around in the grass until he found a rock the general size and heft of a Rocky Ford muskmelon. "When I pitch this rock over to the far side of the house, you be ready to evaporate like a broom-swatted cat, you hear?" he asked the boy. "I hear," replied the latter, and Sundown rose up and pitched the rock over the house.

The rock fell, just so, on the far side of the house. It made a good crackling noise in the matted-dry weeds over there and the killer was off the porch and crouching toward the sound like a big, dark-bearded cat walking down a covey of fledgling quail. He moved so quickly that Sundown had to remind the boy to run, before he might smell out the decoy rock and come for them, full tilt.

They made it to the barn, slipping in the rear through a broken wallboard the boy knew of. The doors were hasped and locked, and the killer had not heard them across the barn lot. They had, perhaps, five minutes to find the old hayfork, and to figure out what to do with it when—and if—they did find it.

"Boy," said Sundown Smith, "he'll be here soon. There ain't but just so many places he'll look afore he *knows* where we are. Two sides, and back and front of the house, and that's it. He's been front and one side. We ain't no world of time."

"You wait here, Mister Sundown."

"No, we dassn't separate for a minute. Here's my hand."

The boy took his hand and, together, they went through the musty gloom of the empty barn to the stall head where the lad remembered his father putting the rusted head of the old hayfork. The fork was there; the fork and about two feet of the broken, spear-pointed, hickory haft which was all that remained of its once five-foot handle.

"She'll do," said Sundown Smith, taking the wicked tines from the boy, and feeling them, and the remnant of handle, in the darkness. Then, softly. "Boy, is there nothing else you can think of? Anything at all, we might use for—well, you know."

"No," said the boy, "nothing."

"She'll *have* to do, then," said Sundown, hefting the fork. "Let's go, boy."

"Mister Sundown, I got a name. It's Bobbie. Bobbie Bromley. Junior."

"All right, Bobbie. We still got to go. Fast."

"You going to stab him with the fork? Hide behind the door, maybe, and get him when he comes in?"

"I wouldn't dast risk it. Not with his kind. He's like a wild critter, boy. He'd smell me out."

"Well, what you aim to do then? If you're afraid to use the fork on him, how's it to do us any good?"

"We got one chance, boy. Is that a loft ladder yonder?"

"Yes, sir."

"Is there a hay trap in the loft?"

"Yes, sir; over this here front stall, right where we're at. Paw used this stall for hay storage."

"All right, boy. You skin up that ladder and you keep an eye peeled on the house. When you see him coming you knock twicst on the loft floor. You hear?"

"Sure. But we can see him coming from here. Them wallboard cracks is half an inch wide. They'll let that lamp shine through, easy."

"Boy," said Sundown, "when he figgers we're out here in the barn, he ain't going to be coming after us with no lamplight to let us lay for him by. He'll be coming in the pitch dark, and all you'll see of him is his shadow floating 'crost the barn lot. Now you get!"

"Yes, sir!" gulped Bobbie Bromley, and got.

The earth in the bed of the stall was loamy and soft and deep with the working of many an unshod hayrig pony's hooves. Sundown was able to get the sharp-pointed stub of the handle well down into it. Almost, in fact, halfway down to the iron of the fork head itself. He set it as precisely beneath the frame of the trapdoor in the loft floor directly above, as he was able to guess at in the nearly blind gloom of the barn. He had only the slightly less black square of the opening to work by, but that had to suffice. And to suffice fast.

Above him, now, he heard the two sharp raps on

the floor, and his heart came up against the base of his throat, cutting off his breath.

More than one sound came to him in the ensuing silence.

Up-valley, the hounds were drawing nearer, their belling taking on a fierceness it had not held before. Sundown recognized it as the same change in their cry he had heard upon the mountainside, just before reaching the logging flume. They had been unleashed again, and were running.

Time again: time was trying to kill him and the Bromley lad as surely as was that black shadow floating toward them across the barn lot. If that posse took him, Sundown, now, the true murderer would need only to shy off and hide out until the Carbide men had gone on. He would then be free to continue his stalk of the boy. For whether the men took Bobbie along with them or not, they would leave the ranch convinced they had destroyed his mother's killer, and that he was thus removed from danger. True, the lad might try to defend him. But no convincing he had forced on the latter by knocking in that kitchen window and blowing out the lamp would hold up with those tight-jawed men who had been running his track since early dawn and who, certainly, when they now came up to him, would be in no mood to listen to the thin stories of either a homeless drifter, or a big-eyed, weanling ranch boy. The old woman, now, Aunt Martha, she would have been a different pot of pepper. Her word would have held off the rope long enough for the men to fan out and put the dogs on the real killer's track. And had her word been not enough, she likely would have taken up a whiffletree or a churn handle and impressed the Carbide committee directly. But Aunt Martha was long gone, and the chances of her getting back from town in time to take a stand in favor of Sundown Smith were about equal to an Apache Indian's winning a popularity contest in Yavapai County, Arizona.

No. It was still Sundown Smith against the Beast.

And soon.

Outside the locked barn doors, now, he heard the scrape of a boot. Then the snuffling, exactly like that of an animal, at the three-inch crack between the sun-warped doors. The Beast was trying to smell him out.

The quality of the outer night's darkness was now being thinned by the climb of the moon. When the killer left the doors to slide around the barn wall, pausing every few steps to sniff anew at some new separation of the sliding boards, Sundown could clearly follow the blot of his shadow. In this way, he knew when he had reached, and glided through, the missing board at the back of the barn. Now it was up to Sundown.

Deliberately, he ran for the foot of the loft ladder. Having the jump on the killer, he beat him to the rickety steps, and up them, into the loft. At the foot of the ladder, the Beast stopped, staring upward into the absolute pitch-dark blackness of the haymow.

When Sundown heard the creak of the first rung, he moved two steps away from the ladder's head. And only two steps.

From then, he counted each rung creak until there was utter stillness again. The Beast was in the loft, at the ladder's head—holding his breath, waiting for his eyes to adjust to the greater darkness. Sundown held his own breath, praying he could outlast the other. He could. Presently, he heard the labored indrawing of the killer's heavy breath begin again. Instantly, he spun about and leaped away from the ladder head, toward the loft hay trap and Bobbie Bromley. As instantly, the Beast snarled and lunged after him.

Sundown counted his steps away from the ladder, as he had counted them running toward it in the barn below. When he had taken the same number, he jumped as hard as he could to clear the yawning hay trap. He alighted safely on the far side, colliding in the soft mat of hay beyond with the hidden boy. In the same instant he heard behind him the killer's startled gasp, as his reaching feet found, and treaded wildly, the empty air of the open trap.

There followed a silence that seemed interminable but could not, in fact, have lasted more than fractions of a second. The period to this dread pause was a single wrenching cry from below. After that, there was no sound at all in the old barn. None, that is, save for the whisper made by the lips of Sundown Smith moving in fervent thanks to Providence for a delivery from evil which could not, surely, or solely, be explained by his own small, desperate craft.

The hounds came up to Sundown, with the posse at their bawling heels, just as he and the boy emerged from the darkened barn. The exhausted posse men would not listen to any protest, either of Sundown's or Bobbie Bromley's. They had the evidence of their own eyes, and that of the hounds' noses. It was enough. They had the rope shaken out and flung up over the hay-winch beam almost before the drifter or his new friend could utter an intelligible word, and certainly before the ranch boy could comprehend that they truly meant to hang the gentle man who had saved his life. When they had rove the coarse noose about Sundown's neck and tightened it testingly over the hayloft beam, he understood, and then he rushed forward crying his outrage between choking sobs and blows of his small fists at the braced legs of the rope men.

Still, the leader of the posse would not listen. Signaling one of the men to subdue the boy, he brought from his saddlebag the piece of trouser-leg torn from Sundown's faded Levi's upon the mountainside above. He fitted it into place on the drifter's leg and said to the boy, "Bobbie, this is the man who hurt your mother. He has lied to you but you must not believe him. You must believe us. We know what we are doing."

"You don't! you don't!" cried the boy, but the leader made a grim sign to his men, and they stood back to make room for their fellows on the rope's end.

"Take the boy around the corner of the barn," ordered the leader, and the man who had Bobbie nodded and dragged him out of sight, as instructed.

But the boy would not quit; not any more than the drifter had quit when he had the opportunity. Once the barn's corner hid him and his captor from the other men, he kicked hard and sure through the darkness, and his sharp boot toe did not miss the mark. The posse man yelled out a curse and let go of the boy to grab his injured shin.

Bobbie shot away from him like a stomped-on cottontail. Scooting on around the barn, he found the broken board at the rear, slid in and dashed through the darkness toward the front stall. The shadow man had still had the shotgun when he had fallen through Sundown's trap. If Bobbie could find that weapon, now, maybe he could use it to make the posse men understand that being seven years old and all stirred up did not disqualify a boy from knowing what he knew, and being able to testify to it. Yes sir, if they wouldn't listen to a little boy, maybe they would listen to a big gun.

It took a great deal of courage to go near that stall, and near what lay within it, impaled upon the broken hay fork. But Bobbie Bromley went into the stall, and found the guard's double-barreled, full-choke, Ithica 10-gauge shotgun. And, with the weapon, he returned to the barnfront scene, just as the ropemen lay back on the rough strand, and Sundown's boot toes lifted free of the ground.

With no time to do anything else, the boy shouldered the huge double and triggered the left barrel blasting upward into the night, and into the barn's winch beam and the Carbide posse's tautened rope.

The charge of Number 4 buckshot dissolved the rope and a foot and a half of the end of the winch beam. Sundown fell to earth, unharmed save for a chafing of his five-day beard, and the Carbide posse men swung about to face a seven-year-old ranch boy who still had one shell to go, and didn't hesitate to let them know it.

He devoted the gape of the 10-gauge's bores to the general vicinity of the posse leader's belt buckle, and directed his remarks to the latter in no uncertain terms.

"The other tube's for you, Mr. Hannigan—" he broke off the threat to cock the big outside hammer of the remaining barrel, and in the silence which ensued, he added tearfully, *"—less'n you 'gree to look in the barn like Mister Sundown asked you to. Now you git!"*

Mr. Hannigan was no fool. He did not care to argue points of proper procedure with a small boy and a very big shotgun on full cock. He got.

The rest of the posse men went with him. When they had pried off the hasp of the doors and had flung them wide and stomped inside, holding high the Rochester lamp fetched from where the killer had left it in the house, they all stopped, stark-staring, at what they saw in the first stall.

The leader quickly blew out the lamp and said to his men, "Boys, get out of here; we can come back in the morning with tools and a wagon."

Outside the barn, he put his heavy arm around Bobbie Bromley's shoulders and muttered, "Bobbie, I reckon you know we're sorry. You done a brave thing, boy, and we're all mightily proud of you. Yes," he said, looking up to nod at Sundown Smith, "and of your friend, yonder, too."

He stepped to Sundown's side and said in a low voice, "We mean it, mister. You got a home in Carbide Valley long as you want."

Sundown just smiled in his sad, slow way, and shook his head.

"Thank you, Mr. Hannigan," he said. "But when the boy is rightly settled, I reckon I'll just be drifting on."

In Carbide Wells, it was just a little after sunrise. It was a day shot full of sunshine and good cheer. In front of the local office of the Inter-Pacific Stagelines, a Concord coach was drawn up and a small crowd gathered.

Here assembled were the good folk of Carbide Wells, town and countryside, gathered to say goodbye to little Bobbie Bromley. It ought to have been a happy time, but it was not. Like Sundown Smith, Bobbie Bromley was now without kith or kin in the whole broad world, and he was being sent on the morning stage to San Francisco, where the state authorities would find a home for him.

To one side of the crowd stood Sundown Smith and his wise old horse, Mordecai. Upon the seat box of the stage Bobbie Bromley was perched beside the grizzled driver, trying to be far braver than he was. Neither his heart nor his eyes were in the business. Both were bent across the heads of the crowd toward Sundown Smith. And it became suddenly very doubtful that Bobbie would ever get to San Francisco. Or, indeed, that he would ever start for San Francisco. That last look at Sundown and old Mordecai said more, in silence, than all the noisy wishes of the crowd could ever render in out-loud farewells.

In the final, fateful second before the stage driver kicked off his brake and yelled, "Hee-yahh!" at his waiting horses, Bobbie slid down off the seat box and ran waving, from that high, unhappy perch, toward Sundown Smith. As he reached him, the drifter got down from old Mordecai and gathered the boy up in his arms and held him there, defying the closing crowd like an aging gray wolf brought to bay, bewildered and confused, but determined somehow to defend what was his, and the boy's.

There was some hot talk, then, and loud. But Mr. Hannigan, who was the mayor of Carbide Wells, shut it off pretty prompt. "The question is," he said, "whether the boy goes our way, or his own. We'll put it to a vote." He paused, spreading this thick legs and jutting his big jaw. "Hannigan," he said, "votes for the boy."

Sundown and the boy stood high upon the mountainside looking back and down upon Carbide Wells for the last time.

They were leaving the valley to go over the mountain and look for that job of Sundown's, which it was to be hoped they would never find. On the way, they would seek some new bluejays with which to argue. They would search for another sunlit glade on another lofty slope. They would listen for the laughter of some new, small stream, in some different and distant place. But this time it would not be a lonely place.

With this thought, Sundown nodded to himself, and plodded on up the trail, the boy coming gladly behind him.

On the last rise before the trail bent to hide the town, Sundown paused to wait for the boy, and for the old horse the boy was leading. When they came up, the three of them stood looking back, just for the least, grace note of time. Straightening, Sundown nodded for the final time.

"Indeed," he said softly to himself, and through force of lifetime habit, "the question comes naturally to a man's mind, if there will ever be another lonely place for Mordecai and me. . . ."

When he spoke, the boy smiled up at him and put his hand in Sundown's hand and the two friends turned and went over the last rise, the old horse following them like a faithful dog.

"REACH FOR THE SKY!"

and you still won't find more excitement or more thrills than you get in Bantam's slam-bang, action-packed westerns! Here's a roundup of fast-reading stories by some of America's greatest western writers:

BANTAM'S #1
ALL-TIME BESTSELLING AUTHOR
AMERICA'S FAVORITE WESTERN WRITER

☐	10450	HIGH LONESOME	$1.50
☐	11149	BORDEN CHANTRY	$1.50
☐	11120	BRIONNE	$1.50
☐	10618	THE FERGUSON RIFLE	$1.50
☐	10765	KILLOE	$1.50
☐	10767	CONAGHER	$1.50
☐	10791	NORTH TO THE RAILS	$1.50
☐	10798	THE MAN FROM SKIBBEREEN	$1.50
☐	10822	SILVER CANYON	$1.50
☐	10986	CATLOW	$1.50
☐	10845	REILLY'S LUCK	$1.50
☐	10895	GUNS OF THE TIMBERLANDS	$1.50
☐	10896	HANGING WOMAN CREEK	$1.50
☐	10897	FALLON	$1.50
☐	10901	UNDER THE SWEETWATER RIM	$1.50
☐	10902	MATAGORDA	$1.50
☐	10905	DARK CANYON	$1.50
☐	10906	THE CALIFORNIOS	$1.50
☐	10988	FLINT	$1.50

**Buy them at your local bookstore or use this
handy coupon for ordering:**

Bantam Books, Inc., Dept. LL1, 414 East Golf Road, Des Plaines, Ill. 60016

Please send me the books I have checked above. I am enclosing $_____
(please add 75¢ to cover postage and handling). Send check or money order
—no cash or C.O.D.'s please.

Mr/Mrs/Miss_____

Address_____

City_____State/Zip_____

LL1—10/78

Please allow four weeks for delivery. This offer expires 4/79.

BANTAM'S #1
ALL-TIME BESTSELLING AUTHOR
AMERICA'S FAVORITE WESTERN WRITER

☐	11049	THE KEY-LOCK MAN	$1.50
☐	10741	RADIGAN	$1.50
☐	10782	RIVERS WEST	$1.50
☐	10831	KIOWA TRAIL	$1.50
☐	10829	THE BURNING HILLS	$1.50
☐	10967	SHALAKO	$1.50
☐	10799	KILRONE	$1.50
☐	11119	THE RIDER OF LOST CREEK	$1.50
☐	10768	CALLAGHEN	$1.50
☐	10761	THE QUICK AND THE DEAD	$1.50
☐	10742	OVER ON THE DRY SIDE	$1.50
☐	10691	DOWN THE LONG HILLS	$1.50
☐	02757	TO THE FAR BLUE MOUNTAINS	$1.50
☐	10491	WESTWARD THE TIDE	$1.50
☐	10449	KID RODELO	$1.50
☐	10446	BROKEN GUN	$1.50
☐	10286	WHERE THE LONG GRASS BLOWS	$1.50
☐	2478	HOW THE WEST WAS WON	$1.50

**Buy them at your local bookstore or use this
handy coupon for ordering:**

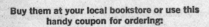

Bantam Books, Inc., Dept. LL2, 414 East Golf Road, Des Plaines, Ill. 60016

Please send me the books I have checked above. I am enclosing $_____
(please add 75¢ to cover postage and handling). Send check or money order
—no cash or C.O.D.'s please.

Mr/Mrs/Miss_____

Address_____

City_____State/Zip_____

LL2—10/78

Please allow four weeks for delivery. This offer expires 4/79.

RELAX!
SIT DOWN
and Catch Up On Your Reading!